The Reluctant Mob Lawyer

A Broken Lawyer Novel

By

Donald L'Abbate

Also by Donald L'Abbate
"Was it Murder?"

And

The Broken Lawyer Series
"The Broken Lawyer"
"A Murder Under the Bridge"
"For One Man's Honor"
"The Chinatown Houdini Bandits"

TABLE OF CONTENTS

Donald L'Abbate

DEDICATION

To my parents, Dominic and Estelle for their never faltering love, patience and support without which I wouldn't the person I am today. Thanks Mom and Dad.

CHAPTER 1

It was supposed to be a quiet Monday with nothing on the schedule. I had planned on doing a little bookkeeping and maybe taking in an afternoon AA meeting. But, as usual, things didn't go as planned.

Joey "Bats" DiFalco, a former client, showed up unannounced. Being a Caucasian lawyer working in New York City's Chinatown, I don't get very many walk-in clients. In fact, I can count on one hand the number of walk-in clients I've had in the last ten years.

Almost all my clients come to me through the New York State Assigned Counsel Plan, or the 18B Panel for short. The 18B Panel assigns criminal cases to attorneys when Legal Aid can't handle the cases. The work is steady, but the pay is lousy which is why I try to snag a couple of private clients whenever I can. Joey "Bats" had been one such client. Now he was back.

Joey is a small-time gangster who doesn't understand that the old time Mafia that he so admired and longed to be a part of was essentially dead. It had been killed by RICO, not the notorious Harlem drug dealer, but the Racketeer Influenced and Corrupt Organization Act passed by Congress in 1970. That law and vigorous prosecution by New York federal authorities spelled the demise of the old-style Mafia. What remained was a far cry from the glory days of the Godfather. Of course, Joey Bats was not about to acknowledge the passing of his beloved Mafia, and I for one, was not about to mention it. After all, he didn't get the nickname, Joey Bats, for nothing.

That being said, the Mafia has had a resurgence after the attacks of 9/11 when the feds had their hands full dealing with counterterrorism. But by then most of the old-time bosses were either dead or in jail, and the few still around were getting old. So what emerged wasn't the Mafia of old, but rather a bunch of knock arounds like Joey.

This new Mafia operates under the same structure and the same rules as its predecessor, but it lacks the finesse of the old Mafia. What the new boys lack in the finesse of the old godfathers, they make up for with violence. If you're not careful when dealing with these guys, you can wind up badly hurt or even dead.

When you practice criminal law, you either learn how to handle unsavory clients, or you risk getting beat up a lot. I began my career working at the District Attorney's Office where personal safety wasn't much of an issue because I had 35,000 New York City cops watching my back. But when I was forced to switch sides after being tossed out of the District Attorney's Office, that changed. Now most of the time the only thing standing between me and my unsavory criminal clients is a desk, or at best, a set of bars.

I won't bore you with the details of my life. First, my life story isn't that interesting, and second, you don't need to know it. Suffice it to say I'm a recovering alcoholic. Knowing that, you can probably guess how I went from a promising career in the District Attorney's Office to a small criminal law practice on Mott Street in New York City's Chinatown.

But back to Joey Bats. I had once represented Joey on a weapons charge and was successful in having the case thrown out of court. That prompted Joey to call me the greatest lawyer since F. Lee Bailey, or as Joey put it, "that Bailey guy with the funny first name." Clearly Joey wasn't the sharpest knife in the drawer.

I hadn't seen or spoken with Joey since we parted on the courthouse steps two years earlier. Either Joey had managed to stay out of trouble, or he got himself a new lawyer. Maybe that Bailey guy. But now he was sitting across from me looking very serious. Of course, with Joey it could have been gas pains because from what I knew about Joey, he rarely took anything seriously.

Being a small-time lawyer, I can't afford to turn away business, but I do draw the line with some clients. I won't represent child molesters, rapists, or sex offenders. There are two reasons I won't take on those cases. First, I'm not sure I could do a good job if I had reason to believe the client was guilty. I believe everyone is entitled to a defense, and a good one, so if I don't think I can give a client a good defense, I won't take the case. The second reason is more personal and pragmatic. My longtime girlfriend, Gracie, with whom I live, is the Sex Crimes Prosecutor in the Manhattan District Attorney's Office, so if I took on one of those cases, we'd wind up going toe to toe in court, and that wouldn't be good. At least not for me. If you have any doubts about that, try watching the old classic movie from 1949, *Adam's Rib*, with Spencer Tracy and Katherine Hepburn.

But Joey wasn't a child molester, rapist, or sex offender, so I had to at least hear his story before I decided if I'd send him packing. It turned out he wasn't there on his own behalf but as an emissary for his goomba, Little Tony Savino who was sitting in Rikers Island Jail while his old man arranged bail. According to Joey, a family friend had represented Little Tony at his arraignment and worked out a bail arrangement. But the family friend didn't handle big criminal cases, so that was why Joey had come to me.

I was starting to think I might be smart not to take the case, yet I still wanted to hear more about it before I decided. Joey was a little vague on the charge, but the terms homicide and killing did work their way into the conversation, so one way or the other this was a major felony case.

Joey said he convinced Little Tony that I was the best lawyer in Manhattan, and I could get him off. Speaking confidentially, Joey said it was an easy case; Little Tony had an iron clad alibi and had done it in self-defense. Obviously, the finer points of the law eluded Joey. Like I said, Joey isn't the sharpest knife in the drawer. To be truthful, I'm amazed he manages to stay alive without full-time adult supervision.

This was a chance for a large fee, and chances like that don't come along often. If you're thinking that I'd take the case just for the money, you'd be right. But what's wrong with that? A fee is a fee. Some fees are big, and some fees are small, but it's all money.

Money is a funny thing. When you have a lot of it, you can afford to be choosy as to where it comes from. But if you don't have a lot of it and you like eating regularly and living indoors, the source of the money isn't quite as important. Still, I didn't take all the cases that came my way. Just most of them.

I told Joey if I took the case, which I wasn't sure I would, I'd need a big retainer, say $100,000, and that didn't include expenses. Joey said that was no problem, and I could just put it on his tab. I reminded Joey that I wasn't running a gin joint, and he didn't have a tab with me. The news seemed to trouble Joey who apparently thought the whole world worked on the cuff. After considering the matter, he said the money wasn't a problem, and Little Tony would make good as soon as he was out of Rikers. I repeated that I hadn't agreed to take the case; I needed to talk with Little Tony before I made up my mind.

Joey nodded and said he'd arrange a meeting as soon as Little Tony was released. In the meantime, I intended to find out as much as I could about Little Tony and the charges he was facing. It was a big fee, but I wasn't sure the money was worth the trouble that came with it. Before I decided if the fee was worth the trouble, I needed to know more about Little Tony and his case.

Joey doesn't always speak in whole sentences, but from what I could piece together, the incident that led to Little Tony's arrest had happened in or near Little Italy. In the past, the case might have been handled by the NYPD's Organized Crime Bureau, but things had changed in the NYPD, and the case was being handled by the Detective Squad at the local precinct which would be the Fifth Precinct.

The Detective Squad at the Fifth Precinct is headed up by Detective Richard Chen, who happens to be a friend of mine. I've known Chen for several years and for the price of a lunch at the Worth Street Coffee Shop, I was sure he'd fill me in on Little Tony's case. That's the kind of relationship we have. I feed him food, and in return, he feeds me information. Over the years, it has proved beneficial for the both of us. Maybe more so for me because as far as I could tell, all Chen got out of it was a thicker waistline.

I gave Chen a call and arranged to meet him for lunch. Then I called my investigator, Tommy Shoo, and asked him to dig up whatever he could on Little Tony Savino and meet me at my office around four o'clock.

CHAPTER 2

When I arrived at the Worth Street Coffee Shop, Detective Chen was already seated at my private table in the back corner. I had seen Chen less than two weeks earlier and with nothing new to talk about, we traded wisecracks as we ordered lunch.

When our drinks arrived, I cut short the chitchat and got down to business. I explained that I was considering representing Tony Savino, but before I made up my mind, I wanted to know how much trouble he was in. Chen asked if I was talking about Little Tony or Big Tony. I told him it was Little Tony, but if Big Tony was in trouble, I wanted to hear about that also.

Chen laughed. He said the Savinos were always in trouble, but they seemed to avoid convictions. At the moment it was Little Tony who was in deep shit. By way of background, the Savinos were soldiers in the Stagliano crew, a faction of the Rucci mob family. Big Tony's association with the Ruccis went way back. All the way back to the early days when Big Tony and old man Silvio Rucci were soldiers in the Gambino mob. Eventually Silvio Rucci took over the family, and Big Tony became his number two man. Somewhere along the way, the two had a falling out. No one knew why, but Big Tony got demoted to his present position in the Stagliano crew.

As for Little Tony, he had been arrested and charged with murdering two members of the Russian mob. The circumstances weren't clear, but for the cops it was an open and shut case.

The bodies had been found a week earlier in the trunk of a car parked in the parking lot under the Manhattan Bridge. A tip from a confidential informer led the detectives to an office in Brooklyn that turned out to be the murder scene.

The medical examiner estimated the two men had been killed three days before they were found shot execution style in the backs of their heads. But it hadn't been a simple execution. Fresh bruises and contusions on the bodies and hands of the two victims suggested they had been in a brutal fight shortly before they were shot. So I asked how it was an open and shut case.

Chen smiled and said the fingerprints lifted by the Crime Scene Unit from both the abandoned car and the murder scene matched those of Little Tony Savino, making him a prime suspect. When the detectives questioned Little Tony, he had several scratches on his face and neck, as well as numerous bruises and abrasions indicative of a recent violent physical encounter. The medical examiner had recovered skin cells from under the fingernails of one of the victims that would presumably be a DNA match with Savino. That, plus Savino's refusal to cooperate, had been more than enough for an arrest warrant.

That was a lot of evidence, but I didn't think it added up to an open and shut case. The bruises on Little Tony weren't a problem. He could have gotten them anywhere. But that would change if the skin under the victims' fingernails was Little Tony's. That would be bad but not fatal to the case. All it proved was that Little Tony and the victims had been in a fight, but it didn't prove he shot the victims. It was the fingerprints that were the problem. But as Joey Bats had said, Tony had an ironclad alibi, and he did it in self-defense, so what was there to worry about?

The only thing to worry about was the involvement of the Russian mob. Not that I was worried, but I knew I'd get an earful from Gracie when she heard the Russian mob was involved. Gracie has a history with the Russians, and it's not a good one.

By that time our lunches had arrived, and we dug into our deli sandwiches. I have had a long-term love affair with pastrami on a club roll, but recently I've strayed. Not that I've abandoned my old favorite; it's more like an infrequent dalliance. Just an occasional beef brisket with mayo on a club roll and French fries instead of a knish. I don't think it's a big deal, but Gertie seems to think so.

In case you haven't figured it out, Gertie is my favorite waitress. She doesn't say anything when I order the brisket; she just gives a little "humph." Who would have thought that pastrami could produce such loyalty in a waitress?

As we finished the last of our sandwiches, Gertie asked if we wanted dessert. Chen looked like he was about to say something, but I threw him a dagger stare and told Gertie to bring the check. Chen knew damn well our arrangement didn't include dessert. I mean, between the deli sandwiches, a couple of Dr. Brown sodas, Chen's knish, my French fries, and the tip and tax, I was in for a good $65. There was no way I was adding cheesecake to the tab, not when all I got in exchange was information that I'd probably find in the arrest report anyway.

In case you're interested, a good pastrami sandwich in New York City is going to set you back somewhere around $20. If you go to the famous Katz's Deli on East Houston Street, expect to pay $22.45 for a pastrami sandwich, a little less for corned beef or brisket, and $5.45 for a knish. You'll pay about the same at the 2nd Ave Deli, and maybe a little less at some of the other delis. But anything costing much less isn't a genuine New York deli sandwich. Trust me on that.

As we were parting, I had one more question for Chen. Who owned the car the bodies were found in? Chen said it was registered to a company run by Silvio Rucci, but it had been reported stolen two days before the bodies were found. Somehow that didn't surprise me.

CHAPTER 3

With nothing on my schedule until my meeting with Tommy Shoo later that afternoon, I decided to drop in on Gracie. Usually I only stop by Gracie's office when I'm in the District Attorney's Office, or if I'm bored and have nothing else to do. But that afternoon I needed Gracie's help, and I wanted her advice.

I met Gracie Delaney over thirty years ago when we were both newly minted lawyers just beginning our careers at the Manhattan District Attorney's Office. Despite our being in competition for plumb assignments, we wound up in a close personal relationship, meaning we were having sex. Then with my career rising like a rocket, I started drinking alcoholically, and as you might suspect, that ended both my relationship with Gracie Delaney and my career in the District Attorney's Office. Of course, at the time I failed to see any correlation between my drinking and the nosedive into the toilet that my life was taking.

As my drinking increased, my life continued its downward spiral until I wound up practicing law from a desk in the back room of Shoo's Chinese Restaurant. In the meantime, Gracie's career in the

District Attorney's Office was steadily advancing. By then Gracie and I saw very little of each other as we were moving in different social circles. That's not exactly true because I wasn't moving in any social circles. I had isolated myself, and the only socializing I did was chatting with other booze hounds in cheap gin mills.

On the rare occasions where our paths crossed, we ignored each other. I can't say that I blame Gracie, or anyone else for ignoring me during my boozing days. I wasn't a "happy drunk." No, if you wanted to be charitable, you might say I had a bad attitude, but you'd be more accurate calling me a miserable bastard.

Finally, after more than a decade of alcoholic drinking, and with my life seriously out of control, I got sober. Actually, it wasn't that simple, and it certainly wasn't by choice. It was an ultimatum; if I didn't get sober, I'd lose my license to practice law. Thanks to AA, my sponsor, Doug, and some others along the way, I'm sober today and happy. Oh, yeah, and as I'm sure you figured out, Gracie and I are back together.

We hooked up again about ten years ago soon after I got sober, and we've been together ever since. We basically live together, but I still keep a place of my own. It's one of those places now in vogue called a micro-apartment. Micro meaning it's smaller than small and even tinier than tiny. I guess calling it a "micro-apartment" sounds better in the ads than calling it a "really, really tiny apartment."

My place is 260 square feet. To give you some comparison, the average parking space in New York City is 162 square feet. So, on those rare occasions when I stay in my micro-apartment, I'm basically living in one and a half parking spaces and paying $2,300 a month for the privilege. It's crazy, but having my own place gives us both a sense of freedom which we seem to need. To us, marriage is like the ultimate nuclear weapon; it's capable of destroying life as we know it and therefore must be avoided at all cost.

I have a buddy who handles divorce cases. He says marriage invariably leads to divorce, so if you want to shortcut the process, simply find a woman you can't stand, give her half of your money, and buy her a house. That way you avoid all the pain between the marriage and the divorce.

But, back to the point. I dropped in to see Gracie that afternoon because some things about the Savino case weren't adding up, and I wanted her take on the situation.

I'm a good criminal defense lawyer, but I'm small-time; I know it and so does everyone else. It doesn't bother me to have a small-time practice; I like it that way. My few private clients, meaning those not assigned to me by the 18B Panel, are generally referrals and usually don't involve high-profile cases. On occasion, a high-profile case has fallen my way, but that's been only by chance. I certainly didn't qualify as a mob lawyer.

Now, suddenly a Mafia made man wants me to be his lawyer? I didn't believe for a minute it was based on Joey DiFalco's recommendation. In the Mafia hierarchy, guys like Joey Bats rank near the bottom, and so Joey's opinion wouldn't be worth shit. So why me? Little Tony had more than a passing acquaintance with the criminal justice system, and I strongly doubted Little Tony had represented himself. The fact that Little Tony was walking around free told me whoever represented him in the past had done a pretty damn good job. I suspected the lawyer was Gene Meyers, a flashy criminal defense lawyer, who had a close association with the Rucci family. Gracie was in a position to confirm Meyers' involvement with the Ruccis, and that was one reason I dropped by her office.

When I explained to Gracie why I was there, she had one of her law clerks run a computer records search. The search turned up twelve cases brought by the Manhattan District Attorney's Office against Anthony, "Little Tony," Savino. In all twelve cases, Little Tony's attorney of record had been Gene Meyers.

As far as I knew, Meyers was alive and kicking, so why would Little Tony switch lawyers? It could be as simple as Meyers being too busy or maybe having a conflict of interest, but that didn't seem likely. Gracie had no better explanation than I had, but she agreed something was odd about the situation, and she took it to be a red flag. Her reasoning, as usual, was solid. She said Meyers was in a better position than me to know about the case, and if he was turning it down, I probably should do the same. If a career mob lawyer was turning down a mob case, something made it too hot to handle. Then she added that I wasn't a mob lawyer, and she asked why I would want to become one so late in my career. That was a thought-provoking question.

There are criminal defense lawyers such as me. Then there's a very small subgroup of criminal defense lawyers known as mob lawyers. Those are lawyers such as Gene Meyers whose entire practice consists of representing mobsters. Granted, all of us in the criminal defense business represent criminals; that's why we're called criminal defense lawyers. But when you represent only mobsters, it doesn't make you a specialist; it taints you as corrupt. Why? Because mobsters have been known to bribe jurors and prosecutors, intimidate, and sometimes kill key prosecution witnesses, even judges. Most reasonable people assume it's done with the knowledge of their lawyers. That's why mob lawyers often share the reputation of their mobster clients.

Answering Gracie's question about why I wanted to become a mob lawyer, I told her that I didn't think taking on Little Tony's case made me a mob lawyer. Maybe technically it did, but I wasn't thinking about that; I was thinking about the $100,000 fee.

Attempting to move the conversation away from the mob lawyer question, I reminded Gracie that there could be an innocent reason for Meyers turning down the case. We didn't even know if Little Tony had gone to Meyers in the first place. Gracie said that was true, but she still thought I shouldn't take the case until I had all the facts and knew why Meyers wasn't handling it. Good advice, but not necessarily what I wanted to hear.

It was getting late, and we both had other things to do, so we dropped the discussion and agreed to meet that night at Ecco for dinner. Then I left and headed to my office for my meeting with Tommy Shoo.

CHAPTER 4

Now would be a good time to mention a little something about my investigator, Tommy Shoo. I met Tommy many years ago when we shared the back room of his grandfather's restaurant on Mott Street. I was running my law practice, what there was of it, from a desk on one side of the room, and Tommy was storing his stock of knockoff Rolex watches on the other side of the room.

For a reason that presently eludes me, I hired Tommy to do some investigative work, and it turned out he was good at it. I kept tossing him business whenever I could, and eventually he gave up the knockoff business, got his PI license, and opened an office on Elizabeth Street. He now employs a couple of part-time investigators and a full-time computer whiz who, according to Tommy, can hack her way into any computer system in the world. I don't know if that's true, and I don't want to know because what I don't know can't get me disbarred.

Tommy is the type of person who everyone loves at first sight. I mean, what's not to love? He's warm, outgoing, looks trustworthy, and can charm the bark off a tree. All of which makes him a good investigator and ironically made him one of Chinatown's top knockoff street vendors back in the day.

Being Chinese and having been raised in Chinatown, Tommy has the trust of the Chinatown community, and over the years, he has built up a network of contacts ranging from gangbangers to local merchants and politicians. He's even managed to charm his way into the Italian community of Little Italy where he's known as the "Chinese pisan."

There's something else you should know about Tommy. Whenever he's about to tell me something he knows I'm not going to like, he gets this look on his face, a half frown, half scowl. That afternoon when he walked into the office the look was there, so I knew something was up. I wasn't sure what, but it was a safe bet it had to do with the Savino case, and I wasn't going to like it.

Getting right to the point, I asked what he had learned about Little Tony Savino. Tommy didn't answer right away. Then waving his finger for emphasis, he said, "You can't take the Savino case."

If you know me, you know I don't like being told what I can and can't do. But in AA I've learned to be more tolerant, so instead of telling Tommy what he could do to himself, I asked why. He said because it involved the Mafia, and I wasn't a mob lawyer.

I already knew that, and I didn't see why it should stop me from taking the case. When I didn't respond, Tommy added, "For God's sake, not only is it the Mafia; it involves the Russian mob as well. The Russian mob!" he repeated for emphasis, then asked, "Don't you understand what that means?"

Truthfully, I didn't. All I knew was the Russian mob was headquartered in Brighton Beach in Brooklyn, and you didn't want to mess with them directly. I recalled a cop once telling me when I worked in the District Attorney's Office that the Russian mob was much more ruthless than the Mafia. He said if you crossed the Italian Mafia, they'd kill you, but they wouldn't hurt your family. If you crossed the Russian mob, they'd also kill you, but not before they killed members of your family and sent them to you piece by piece. But what did that have to do with me taking Little Tony's case?

Tommy said it was complicated. When someone says a question is complicated, it either means they don't know the answer, or they don't want to tell you the answer. I gave Tommy a look, and sensing my growing frustration, he tried to explain. He said it seemed like it was a simple case, but it probably wasn't.

Little Tony Savino was a soldier in Salvatore "Sally Boy" Stagliano's crew, a part of the Rucci mob family. That much I figured, and I knew how the Mafia operated.

You don't live in New York City for as long as I have and not know how the Mafia is organized and operates. That is, unless you live in a cave and have never read the *Godfather* or seen the movie. Me, I've lived near Little Italy most of my life; I've read the book twice; and I've seen the movie three times. I didn't need Tommy to explain the Mafia to me.

Each Mafia crime family is headed up by a boss, usually referred to as the Don. Silvio Rucci was the Don heading up the Rucci family. Next one in the pecking order is the underboss, second in charge and in line to become boss if something happens to the Don or the Don retires. Junior Rucci was said to be the underboss of the Rucci family.

Every boss has a consigliere, or counselor, who advises him and often acts as the family's representative in meetings with other families, particularly in times of conflict. No one was certain who the Rucci consigliere was, although it was believed to be Silvio's second son, Jimmy. Whether that was true or not might be an issue down the road, but at that point I didn't think it mattered.

Below the Don and the underboss, the rest of the family is divided into crews called regimes, headed by caporegimes. Sally Boy Stagliano is a caporegime, or capo for short. A mid-level member of the gang but trusted to handle Rucci family business and run a crew.

Sally Boy's regime, or crew, consists of soldiers and associates who take orders from him, giving the boss a layer of protection. Soldiers in the crew are members of the family but associates aren't. Associates are free lancing criminals, trying to earn their way into the family. If an associate proves himself worthy, he can become a solider by making his bones, meaning killing someone, and taking the oath of Omerta, or silence. Then he is officially a member of the family, or as it's called, a "made man."

Sally Boy ran the Rucci family's gambling, loan sharking, prostitution, and drug business in sections of Brooklyn and Queens, two of New York City's outer boroughs. Little Tony was an enforcer whose job was to make sure people paid their debts on time, and no one moved in on the Rucci family's territories or interfered with their business.

As for the charges against Little Tony, it seemed a couple of Russians had tried taking over a bookmaking operation in Rucci territory and wound up dead. Suspicion naturally fell on the Rucci family, and forensic evidence pointed to Little Tony as the killer.

It sure as hell sounded simple enough to me, and I saw no reason why I should turn down a $100,000 fee. But Tommy again said it wasn't that simple. There was a lot more at stake in this case than simply two dead Russian mobsters. The murders were the flash point for what could turn into an all-out war between the Russian mob and the Mafia.

That didn't sound good, but before I turned down the case, I wanted to know how the murders could result in a mob war. Tommy said it had to do with how the Mafia and the Russian mob conducted businesses in Queens and Brooklyn over the years.

That didn't exactly answer my question, and Tommy, seeing my growing impatience, suggested I sit back, and he'd explain it all.

CHAPTER 5

Before the Russian mob existed in New York, the Mafia controlled both Brooklyn and Queens, with the territories divided among two of the infamous original Five Families. But that changed in the 1970s, when the Cali drug cartel moved into the Queens neighborhood of Jackson Heights, and the first of three-hundred thousand Soviet immigrants moved into the Brighton Beach and Sheepshead Bay sections of Brooklyn.

With the notorious Pablo Escobar and his Medillin cartel in South Florida drawing so much attention, the arrival of the Cali cartel in New York went practically unnoticed by law enforcement, but not by the Mafia. Realizing their business interests were threatened, the Mafia bosses took a closer look at the newly arrived mob. For one reason or another, perhaps the extremely violent nature of the Cali cartel or the small amount of territory it controlled, the Mafia bosses found it was not in their interest to compete and basically withdrew from the area of Queens that the cartel controlled.

Things remained the same until a couple of years later when war broke out between the competing Columbian drug lords. With the escalating violence, the DEA and NYPD stepped in big time and took down the leaders of the Cali cartel. Unfortunately, by that time the Colombians had been joined by the Mexicans and the Dominicans who were equally violent. As these new gangs spread in Queens, the Mafia bosses ceded more territory to them, recognizing that a war would do more harm financially than the loss of territory. Still, at the time, the Mafia controlled large sections of Queens, most notably in the southern part of the borough where John Gotti, the Teflon Don, ruled.

As for the Russians' venture into organized crime, it happened much more slowly. Early Russian crimes in Brighton Beach were small-time and petty, mostly involving fraud. But things changed as the community grew. Within twenty years, Brighton Beach became the largest Russian community outside of the Motherland, earning it the nickname, Little Odessa.

In 1991, after the collapse of the Soviet Union, ex-KGB agents, aided by veterans of the Afghan war, organized and internationalized the criminal gangs in Russia. Criminals thought to be too violent in Russia were sent out of the country, many winding up in Brighton Beach, and the Russian mob was born.

As the Russian mob was quietly growing and expanding, the Italian Mafia and the drug cartels were under increasing pressure from federal prosecutors, and ranking members of both organizations were arrested, prosecuted, and sent to prison. Then after the 9/11 attacks with the FBI turning its attention to terrorism, things began to stabilize for what was left of the Italian Mafia and the drug cartels.

With its ranks thinned and many of the old-time bosses either dead or in jail, what remained of the Italian Mafia wasn't much. But it was enough to control most of the organized crime in New York City. The exceptions being Brighton Beach controlled by the Russian mob, and the sections of Queens controlled by the drug cartels. Everyone seemed content with their own little fiefdoms, and while there wasn't a specific understanding between the groups, it was simply a very pragmatic live and let live situation. Everyone knew if they went to war, not only would they face mutual annihilation, but the public wrath would lead to unrelenting prosecutions that nobody wanted. So, there was a peaceful but uneasy co-existence until Little Tony Savino took out the two Russians.

It was all very interesting, but I was losing patience. I'd heard enough about the history of the Russian mob and the Mafia; now I wanted to know what it had to do with Little Tony's case. Tommy wasn't happy when I told him to drop the history lesson and get to current events. Tossing me a nasty look, he pulled a little notebook from his shirt pocket and gave me a full report.

Word on the street was that the two dead Russians had set up a bookie operation in the Park Slope section of Brooklyn, a territory belonging to the Rucci family. On its face, it seemed to be a small-time rogue operation, but it wasn't. It had been sanctioned and planned by the Russians who viewed the Rucci family conflict as an opportunity to take over Rucci territory. The poaching operation was a test to see how the Ruccis would respond.

If the family problems were as bad as the Russians suspected, the Ruccis might be too distracted or too fractured to take action. If that were the case, the Russians would continue taking over more territory.

But even with the family problems, the Ruccis weren't about to let anyone move in on their territory. When old man Rucci learned about it, he may have mistakenly thought it was simply a rogue operation and not a coordinated effort by the Russian mob. In any event, he sent two of his men to warn the interlopers what would happen to them if they continued to take book in his territory. Of course, the Russians had no intention of abandoning the operation, and to show Rucci they weren't intimidated by his threats, they sent his soldiers back minus their index fingers and one ear each.

The cut off index fingers I understood; they were the trigger fingers, but why the ears? Tommy said it was a message to Rucci that they weren't listening to his threats.

Apparently incensed by the insult, Rucci ordered Sally Boy to send Little Tony to "take care of the situation." It was only after the two were killed that Rucci learned they weren't rogue operators, but they were working under orders from the Russian mob. The Russians didn't take kindly to Rucci whacking two of their soldiers, and everyone had expected a war to break out between the Russians and the Italians, but so far it hadn't.

19

I thought that was good, but Tommy said it wasn't, at least not for me. There was a rumor floating around that a deal had been cut that involved Little Tony being charged with the murders. No one seemed to know the details, and Tommy hadn't been able to learn anything more about the supposed arrangement.

None of what Tommy had just told me made sense to me, and I told Tommy so. How was some suspected peace arrangement between the Russian mob and the Mafia tied up in Little Tony's murder case? Tommy admitted he didn't know how they were connected, but he believed they were.

Then he asked me two questions: Why had Little Tony come to me? And, why hadn't he gone to Gene Meyers? They seemed be the questions of the day. I didn't know the answers, and maybe I didn't want to know the answers. It was beginning to look like there was more to Little Tony's case than met the eye. But I wouldn't know until I met with Little Tony.

CHAPTER 6

Tommy and I were still talking when Joey Bats called and said a meeting with Little Tony was set for the next day at the Italian American Bocci Club on Hester Street. I was to meet Joey on the corner of Baxter and Canal Streets at three o'clock and he'd take me to the club.

I knew about the Bocci Club. It was the Rucci gang's hangout, a private club in an old storefront on Hester Street. It was strictly members only with the occasional invited guest. I had never been in the place, but I was willing to bet nobody inside was playing bocci. Hangouts like the Bocci Club were common during the Mafia's hay days, but only a few still existed, and none of the ones still around were as notorious as those of the past.

Perhaps the most famous of the old social clubs was the Ravenite Social Club at 247 Mulberry Street, where the Gambino gang hung out and where the infamous "Teflon Don," John Gotti, ran his operation. Now the once fortified storefront is a high-end shoe store. From high crimes to high heels, go figure.

The Mafia's social clubs weren't located just in Little Italy. Gotti also frequented the Bergin Hunt and Fish Club in Ozone Park, Queens, which today houses a medical supply store and pet grooming salon.

The Genovese gang boss, Vincent "the Chin" Gigante, also known as "The Oddfather," for his propensity to walk around the streets in his bathrobe feigning mental illness, hung out in the Triangle Civic Improvement Association on Sullivan Street in Greenwich Village.

Back in the day, the Mafia bosses conducted their business in these "social clubs." It was where the bosses met with their capos and underbosses to plan operations and make deals. When business was finished, they hung out, played cards, drank wine, and gossiped. It wasn't unusual to see NYPD detectives or FBI agents sitting in cars outside the clubs taking pictures of everyone who went in or came out.

The cops and the FBI probably ran out of film when 200 members of the Gambino crime family came to the Ravenite Social Club on Christmas Eve 1985 to pay their respects to John Gotti, the new head of the family. Just days earlier Gotti had masterminded the assassination of the prior boss, Big Paul Castellano, outside of Sparks Steakhouse.

The attention the cops and the FBI were giving to the social clubs should have been a tip-off to the bosses that their clubs weren't as secure as they thought. It was a lesson John Gotti learned the hard way when a bug planted by the FBI recorded his conversations in the room on the second floor of the Ravenite Social Club. The tapes played a key role in sending him to prison for life.

I heard the current crew of Mafia bosses are more careful about what they say and where they say it. Still, business must be conducted somewhere, and that's why some of the old-style clubs still exist. But now the places are swept electronically for bugs on a regular basis.

Truthfully, I would have preferred meeting Little Tony in my office, but I understood why he wanted to meet at the Bocci Club. He didn't know me from a hole in the wall, so he wanted to meet on his turf where he was safe. I wasn't worried about my own safety because Little Tony had no reason to kill me, at least not yet. To be honest, the idea of going into a mob hangout excited me. Maybe I watched the Godfather movies too many times, or God forbid, I was becoming like Joey Bats.

Tommy didn't share my enthusiasm about the meeting, and he certainly didn't want me going to the Bocci Club. But he wasn't going to change my mind, and I needed to meet Gracie at Ecco. So I ended our meeting by getting up and walking out of the office while Tommy was still talking. After all these years, Tommy has become accustomed to my rudeness and doesn't make an issue of it, although I have caught him giving me the finger behind my back a number of times.

CHAPTER 7

It took about ten to fifteen minutes to walk from my office to Ecco on Chambers Street, and I was already ten minutes late. I would have taken a taxicab, but it was rush hour which meant taxicabs were at a premium. Even if by some miracle I found one, with all the traffic, the trip would have taken twice as long as walking. I just had to walk fast and hope for the best.

With Little Tony Savino's case up for discussion, the last thing I needed was for Gracie to be in a bad mood, and me being late wasn't going to put her in a good mood. Even in a good mood, she wouldn't be happy about me going to the Bocci Club, and I had no doubt she'd tell me not to go. But I had made up my mind to go, and nothing Gracie could say was going to change that.

Back in my drinking days, none of this would have been a problem. I'd have just walked in late, copped an attitude, downed a couple glasses of scotch, and told Gracie to mind her own damn business. Now you know why we broke up back then. It only took me a decade to figure it out myself.

But I was sober now, so I hoped Gracie had already ordered a glass of wine and had mellowed enough not to make an issue of me being late. Better we start off on the right foot.

Walking as quickly as I could, I managed to arrive only twenty minutes late.

Ecco had become one of my favorite Italian restaurants, and other than her sushi restaurants, it was one of Gracie's favorites as well. It is absolutely old-style Italian from its classic storefront entrance to its tile floors, its mahogany mirrored walls, and its small tables, it screams Italian. The Italian doesn't stop with the decor; the food is truly old country style Italian. It's what my mother would have cooked if she had been Italian, and she could cook. I love my dearly departed mother with my whole heart and soul, but as saintly as she was, she couldn't cook worth a damn.

But back to Ecco and Gracie. Walking through the front door, I saw Gracie seated in one of the small booths sipping a glass of wine, so maybe me being late wasn't going to be an issue. I hoped not because I was hungry and arguing with Gracie tends to ruin my appetite.

Things started off well enough with small talk about how our day had gone. Then after our appetizers arrived, Gracie dove right into the deep end and asked what I had decided to do about Little Tony's case. I said that I hadn't made up my mind yet, but I was going to meet with Little Tony, after which I'd make my decision. I didn't mention that the meeting was at the Bocci Club or that the Russian mob was involved. I was hoping to get at least halfway through my penne arrabiata before we got into the main event.

Gracie's smart, and she can read me like a book. The antipasto plates were barely off the table when she asked me when and where I was meeting with Little Tony. The remainder of the meal didn't go well at all. It started downhill when I told Gracie that I was meeting Little Tony at the Bocci Club. Then after I mentioned the Russian mob could be involved, the conversation went completely off the rails.

After arguing about it for half the meal, I said that I was going to the meeting, and that was it. From that point on, Gracie refused to talk to me which was fine because we hadn't even started arguing over the Russian involvement.

Gracie still wasn't talking to me when we got back to her place, so when she went off to the bedroom, I knew enough not to follow her. Instead I went into the den to watch a little television, but I was too distracted. I couldn't help but wonder why Little Tony wanted me to represent him.

When you represent a Mafia made man, you run the risk of pissing him off and getting yourself killed. In this case, there was the additional risk of pissing off the Russian mob which could also get me killed. I couldn't recall another time in my life when I had to worry about so many people wanting me dead. Maybe during my drinking days, but back then I didn't take things seriously. I call that period of my life my bulletproof days because I thought nothing could take me down. Nothing except myself as it turned out, but that's another story.

As I sat there alone in the den, I began to think maybe Gracie and Tommy were right. Did I really want to get involved in a case that could get me killed two ways? I'd done some stupid things in my life, mostly when I was drinking, but screwing around with the Russian mob and the Mafia at the same time might top the list.

On the other hand, $100,000 or more was on the line, and that much money doesn't come along very often. I've always said money wasn't important to me, and it hasn't been, but you reach a certain age and you realize you can't work forever. What then? Gracie says I shouldn't worry because she has a pension, but I can't live off her. Call it pride; call it what you want; I just couldn't do it. So it's either accumulate some retirement money, or work until I drop or burn out.

When I get myself all twisted up like that, I call my AA sponsor, Doug. That night we spoke for an hour. As usual, Doug was no help at all; he wouldn't tell me what to do. Doug never tells me what to do; he simply keeps asking me questions until he has me pointed in the right direction. That's what he did that night.

One of Doug's favorite questions is, do you want to be right or do you want to be happy? Sometimes you can't be both. Choose your battles and avoid overkill. Simple advice, not always easy to follow, but usually effective.

After talking to Doug, I went into the bedroom and had a long talk with Gracie. I tried to explain why the case was important to me, and while I valued her opinion, the decision was mine.

Donald L'Abbate

I thought it had gone well until Gracie tossed me my pillow which meant I'd be spending the night on the couch.

CHAPTER 8

The next morning Gracie was talking to me, but in a tone of voice that wasn't exactly warm or even friendly. It was more a "matter of fact" tone, if you get my drift. But it was better than the cold silent treatment of the night before. The situation was improving, but that could quickly change if I took on Little Tony's case. I still hadn't made up my mind, but I was definitely leaning in that direction.

I had a sentencing hearing that morning that left me little time to think about Little Tony. The sentencing was before Judge Paul O'Donnell, better known at the bar as "Hang 'em high Paul." O'Donnell is old school; he believes the criminals, not society, are responsible for the crimes they commit, and he has no problem sentencing violent felons to maximum sentences. Most criminal defense lawyers hope to avoid his courtroom, but cases are randomly assigned by the computer, so it's simply the luck of the draw.

For my client, Fabian "Demente" Flores, it was really bad luck. Demente, as he insisted I call him, was a member of the notorious MS-13 gang and had been charged with murdering two men with a machete in a midtown parking garage during an argument over a parking space. According to the medical examiner's report, Flores wasn't content with simply killing the two men; he had chopped up their bodies while they were still alive. The district attorney deemed that to be a "cruel and wanton" act, raising the charge to first degree murder with a potential sentence of life in prison.

There were four eyewitnesses to the crime that made the case a slam dunk for the district attorney and left me no room to negotiate a plea deal. But as the case progressed, three of the eyewitnesses suddenly developed amnesia and refused to testify. I think their reluctance to testify resulted in no small part from the press coverage that the case was receiving. The brutality of the crime had drawn national media coverage, with many of the stories describing in detail the ruthless, violent, and often inhumane behavior of the MS-13 gang. The stories were enough to scare even the bravest witness, so I couldn't blame any of them for refusing to testify.

With only one witness left, the prosecution was forced to offer a plea deal which I advised Demente to accept. But he refused, believing the last witness would eventually fold. But the stars were aligned against Demente.

The prosecution's final witness was the uncle of a girl savagely raped by a half dozen of Demente's fellow gang members, and nothing in the world was going to keep him from testifying against Demente. Faced with that reality, Demente finally, although reluctantly, agreed to a plea deal and pleaded guilty to two counts of first degree manslaughter, a class B violent felony, with a maximum sentence of twenty-five years in prison. It was no bargain, but it beat a life without parole sentence.

Demente Flores was a career felon with a long record, so it wasn't surprising that the Probation Department report contained nothing that I could even remotely argue warranted a mitigation of the sentence. Demente's situation wasn't helped by his tattoos, particularly the facial tattoos, identifying him as a MS-13 member having more than a passing familiarity with murder.

If there are two things that Hang 'em high Paul hates, they are gang members and defendants with facial tattoos. Demente was starting off in the hole, and his normally belligerent attitude wasn't likely to improve his situation. Everything about the man was screaming, "lock me up forever."

There wasn't anything I could do to change things, and frankly, I didn't want to change anything. The moment I looked into Flores' dead eyes, I knew he was a psychopathic killer. I had seen enough of those dead eyes to know a psychopath when I saw one, and Flores was definitely a psychopath who had likely killed before and would kill again if he wasn't put away. I mean, the guy had chopped up two human beings in a dispute over a parking space. I didn't see him as likely rehabilitation material.

But I had a job to do, and I did it. I had gotten Demente the best possible deal under the circumstances. Had the sentencing been before a more lenient judge than Hang 'em high Paul, maybe Demente might have gotten off with fifteen years. That is, if he was really lucky. But he wasn't lucky, and his sentencing was before Hang 'em high Paul, so I was sure Demente was going away for the max.

I was good with that, but I was worried that with everything Demente had going against him, the judge might overstep his bounds when sentencing him. Since Demente was being sentenced on two counts of murder, the judge could order him to serve the sentences consecutively, which would mean one after the other for a total of fifty years. But that would be grounds for an appeal, and the last thing I wanted to do was deal with Demente during the appeal process, or even worse, having to go through the whole process all over again if the appellate court threw out the conviction.

When the court officers brought Demente into the courtroom, he sat down next to me without saying a word. He pushed his chair back so he could slouch down, and then he stuck his legs straight out and spread apart, all the time glaring at Judge O'Donnell. It was Demente's childish way of showing disrespect for the proceedings and for the judge. Judge O'Donnell wasn't going to take any crap from a punk like Demente, so he glared back, shaking his head and smiling, knowing he would soon have the last laugh.

The judge asked if I had anything to say before he pronounced sentence. I said that I did and proceeded to offer what little I could to mitigate the sentence, knowing it was all bullshit and to no avail. The judge was good enough not to laugh out loud at my comments. When I was done, the judge asked Demente if he had anything he wanted to add. Without standing, and while staring at the judge, Demente spat on the floor.

Demente was waiting for what in his twisted mind he thought would be his moment of glory. It would be the moment everyone would know what would happen to them if they disrespected Demente.

It was the distorted thinking of a psychopath who had hacked up his two victims because in his words, "they had disrespected him." In his sick twisted mind, it had been all about honor, and he was proud of what he had done. He sat waiting for the judge to talk about his crime and to give the gruesome details. That would be Demente Flores' moment of glory.

But Judge O'Donnell was two steps ahead of the demented one, and without a word said about the crime, he sentenced Demente to the maximum of twenty-five years in prison on each count. But much to my relief, he ordered the sentences be served concurrently.

Demente, furious over not having had his moment of glory, was dragged shackled and screaming from the courtroom while Judge O'Donnell looked on, smiling. In all the commotion, I don't think Demente heard me say, "Goodbye, see you in twenty-five years."

Actually, I doubt he'll make it out at all. He's the type that will kill or be killed in prison, so either way he'll never leave the place alive. Bad news for Demente, but good news for the rest of us.

As I packed up my papers and prepared to leave the courtroom, I glanced up at Judge O'Donnell, and we nodded to each other. Justice had been served.

CHAPTER 9

At three o'clock I met Joey Bats on the corner of Baxter and Canal Streets. Joey was wearing one of those velour warm-up outfits that were all the rage among the mob boys two decades ago. Apparently, Joey hadn't gotten the memo that warm-up suits were out. But it didn't matter because he was just the delivery boy.

As we walked north on Baxter Street toward the Bocci Club on Hester Street, I asked Joey who'd be at the meeting. Joey said that was confidential information, so he couldn't say. Of course, that didn't make sense since I was going to the meeting. But I didn't say anything because I realized Joey had no idea who'd be there. He wasn't high enough up in the ranks to be told, so rather than embarrass him, I just kept my mouth shut.

The Bocci Club is located on the south side of Hester Street between Baxter and Mulberry Streets. The front window is painted black so it's impossible to see inside. The glass paneled front door had been replaced with a solid metal door. The only marking identifying the premises was a small plaque on the door that read "BOCCI CLUB - PRIVATE - MEMBERS ONLY." Joey used an intercom and speaker box mounted on the wall next to the door to get us admitted.

Inside there was a bar along the right wall and six or seven tables scattered around the remainder of the room. Seated at the tables were nine or ten guys, some playing cards, others just bullshitting. A couple of the guys looked up when we entered and nodded to Joey. No one said anything.

Joey led me to a door in the back wall. After knocking, he opened the door and motioned me inside. Joey followed me in, closing the door behind him. Three men were sitting at a table. As I approached, they smiled and stood to greet me. I recognized Sally Boy Stagliano from his mug shot that I'd seen recently in the *New York Post*. The *New York Post* regularly published articles about the mob, including the latest available mug shots.

Next to Sally boy was an older man who introduced himself as Big Tony Savino. The last of the three to greet me and shake my hand was Little Tony Savino.

Little Tony was anything but little. Imagine a refrigerator with arms and a head, and you have a pretty good idea of what Little Tony looked like. His nickname, Little Tony, had been given to him when he was a kid to distinguish him from his old man Big Tony Savino. As fate would have it, Little Tony grew to be twice the size of Big Tony, which often led to confusion. So it wasn't unusual to hear someone ask, "Do you mean big Little Tony, or little Big Tony?"

When the introductions were done, Joey Bats was dismissed, leaving me alone with the three made men. I wasn't nervous because these guys had no reason to kill me, at least not yet, and I had promised Gracie I wouldn't give them a reason to do so.

Sally Boy asked if I'd like a coffee or a drink, and after I politely declined, he got down to business. He said Little Tony had gotten himself into a bit of a jam, and he needed a lawyer. Unfortunately, his usual lawyer, Gene Meyers, was unavailable. That last bit of news made me wonder if Gene Meyers was still walking amongst us. Being a full-time mob lawyer was a dangerous occupation. You learned things which, if made public, could put a lot of people in prison. Need I say more?

Sally Boy said he had heard good things about me and that I came highly recommended. I figured I had Joey Bats to thank for that, although I doubted Joey's word carried much weight. Not knowing what Joey told the boys, I said I hadn't yet agreed to take the case; I needed to talk with Little Tony first. Sally Boy didn't seem to take the news well. He looked either puzzled or annoyed. I couldn't tell which, but I was hoping he was puzzled because I sure as hell didn't want to annoy him on our first date.

Sally Boy shook his head and said, "Okay, ask him what you need to ask him."

When neither Sally Boy nor Big Tony moved to leave the room, I said that I needed to talk to Little Tony in private. That look came back on Sally Boy's face, and I started to regret taking the meeting.

I'm not a fighter. I'm a talker, so rather than let Sally Boy stew over whatever it was that was bothering him, I jumped in and explained the finer points of attorney-client privilege. If nothing else, I thought it might put Sally Boy to sleep.

When I finished my little speech, Sally Boy elbowed Big Tony, gave him a nod, and both men left the room. As soon as they were gone, Little Tony said, "I didn't kill those two guys. I messed them up pretty good, but I didn't kill them."

Okay, I hadn't planned on getting there so quickly, but there it was.

Did I believe him? Probably, because he had no reason to lie to me. To cops, he had a reason to lie, but there was no reason to lie to his lawyer. I mean, killing people was what he did for a living. I knew that, and he knew that I knew. So, if Little Tony said he didn't kill the two Russians, he probably didn't. But I still needed the details.

It turned out Little Tony wasn't shy when it came to sharing the details, and he poured out his story in a string of short and almost coherent sentences. Rather than give you a word for word recap and let you figure it all out on your own, I'll give you the cleaned up condensed version. On the instructions of the boss, who I took to be Sally Boy, he had gone to see these two Russians who had horned in on the Ruccis' bookmaking operation in Park Slope.

Two of Rucci's guys sent earlier had come back beaten up, so this time the two jerks had to be taught a lesson. They were tough, but in the end, they were no match for Little Tony. He did as he had been told and taught them a lesson; then he left them unconscious, but alive, in the ruins of what had been their office. That was all he knew about the case.

The story rang true, and it explained all the damning evidence against Little Tony. Of course, it still left Little Tony in a big hole, along with several unanswered questions. Like who shot them in the head, and how did they wind up in the trunk of a car in Manhattan?

If I took the case, I'd need to figure all of it out or at least come up with a story to tell.

When Sally Boy and Big Tony rejoined us, Sally Boy dropped a Manila envelope on the table in front of me. I didn't need him to tell me it contained $100,000 in cash, the retainer I had asked for. It was time to decide. Did I take the envelope and leave, or did I just leave?

Taking the envelope, I shook Little Tony's hand; for better or worse, I was now his lawyer, or as Sally Boy would say, his mouthpiece.

I walked out of the Bocci Club that afternoon $100,000 richer than when I walked in, but I wasn't looking forward to dinner that night with Gracie.

CHAPTER 10

On my way back to the office after my meeting with Little Tony, I passed a gin mill where I used to hang out during my drinking days. Passing it, the thought crossed my mind that a decade ago, if I had $100,000 in cash in my pocket, I'd be in there buying rounds for everybody. Of course, that was a fantasy because a decade ago I had no shot at having even a hundred bucks in my pocket. Still, I could almost envision what it would have been like, and the thought brought a smile to my face.

When I realized what I was thinking, it scared the crap out of me. The fact that I was even momentarily pleased at the thought of being in a gin mill buying drinks wasn't good. It meant my memory of what life was like back then was becoming distorted, and that was the first step on a quick trip back to hell.

There was nothing pleasant about my life when I was drinking and certainly nothing that should trigger fond memories. What was the big deal about a little fond memory, even if it wasn't exactly the truth? I'll tell you. Alcoholism is a funny thing; it's never done with you. Give it the chance, and it will seduce you again.

In the first step, you admit you're powerless over alcohol, and you surrender to the idea that you're an alcoholic. Even though you surrender, alcoholism never surrenders. It comes after you forever, and that's why I need Doug and why I go to meetings. If I forget the horrors I lived through and created when I drank, I'm likely to go back and do it all again. It's a simple little thing, but once you forget your history, you're doomed to repeat it.

I checked the AA meeting schedule I carry with me and found a nearby meeting. You may think that's crazy and that I go overboard with this AA stuff, but unless you're an alcoholic and gone through it, I don't think you can appreciate what being an alcoholic is like. As baffling as it might be to you, it was as baffling to me until I got into the program. Before that, I thought AA was a bunch of crap, just a group of crazy drunks going to meetings. But truth be told, AA saved my life and continues to save my life. I'll die an alcoholic because the disease never goes away, but I'm determined to die sober, and that's why I go to meetings.

After the meeting, I had just enough time, if I hurried, to get to the sushi restaurant early enough for dinner with Gracie. Going to a sushi restaurant was part of my penance for simply thinking about taking on Little Tony's case. Now that I had actually taken the case, God only knew what was going to happen. I might be eating sushi dinners for the rest of my life, or I might be eating alone.

One thing was certain, being late two nights in a row wouldn't make things any easier. Walking quickly, I managed to arrive at the restaurant at the same time as Gracie. Luck was with me, at least that far.

Once seated, Gracie asked how my day had gone. I said, "Well, I have $100,000 in cash in my jacket pocket because I decided to take the Savino case, and if I live through the case, we'll go someplace really nice on vacation. How's that?"

It was the shock and awe approach, and for the moment it seemed to work. Gracie was speechless.

Then after a long pause, she simply said, "You're not kidding, are you?"

I confessed that I wasn't kidding and waited for Gracie's reaction. I thought for sure she'd argue with me, but she didn't say a word. She hadn't given me her approval, but she hadn't taken issue with my decision, so we were apparently in what I call the thaw stage of our argument. That's the stage where I can return to the bed, but there'd be no sex.

Later that night as I lay in bed, something dawned on me. I realized that in the past I had only taken on private clients when I felt I could help someone. There was always a fee involved, but it was never the reason I took the case. This time it was different; I was taking the case strictly for the money. Maybe that had something to do with those dangerous feelings I got when I passed the gin mill earlier that day.

But it was done; I had taken the case, so there was no sense dwelling on it. I'd just have to be careful, not only for my physical well-being but my sobriety as well.

Maybe I was worrying for nothing. I had Doug and *The Big Book*, and now that I was a mob lawyer, I could always get a gun. No, getting a gun would only give me something else to worry about.

CHAPTER 11

The next day I was in the courthouse having just filed my Notice of Appearance in Little Tony's case when I saw Gene Meyers in the hallway. Obviously, Gene was alive and kicking, and still working, so why wasn't he representing Little Tony Savino, and more importantly, why was I hired to represent him?

They were nagging questions, and they had me wondering if I'd made a mistake in taking the case. Maybe I had acted too rashly, or maybe the money had blinded me to what was really going on. But it was too late to worry about it now; I had taken the money, filed my Notice of Appearance, and there was no turning back now.

I knew Meyers in a passing way, but not well enough to walk up and ask why he wasn't representing Little Tony. For the time being, I'd have to look elsewhere for an answer. I wasn't sure where, but the question needed answering. Like I said, I'm not one to look a gift horse in the mouth, but when something comes along too easily, there's usually a catch to it, and I was sensing there might be a catch to this one.

There were only two reasons why Meyers wouldn't be handling Little Tony's case; either Meyers turned it down, or Rucci didn't want him to have it. I couldn't see Meyers having much of a choice in the matter, so that meant Rucci didn't want Meyers handling the case. But why? And why hand it to me?

I was sensing trouble, and trouble with the Rucci mob was the last thing I needed. I doubted my buddy, Joey Bats, knew anything more than I did, but not knowing where else to turn, I gave Joey a call.

Joey is a fringe player in the Stagliano crew, not a "made man" in the Rucci mob. Joey is a tough guy, but I doubted he ever killed anybody. He'd earned his nickname Bats because he had beaten a couple of people with his Louisville slugger, but I suspect that was a far as it went.

At one time, Joey carried a gun which is how I came to know him when the cops found it in his car. But the cops kept the gun, and as far as I knew, he never replaced it. When I was representing him on the gun charge, he admitted that he had never even shot the thing. He carried it simply to look cool and impress women. Never having seen Joey in the company of a woman, I don't think that strategy worked out too well for him.

As I suspected, Joey was no help. All he knew was that Sally Boy had asked him if he knew any lawyers, and he had given Sally Boy my name. Joey had no idea why Gene Meyers wasn't representing Little Tony.

Rather than ask Tommy to check it out and face another argument over me taking the case, I dropped in on Marty Bowman at the District Attorney's Office, hoping he might have some information he was willing to share. Marty had recently been promoted to Chief of the Rackets Bureau which investigated organized crime groups.

The Savino case was a simple murder case, so it wouldn't be in his bureau's jurisdiction, but Marty might know what was going on inside the Rucci mob. If he had any information that he was willing to share, it would probably cost me a lunch to get it.

Marty Bowman and I have a history together. We've crossed swords numerous times, and I've come out on top most of those times. But Marty's a decent guy, and I respect him, so we get along well. That doesn't mean there weren't times when we wanted to kill each other. Figuratively, of course, not literally.

Now with Marty heading up the Rackets Bureau, our days of dueling are probably over. Most of my 18B clients aren't smart enough to do anything that warrants the attention of the Rackets Bureau, so the likelihood of Marty and I facing off in court are slim. I was hoping the thought of never seeing me again in court would make him happy or at least put him in a good mood.

I found Marty at his desk in his new office which was about three times the size of his old office, and it had windows. In the District Attorney's Office, you know you're moving up in the world when your office has windows, and Marty's office now had two windows. Gracie's office also has two windows, but her windows overlook Columbus Park, while Marty's overlook Hogan Place. Marty may have been on the rise, but Gracie was still ahead of him.

Surprised that I had managed to get past his secretary in one piece, Marty smiled and asked what I wanted. It wasn't the warmest or friendliest of welcomes, but it beat him calling for security.

Sizing up the situation, I decided a little small talk would be best before asking a favor. So I lied and said that I had stopped by to congratulate him on his promotion. Marty's no fool, and I could tell from the look on his face that he wasn't buying my bullshit. But he was courteous enough not to call me on it.

With the pleasantries out of the way, I asked what was going on with the Rucci mob. Of course, Marty wanted to know why I was suddenly interested in organized crime. I explained that I had been hired to represent Little Tony Savino, and I couldn't figure out why I was chosen over Gene Meyers.

Marty, never at a loss for a smart-ass comment, said, "Now that you've become a mob lawyer, I would have thought you'd know that."

I wanted to hit back with a smart-ass comment of my own, but I didn't want to antagonize Marty since I still needed his help. Besides, to be honest, I couldn't think of one, so instead I said, "I'm only a junior mob lawyer, and the bosses don't tell me anything."

Marty laughed; then he started to stare at the ceiling. Staring at the ceiling was something Marty did often. It was a signal that he was thinking. I don't know if it helped him think, but I've learned it's best not to interrupt the process, so I just sat and waited. Finally, after what seemed like forever, he said that he didn't want to talk in the office, but if I met him at the Whiskey Tavern on Baxter Street at six o'clock, he had a story he thought would interest me.

I couldn't tell if Marty had information to share, or he was setting me up to buy drinks, but either way, I'd be there at six o'clock.

CHAPTER 12

After leaving Marty's office I dropped in on Gracie. I wasn't eager to see her, but my instincts told me I'd be in trouble if she found out I had been in the building and hadn't stopped by her office. With things between us slowly getting back to normal, I wasn't about to add fuel to what I hoped was a dying fire.

It had been two days since our argument, and we were still in the thaw stage of things. As I mentioned before, that's the stage where we're being mostly civil, and I'm allowed back into our bed, but I have to stay on my side.

It's the stage that has me completely baffled. The only thing I know to do is to offer to eat sushi without the expectation of sex afterward. I'm very uncomfortable when we get to this point. I do better when Gracie's giving me the silent treatment because then I can justify my own anger and act stupidly. I know doing that is wrong, but I do it anyway. Doug tells me that I'm childish when I do that. But I don't care. Actually, I shouldn't say that because I do care. As much as I hate to admit it, it hurts when Gracie won't talk to me. I've shared my feelings at AA meetings, and it's helped me get over the pain and the anger. What I've learned is that sometimes love hurts, but if it's the right love, it's worth it. Gracie is worth the pain, but I'm not a masochist, and I don't like it, so sometimes I rebel.

Gracie was busy preparing for a staff meeting, but she said that she had time for a quick cup of coffee. That I understood, and it was good. It was Gracie's way of letting me know that things between us were improving. That's how Gracie operates. She doesn't always say what's on her mind, but she sends signals, or at least I think she's sending signals. I might be reading too much into what Gracie does, but after all these years, I don't think I am.

Maybe that's something all women do. Sending signals, that is. I don't know because I haven't had a close enough relationship with any woman other than Gracie. My mother doesn't count, but she did send signals. When she put her hand on the top of her head and gave me that evil eye look, it was time to run for my life. Unfortunately, Gracie's signals are not as obvious as were my mother's signals. Most times I find Gracie's signals confusing which explains how I wind up in trouble.

I admit that I don't understand women, but it might not be my fault. Allow me to explain. Not long ago Gracie forced me to attend an off Broadway production of *My Fair Lady,* the musical based on George Bernard Shaw's novel, *Pygmalion.* I enjoyed the show, and I found one particular tune very insightful. The song is, *"A Hymn to Him, Why Can't a Woman Be More Like a Man?"*

It's a simple question, the answer to which could end the age-old battle of the sexes. Obviously, it doesn't mean anatomically; it means simply that if women thought and acted like men, we'd understand them better, and life would be a lot easier for all of us. I admit that I haven't thought through all of the consequences, and perhaps I should before I make such a wish.

Anyway, Gracie and I had a cup of coffee, and I explained why I was in the building and the dilemma I was having with the Savino case. To her credit, she didn't start rehashing our old argument. Instead, she said that she'd poke around and see if she could come up with anything on the Rucci mob. Even though she said that she was unlikely to learn anything more than Marty knew, I was still grateful for the offer. I wasn't counting on Marty telling me anything useful.

Marty was a good guy, but he played things close to the vest which I couldn't blame him for doing. If I was in his shoes, I'd play it close to the vest too. I was hoping the information he was willing to share would shed some light on the situation, but I didn't expect it to explain away everything. I needed another source which meant I'd have to call Tommy.

Figuring I'd be in for another argument with him, and not relishing the prospect, I decided to wait until after my meeting with Marty. Maybe Marty would surprise me by telling me everything I wanted to know. I didn't believe that, but hope springs eternal, especially if it meant I didn't have to argue with Tommy.

It was just past noon, and I invited Gracie for an alfresco lunch. She knew that meant Sabrett hot dogs under the umbrella, but she declined. She said that she and her staff were having lunch in. I think that was just a dodge to avoid the hot dog stand. But it was fine; I didn't need company to enjoy my hot dogs. So, we made plans to meet for dinner that evening, and of course, it was sushi. I still wasn't completely out of the doghouse, but that was okay; the door was open, and I was mostly out. The situation was definitely improving, and I went off happily to enjoy my lunch in the park.

With nothing on my schedule until my meeting later that evening with Marty, I thought that I'd have a nice leisurely lunch followed by a quiet afternoon, but boy, was I wrong!

CHAPTER 13

I had taken my two hot dogs and my Dr. Brown's Cream Soda to a bench in Thomas Paine Park across from the courthouse, intending to have a quiet lunch. I had barely taken the first bite of my hot dog when a very large man sat down next to me and said hello. I knew immediately it was trouble. In the first place, New Yorkers don't just walk up to strangers and say hello. In the second place, he said hello with what sounded to me like a Russian accent.

Hoping it was merely a coincidence that a large Russian man had taken a seat next to me on a park bench, I smiled and said hello. My new friend said nothing; he simply sat next to me while I ate my lunch.

When I was done and stood to leave, the man said, "Sit down, counselor. We must talk."

The accent was definitely Russian, so I had a damn good idea what he wanted to talk about. When I made no move to sit, he pulled open his jacket, just enough to reveal a large gun. The gun didn't bother me because I knew he wouldn't use it, at least not there in the park. It was crowded, and it was just around the corner from One

Police Plaza and across from the Federal Building, so there were lots of law enforcement types in the crowd.

I had a choice. I could sit and find out what he wanted or leave and run the risk of him cornering me in a more private location. Most likely a location where he wouldn't be inhibited in using his gun. Weighing the choices, I sat back down.

Looking squarely into my eyes, he asked simply if Little Tony was guilty. Getting right to the point is a quality I admire, but not necessarily in someone carrying a gun. Rather than mentioning client confidentiality, which I was pretty sure my new friend didn't care about, I said that I didn't know. Apparently that wasn't the answer he was looking for because his eyes grew dark, and he repeated the question.

For the life of me, I couldn't figure out what the hell this inquisition was all about. Why were the Russians asking me if Little Tony was guilty? They should have been able to figure that out on their own.

Maybe I was in this deeper than I thought. Maybe I should have listened to Tommy and Gracie. But I hadn't, and here I was in Thomas Paine Park sitting next to a large Russian man with a gun asking me a question I couldn't answer. Being a mob lawyer wasn't all it was cracked up to be.

I was under no obligation to tell the truth and would have happily lied, but I didn't know what answer would make my Russian friend happy. If not happy, at least satisfied enough to leave me alone. I tried answering again, this time saying I wasn't sure. The Russian just shook his head, so that wasn't the answer he was looking for. Rather than chance another wrong answer and risk getting disqualified from whatever game we were playing, I stood up and walked away.

The Russian didn't bother to follow me, which was good, but not knowing why he was asking me the question in the first place was still bad. If I didn't think it might get me killed, I'd have given the $100,000 retainer back to Sally Boy and called it a day. But knowing what I already knew from talking with Little Tony, I didn't think the boys would let me off the hook that easily. Besides, the further I got from the park, the calmer I felt and the less willing I was to give back the cash.

By the time I reached my office, I had convinced myself the whole incident was nothing more than a meaningless encounter. So what if the Russians wanted to know if Little Tony was guilty? They'd find out soon enough when we reached a plea deal or went to trial.

Even though I'd convinced myself there was nothing to worry about, I thought it best not to mention the encounter to Gracie.

CHAPTER 14

The Whiskey Tavern was apparently the new after court hangout for local lawyers. It was one of the few downtown bars I wasn't familiar with, only because it opened a couple of years after I got sober.

I love anything with New York City style, and the Whiskey Tavern has it in spades. It's everything a New York City bar should be and more. It was dark, loud, and down to earth. Nothing about it was pretentious. It was a simple old-fashioned gin mill. If I was still drinking, it would definitely be my hangout. At least until I wore out my welcome which happened a lot when I was drinking.

Walking past the crowded bar, I spotted Marty sitting at a small table in the back corner. He waved, lifting his empty beer glass. Passing the barmaid on my way to the table, I asked her for club soda and a refill for Marty.

The table was small which was good because with all the noise, we needed to be close to hear each other. The noise also made it impossible for anyone to eavesdrop on our conversation, not that anyone had a reason to.

Before long, the barmaid arrived with our drinks, and Marty started telling me what he knew about the Rucci mob. The Ruccis had been under heavy surveillance by the District Attorney's Office and the NYPD for months after rumors surfaced that there was dissension in the ranks, and there could be a change in leadership. Silvio Rucci, the last of the old-time mafioso, was still head of the family, but he was considered by many to be a dinosaur, and rumors had it that he was getting senile. That was supposedly why his two oldest sons, Junior and Jimmy, were trying to take over control of the family.

The NYPD and the District Attorney's Office weren't particularly concerned about the internal problems that the Ruccis were having. If the Ruccis wanted to kill each other, the DA and NYPD were fine with that. It was a possible war between the Ruccis and the Russian mob that had them worried. Recently the Russians had taken advantage of the turmoil to move in on Rucci territory in Brooklyn. The Ruccis had retaliated, and Marty's people believed a full-scale mob war could be brewing.

When I asked Marty if the recent retaliation was the murder of the two Russian mobsters, he laughed and said maybe I was actually a mob lawyer. According to a NYPD confidential informer, the killings had brought the tension level between the two mobs to the boiling point. But then for some reason, the situation cooled off. No one knew if the cooling off was because an accord had been reached, or if it was simply a temporary lull in hostilities.

Marty once again pointed to his empty glass and said there was more to the story. I ordered another beer for Marty and waited.

In addition to the rift between old man Rucci and his sons, there seemed to be something amiss between the three brothers. No one knew for certain what it was, but they believed it involved Willie Rucci, the youngest of the brothers, nicknamed the Worm. What they had heard from their confidential informants was that Willie the Worm was in deep shit with his two older brothers. There had even been rumors that Willie might get whacked, but nobody would say why. It seemed that as of late, a lid had been put on the situation, and no one, not even the confidential informants, were talking.

Marty didn't know why there had been this sudden lockdown on information, and he didn't seem to care. As he put it, so long as there was no gang war between the Russians and the Mafia, no one on his staff or with the NYPD was going to lose sleep if Willie got whacked by his brothers.

As for the murder of the two Russians, all Marty knew was that the case was being handled by Sarah Washington's group. He'd heard it was a slam dunk on the forensic evidence, and Sarah was expecting an early plea deal. Marty had no idea why Gene Meyers wasn't handling the case. I think he liked the idea that I had the case, figuring I was headed for a beatdown.

I signaled the barmaid for another round, hoping Marty had more to tell, but all I got for my effort was a bigger bar bill. Marty was done talking business. Either he didn't know anything more about the Ruccis, or if he did know more, he wasn't going to tell me what else he knew.

After dropping $55 on the bar, all I learned was that the Rucci mob was in chaos, and Willie the Worm might be on his brothers' hit list. On the surface, none of that seemed relevant to Little Tony's case, but my gut was telling me otherwise. If, as Little Tony claimed, he hadn't killed the two Russians, then who had? This wasn't a random killing, and the only people with a motive to kill the Russians were members of the Rucci mob. Maybe Willie the Worm had done the murders, and that's why he was on his brothers' shit list. Why after the murders did things calm down between the Russians and the Ruccis? I just couldn't fit it all together. I needed more information, and I wasn't going to get it from Marty Bowman.

Leaving the bar, I called Tommy Shoo. I asked him to find out what he could about the Rucci family feud and what was going on with Willie the Worm. I specifically didn't mention my encounter with the Russian that afternoon, and I didn't ask him to investigate the Ruccis' dispute with the Russian mob because I didn't want him anywhere near the Russians. A couple of years earlier, I got Tommy involved in a drug case that I was handling, and he wound up being shot. I vowed at the time never to put the kid in harm's way again, so I wasn't going to let him get anywhere near the Russian mob.

I was still thinking the encounter in the park was essentially meaningless, but not being able to put all the pieces together bothered me. Why was there a lull in the hostilities between the Russians and the Italians? If they struck a deal over the killing of the two Russians, why would the Russians care if Little Tony was guilty? A deal was a deal.

If there was no deal, then why question me about Little Tony's guilt? The Russians wouldn't be troubled if they killed Little Tony, and it turned out he wasn't the killer. They weren't known for having a conscience. If they killed the wrong person, they'd just keep killing people until they got the right one. Hopefully, I wouldn't be representing anyone else on the list.

CHAPTER 15

The next morning when I arrived at the office, Connie handed me a message. Sarah Washington had called and wanted me to call her back. Since I didn't have any pending cases with Sarah at the time, I was guessing it had something to do with the Savino case. Marty had probably mentioned his meeting with me to Sarah, and now Sarah was curious as to why I was representing a Rucci mob member.

Sarah Washington is a senior deputy district attorney who I've known and worked with over the years. She's a top-notch prosecutor, smart, savvy, and tough. We first met when Sarah was a rookie assistant district attorney, and I was new to sobriety. Both of us were feeling our way, me learning to live soberly and her learning to be a prosecutor. Maybe that was why we took a liking to each other. Whatever it was, we became friends and have worked together on dozens of cases since.

Don't get the wrong idea; Sarah is a straight shooter all the way and would never cut me a break that I didn't deserve. Still, it doesn't hurt to have the ear of a friendly prosecutor.

As I suspected, Sarah was calling about Little Tony's case. As deputy chief of the Trial Division, Sarah wasn't handling the case personally; that job fell to one of her underlings. But she had gotten word that I had filed a Notice of Appearance in the case and wanted to let me know the case was going to the Grand Jury the next day.

I laughed, knowing that wasn't why she had called. I had already gotten notice of the Grand Jury hearing, and besides, assistant district attorneys don't call defense attorneys to tell them such things; even when the ADA and the defense attorney are friends.

Hearing my laugh, Sarah knew she'd been called out, and she tried a new tack. She said since Gene Meyers always represented the Ruccis, she wanted to make sure there hadn't been a screwup in the Clerk's Office. That probably wasn't true either, but I let her off the hook, assuring her there had been no screwup, and I was indeed representing Mr. Anthony Savino, the younger. Sarah was kind enough not to ask why, and I was smart enough not to volunteer any further information.

That could have been the end of the call, but hoping to get something more out of it, I asked Sarah what evidence she had on the case. Technically she wasn't required to tell me anything, and most prosecutors wouldn't give up that information until forced to do so. But Sarah isn't like most prosecutors; she's fair and open-minded. Knowing I'd be filing a Brady demand that would require her to disclose all the evidence she had against Little Tony anyway, Sarah shared it with me. She said that she had everything from forensic evidence to eyewitnesses.

The eyewitnesses didn't trouble me as much as the forensic evidence, that was unless the eyewitnesses witnessed the murders. Even then eyewitnesses can prove to be unreliable but forensic evidence rarely is.

I asked about the eyewitnesses first, holding my breath and praying they hadn't witnessed the actual murders. Sarah said two witnesses had seen Little Tony enter the office when the two dead Russians were last seen alive at their place of business. Okay, that wasn't good, but it was far from earth shattering. Seeing him entering the victims' office simply put him on the scene, if that. It wasn't as though the witnesses had seen Little Tony roughing up the victims or shooting them. That would have been earth shattering.

Next, she told me about the forensic evidence. The crime scene investigators found Little Tony's fingerprints all over the office where the two Russians were presumably killed, and all over the car in which their bodies were found. Again, troubling but still explainable.

Also explainable, but more troubling, was Little Tony's skin under the victims' fingernails. To that point, everything Sarah mentioned I already knew from my lunch with Detective Chen. But then she told me something I didn't know. Sarah expected ballistic reports would match the slugs that killed the two Russians to the gun Little Tony was carrying when arrested. That I wasn't prepared for. Little Tony had failed to mention that he was carrying a gun when arrested. We'd definitely be talking about that the next time I saw him.

I asked if there was anything else, such as statements that Little Tony may have made to the police. I was relieved to hear there was nothing else. Still, Sarah believed she had enough to put Savino away on murder charges.

I didn't agree, but I wasn't about to argue with her. Instead, I asked when I could expect to receive copies of the coroner's report and the forensic reports. Most prosecutors hold on to the reports for as long as possible, but Sarah always gave me copies right away. I was hoping that would hold true in Little Tony's case, and it seemed like it would. Sarah said she'd tell Assistant District Attorney Johnny McAvoy, who was handling the day-to-day details, to send me copies of the reports as soon as they were available.

I hadn't worked with McAvoy before, but I'd heard from other lawyers that he had a real edge to him. He was young, ambitious, and full of himself. Some of the older defense lawyers claimed he was a lot like me back when I was the Golden Boy of the District Attorney's Office. That was before my drinking derailed my career.

The case against Little Tony was strong, but it wasn't a slam dunk. Not unless the slugs from the gun Little Tony was carrying when arrested matched the slugs that killed the two Russians. I'd have to await the ballistic reports, but my gut was telling me there'd be no match. Little Tony knew enough not to carry around a murder weapon. Without the ballistic match, there was plenty of room to argue reasonable doubt. Still, the gun was a problem, mostly because its existence came as a surprise.

As things stood, it was a little unsettling. Normally at that stage of a case, I have a pretty good idea of what's going on and what I'm up against. There might be some outstanding legal issues to resolve, but I usually have a strategy for going forward. But with Little Tony's case, I had more unanswered questions than I had answers, and the list of unanswered questions was growing. Not only did I not know why I was on the case and not Gene Meyers, I didn't know who in the Rucci crew I could trust and who I couldn't.

The only thing worse than unanswered questions are surprises, and now on top of the unanswered questions, I had just been surprised to learn that Little Tony had a gun in his possession when he was arrested. Any lawyer will tell you that unanswered questions and surprises can, and most times, do hurt you, and they can hurt you a lot.

But I had an evidence hearing in another case scheduled for ten o'clock that morning in Supreme Court, so I didn't have time to dwell on the problem.

CHAPTER 16

When I arrived for the evidence hearing, I learned that the assistant district attorney handling the case had a scheduling conflict, and so the hearing was adjourned. Leaving the courtroom, I spotted Gene Meyers sitting on a bench down the hall. I figured it was time that he and I had a little friendly chat. I didn't know the man, so it would be an awkward situation, but I was used to being in awkward situations, most times self-created. When I was drinking, my whole life was an awkward siltation.

Sitting down beside Gene Meyers, I introduced myself. He surprised me by saying he knew who I was, then he asked what I wanted. I knew from the bluntness of his question that our chat wasn't going to be friendly or long.

I can be as blunt as the next guy, so I said that I wanted to know why he wasn't representing Little Tony Savino in the two murder cases. He said that he wasn't asked, and he didn't know why. I believed the first part but not the second part.

If he was asked to handle the case but was unable to do so, he would have helped the Ruccis find another lawyer, and it wouldn't have been me. From that, I could safely conclude he hadn't been asked to handle the case, and I was beginning to think I knew why.

The case against Little Tony was strong but not airtight. Even I could see that, so I had little doubt that Meyers would see things the same way. With his talent and experience, Meyers would certainly be able to find the cracks in the case and put together a decent defense. It might not be good enough for an acquittal, but it would be good enough to warrant a decent plea bargain.

But the Ruccis chose to keep Meyers on the bench, hiring instead someone they believed to be a less experienced and very possibly an incompetent lawyer. The Ruccis would only do that if they wanted Little Tony convicted, not acquitted.

Meyers stood to leave, but before he turned away, I asked if it was a conflict of interest that kept him from representing Little Tony. It was a polite way of asking if the Ruccis expected him to tank the defense if he took the case. Meyers didn't have to answer my question, and for a moment I thought he wasn't going to, but then he smiled and said, "It could be. I always liked Little Tony; give him my best." Maybe the rumors that Meyers didn't have an ethical bone in his body weren't true.

When Meyers wouldn't take the case, the Ruccis probably realized it would be hard finding a lawyer willing to throw a client under the bus. I know a couple of lawyers who have what I'll call marginal ethics, but I doubted even they would go that far. Assuming the Ruccis found a lawyer willing to throw the case, they'd have to wonder if they could trust him. After all, if he was willing to sell out one client for money, why wouldn't he sell out the Ruccis if offered more money?

The next best thing to a corrupt lawyer is an incompetent lawyer or maybe a lawyer with a dubious history. Say, for instance, a lawyer with a history of alcoholism who handled 18B Panel cases. Get the picture?

Now I knew why I was hired, to blow Little Tony's defense. But I believed Little Tony was telling the truth; he hadn't killed the two Russian mobsters, and I intended to give him the best defense possible. To do that, it would help to know who had killed the two Russians. Based on what I learned from Marty the night before, the most likely candidate was Willie "the Worm" Rucci.

Donald L'Abbate

The way I figured it was that Willie had done the deed without permission, and the murders had created a big problem which threatened the long-standing peace between the Ruccis and the Russian mob, the last thing the Ruccis wanted.

A mob war is bad for business, and knowing how vicious the Russians were, it was unlikely that the Ruccis were anxious for a fight, particularly with a family squabble going on. They needed a way out of the jam but finding one wasn't easy.

As Tommy said, the Russians are driven by revenge and don't care about the consequences. As long as the Russians believed the Ruccis were responsible for the murders, they'd want revenge. The Ruccis' only way out was to convince the Russians that they had nothing to do with the murders or offer up the murderer. Convincing the Russians they had nothing to do with the murders was a long shot at best, and I doubted the family was willing to throw Willie under the bus.

The only other possibility that made sense was making Little Tony the fall guy. So they framed Little Tony, hoping a conviction would give the story credibility. But an acquittal would spoil everything, and that was why they needed a lawyer who was willing to throw the case or one too stupid to win it. For whatever reason, the Ruccis thought I was that lawyer. Whether they thought I was stupid, or they could buy me didn't matter because I was neither.

I called Joey Bats and told him I needed to see Little Tony as soon as possible. Joey suggested we meet at the Bocci Club, but I said no, I wanted to see Little Tony in my office. Realizing that not everyone in the Rucci crowd was looking out for Little Tony's interests, I needed to keep things close to the vest until I knew who I could trust, and the only one I trusted at that point was Little Tony. I wasn't sure where Joey Bats stood in all of this, but I'd soon find out.

If Joey wasn't in on the frame-up, he'd pass along my message to Little Tony only. If he was in on the frame-up, he'd pass the message on to the Ruccis as well. I was sure that the Ruccis wouldn't let Little Tony show up for a meeting by himself, and they'd probably demand the meeting be held at the Bocci Club. If Little Tony agreed to come alone to my office, chances were good that the Ruccis wouldn't know about the meeting.

The wild card in all of this was Big Tony. Other than meeting Big Tony at the Bocci Club, all I knew about him was what Detective Chen had told me, and that wasn't much. Still, I found it hard to believe that Big Tony would sell his own son down the river. When Joey called me back, some of my questions would be answered.

CHAPTER 17

An hour later the call came from Joey Bats. He said Little Tony could meet me at my office that afternoon, but he wanted to know if he should tell Sally Boy about the meeting. It was an interesting question full of implications. It probably meant Joey hadn't passed on the message to the Ruccis. If he had, there'd be no meeting at my office. Period. But, more importantly, reading between the lines, the question seemed to be a test much like my message had been. If that was true, then the question hadn't come from Little Tony. More likely it came from his old man, Big Tony.

There was no doubt in my mind that Big Tony was smart because you don't get to be that old in the Mafia if you're not smart. That's why Joey Bats was more likely in need of a cemetery plot rather than a retirement plan.

Not only was Big Tony smart, he was smarter than his son, Joey Bats, and Sally Boy Stagliano combined. If not smarter than the three of them, at least more cunning, and that was just as important in the Mafia.

Assuming Joey had passed on my message to Little Tony alone, which seemed to be a safe bet, then it was Little Tony who passed it on to his father. I had to believe that Big Tony knew something was amiss when he learned Gene Meyers wasn't handling Junior's case. Being kept in the dark, he'd be suspicious and unsure who he could trust. So what would he do? A smart guy like Big Tony would distrust everyone, especially the bosses.

As much as he was a wild card in my deck, I was a wild card in his deck. He couldn't be sure where I fit into the picture, and he had to wonder if I was part of the frame-up. By asking if Sally Boy should come to the meeting, he was trying to find out if I was in Sally Boy's pocket. If I was in Sally Boy's pocket, the answer would be yes. Saying not to bring Sally Boy to the meeting wouldn't prove that I wasn't working for Sally Boy, but it would at least shift the odds in that direction.

But now I had another problem. If Sally Boy and the Ruccis were using me to set up Little Tony to take the fall for a couple of murders he didn't commit, they wouldn't be happy with me working hard to get him off. Plus, if the Ruccis were turning on the Savinos, I might be walking into the middle of a Mafia civil war. Marty Bowman had mentioned the Rucci brothers were fighting each other for control of the family. Maybe Big Tony Savino had picked the wrong side. Or maybe Sally Boy was worried he had picked the wrong side, and Big Tony might replace him at some point.

From what Joey Bats had told me, Little Tony was the best enforcer the Rucci family had, very much like the fictional character Luca Brasi in the book, *The Godfather*. In a civil war, you'd want Little Tony on your side, and if you couldn't get him on your side, you'd want him dead or at least out of the picture. That was one possibility, but I was sure there were more.

There were a lot of pieces to this puzzle, and so far, I hadn't been able to put any of them together. Maybe a private meeting with Little Tony and his old man might help, so I told Joey Bats that he shouldn't bring Sally Boy along, but Big Tony was invited if he wanted to attend. Joey said he'd pass on the message, and he and Little Tony would be in my office at three o'clock that afternoon.

My life was getting more complicated by the minute. I had been a mob lawyer for less than a week, and already my life was in danger.

Donald L'Abbate

First, I get confronted by a Russian mobster, and now I might be in the middle of a Mafia civil war. I could see the headline in the *New York Post*, *MOB LAWYER SHOT DEAD ON MOTT STREET - VICTIM OF THE RUSSIAN MOB OR MAFIA CIVIL WAR*. All for a lousy $100,000. At least if I was killed, I wouldn't have to listen to Gracie telling me she told me so.

CHAPTER 18

By the time Joey Bats and Little Tony showed up, I had convinced myself I was blowing things way out of proportion. I knew that I wasn't, but I needed to think I had in order to keep my head from exploding. I still hadn't decided what to tell Gracie, but I'd worry about that later.

I can't say that I was surprised when Big Tony showed up with Joey and Little Tony. I still wasn't certain where Joey Bats' loyalties lay, and not wanting to take a chance he was Sally Boy's spy, I told him to wait in the reception area. Knowing Joey wouldn't like being left out, I explained it had to do with attorney-client privilege, and while he still looked a little miffed, he didn't argue.

With Joey gone, I turned to Little Tony and got right to the point. I asked why he hadn't told me he was carrying a gun when he was arrested. He said that he always carried a gun, and I should have known that. Okay, I could see his point. I mean, to him, carrying a gun was like wearing underwear; it's something he did all the time, so he saw no reason to mention it.

I said the cops were doing ballistic tests on the slugs retrieved from the two dead Russians and looking to match them to his gun. Little Tony shrugged and said it didn't matter because he hadn't killed the two guys. He had just beat the crap out of them and kneecapped the one guy who had really pissed him off. So, now another surprise, he had kneecapped one of the Russians.

Again, I asked why he hadn't told me about the kneecapping to which he replied simply, "You never asked."

Hoping to avoid further surprises, I asked if he had done anything else to either of the two Russians before, during, or after his visit to their office. Little Tony said no, so I moved on to the matter of the skin under one victim's fingernails and the scratches on Little Tony's neck. When I asked how that happened, Little Tony said one of the guys tried to strangle him but couldn't get his hands around his neck. Looking at Little Tony's neck, I could see why. His neck had to be twenty-two inches around, so anyone trying to strangle him was more likely to scratch him than kill him.

Matching the skin cells to Little Tony didn't prove him guilty of murder. It just proved he had physical contact with the victims. Of course, when you added that to the other circumstantial evidence, you do start building a case for murder. But we'd take it one step at a time. I asked Little Tony if his DNA was on record, and he said it was. His DNA had been taken a couple of years earlier when he was arrested for assault. He was quick to point out that the case never went to court and charges were dropped. I figured that I knew why, but I kept my mouth shut.

The fact that Little Tony's DNA was on record didn't matter. If it hadn't been on record, McAvoy could easily get a court order requiring Little Tony to provide a DNA sample. So, one way or the other Little Tony's DNA was coming into the case.

You might think that requiring someone to provide their DNA violates their Fifth Amendment right against self-incrimination, but you'd be wrong. The United States Supreme Court ruled that the Fifth Amendment applies only to testimonial evidence and not DNA which, like fingerprints, is non-testimonial evidence.

When I asked Little Tony how his fingerprints wound up all over the car in which the bodies were found, he said the car belonged to old man Rucci, and he and Sally Boy used it all the time. In fact, the day after he beat the crap out of the Russians, he and Sally Boy drove the car to Brooklyn to make a couple of deliveries.

With that, I looked over to Big Tony and said that Sally Boy's fingerprints weren't found on the car, just Little Tony's fingerprints. Big Tony nodded, but I couldn't tell from his nod if the news came as a surprise, or he already knew Little Tony was being set up by the Ruccis.

It was a game of cat and mouse, only I didn't know which of us was the cat and which of us was the mouse. I didn't know if I could trust Big Tony, and he didn't know if he could trust me. For all he knew, I was just a flunky lawyer working for the Ruccis. I hoped my little ploy of pointing out the possible frame-up had changed all of that. But even if it had, I still couldn't be sure if I could trust Big Tony. Was Big Tony a part of the frame-up and playing me?

I didn't think asking Big Tony outright if he was in on the plan to frame his son was the smartest way to approach the subject. It was a touchy question to begin with, and even more touchy when you're asking a mafioso. Unless you want to end up dead in an alley, you don't just throw it out there. The subject needed to be broached with finesse which, in case you hadn't noticed, isn't my strong suit. But the circumstances inspired me to do my best.

Addressing both Little and Big Tony, I eased into the subject. I said the district attorney had a lot of evidence, but I thought it could all be explained away. I thought it best to start off with something positive. Then came the loaded question. Did they want me to explore a plea bargain?

It was my way of asking Big Tony if he was willing to let his son take the fall for the murders. With the evidence such as it was, a plea bargain was definitely the best choice. It didn't mean we couldn't do better at trial, but with the odds against us, a plea bargain capped the risk. Big Tony knew it and had probably figured out by then the only reason that I was on the case, and not Gene Meyers, was because the Ruccis thought I was incompetent and couldn't win the case at trial. So, by saying no to a plea bargain, Big Tony would be assuring his son's conviction.

Little Tony looked to his old man which confirmed what I suspected. Both men understood the question, and Big Tony was calling the shots.

After a minute, Big Tony asked, "Can you win this case, counselor?" It was a typical question, but it wasn't asked in the typical way. Big Tony wasn't asking for an evaluation of the evidence; he was asking if I had the balls to take the case to trial and to win it.

I don't usually make predictions because you can never be sure what a jury is going to do, but in this case, I felt like I needed to make an exception. I said so long as the ballistic reports confirmed the slugs that killed the two Russians hadn't come from Little Tony's gun, I thought we could win or at least get the charges substantially reduced on a plea bargain down the road.

Big Tony nodded and said, "No plea bargain, at least not yet. You just go out there and win this case, counselor. Got it?"

Big Tony's answer of "not yet" left me in the dark. It wasn't no, but it wasn't yes either. I had thought my question called for a "yes" or "no" answer, so I hadn't anticipated an inconclusive answer. If that had happened in court, I would have pressed the witness until I got a straight answer. But it wasn't court, and Big Tony wasn't on the witness stand, plus I didn't have a couple of armed court officers standing nearby.

I decided to give it one more try, approaching the question from a different direction. I reminded Big Tony that if I won the case, the Ruccis were likely to kill me. To which Big Tony replied, "If you don't win, and I think you lost on purpose, I'll kill you." He was smiling when he said it, but somehow I didn't believe he was kidding. That led me to believe he wasn't okay with Little Tony being framed.

Then he said something that puzzled me. He said, "There are things going on that you don't know about and don't need to know about now. You just lay low for the time being, and things will work out."

When someone like Big Tony Savino tells you something like that, you don't ask questions, you just listen. I had no idea what he was talking about. I just hoped it meant that I wasn't going to be killed.

That night over dinner, I tried to explain to Gracie what had happened earlier and the possible railroading of Little Tony. I think in the retelling it might have come out sounding a lot worse than it was, although I admit there wasn't much positive in the story to begin with. I did my best to put an optimistic spin on everything, mentioning the big fee several times. But Gracie's constant reminder that I might be killed by the Mafia or by the Russian mob took much of the optimism out of the conversation.

I reminded Gracie that I promised to take her on a very long and expensive vacation when the case was over, assuming I was still alive. She said if I wasn't, she was going anyway. She'd miss me, but she was still going.

I asked if she'd bring another man with her. I was happy when she said, "Don't be silly. I wouldn't bring another man with me."

But my happiness was short-lived when she added, "There'll be lots of single men where I'm going."

I think she was kidding. Actually, I know she was kidding. That was just Gracie's way of punishing me for not listening to her when she said I shouldn't take the case.

CHAPTER 19

Little Tony's case had provided a nice influx of cash which meant I didn't have to hustle to stay in the black. It also meant I could take a little breather and turn down a couple of 18B assignments. But now expecting a lull in Little Tony's case, and with Big Tony telling me to lay low, Connie convinced me to accept a new case the panel had just sent over.

Handing me the assignment email, Connie said it was an interesting case, one I would like. I had just started to read the email when my cell phone rang. Glancing at the caller ID, I saw it was Tommy on the line. Figuring the call was about the Ruccis, I pressed the answer button and handed the assignment email back to Connie, telling her to accept the case. That was my first mistake of the day; unfortunately it wouldn't be my last.

Tommy had been busy checking out the Rucci situation but had come up against a brick wall. Whatever was going on with the family, it was staying with the family, or as Tommy put it, "what happens in Rucciland stays in Rucciland."

In the past, spreading a little cash around had loosened lips, so I suggested Tommy try that approach. He said that he'd considered doing that, but it wasn't going to work this time. Nobody was talking about the Rucci family, and when he said nobody, he meant nobody. He had a couple of solid contacts, low level guys who tried coming off as big shots by running their mouths, but even they weren't talking family business. If those guys weren't talking, clearly the word was out, "talk and you're dead."

Tommy did have one piece of information I found interesting. Linda Chow had been examining the Rucci family's phone records. I didn't want to know how she was able to do that, but what she discovered was intriguing. Over the last couple of weeks, since the two Russians were murdered, one of the Ruccis had made several calls to a burner phone in Brighton Beach, Brooklyn, home of the Russian mob. She couldn't be certain who made the call but based on the pattern of other calls made from the same phone, she suspected the phone belonged to old man Rucci. Of course, Linda had no way of knowing who was on the other end of the line when the calls to Brighton Beach were made. The calls could have been to someone in the Russian mob or to Rucci soldiers spying on the Russians.

I thanked Tommy for the report and told him to keep working his contacts. Maybe something would break somewhere. In the meantime, I took a closer look at the new 18B case. I figured it would take my mind off Little Tony's case.

The first thing that caught my attention were the charges. The defendant was charged with violating Sections 190.83 and 190.85 of the Penal Law Code, both of which had to do with fraud. That made the case unusual because nearly all my 18B Panel cases involved drug dealings, robberies, murders, or other violent crimes. The Penal Law Code sections for those crimes I knew by heart, but I wasn't familiar with the fraud charges.

The defendant's name was Devon Matthews. He was seventeen, lived in one of the city's housing projects in the Two Bridges Section of Lower Manhattan, had no criminal record, and was a full-time student at HSMSE at CCNY. That was a lot of letters, very few of which I was able to decode.

That's another thing that pisses me off. Why have we gotten so lazy that we must reduce everything to acronyms? And what the hell is a "smartphone?" Were my old phones stupid phones? When I got my first so-called smartphone, Connie sent me text messages that I couldn't understand. At first, I thought the phone was broken, then I thought maybe Connie was using some code. No, it was the damn acronyms. When I complained to Connie, she said I had to come into the Twenty-First Century. I said that she had to stop using the acronyms, or she'd be fired.

To be fair, some acronyms I knew. Like I knew CCNY was City College of New York, and given Matthews' age, I assumed the HS stood for high school. As for the MSE, I had no idea what those letters meant. I did know one thing; the kid's pedigree made him a unique client. I could count on one hand the number of times I had an 18B Panel defendant without a criminal record, not to mention being a full-time high school student. As I said, everything about this case was unusual.

Grabbing my copy of the New York Penal Law Code, I quickly learned that Section 190.83 was Unlawful Possession of Personal Identification Information in the First Degree, a class D felony, and Section 190.85 was Unlawful Possession of a Skimmer Device in the Second Degree, a class A misdemeanor.

Obviously, this was some sort of high tech crime which I was definitely not equipped to handle. Identity theft I understood, but as for a skimmer I had no idea what that was, and I was pretty sure I didn't want to know. I called out to Connie and told her to send back the case with my apologies. But it was one of those days when Connie thinks she runs the office, and I work for her.

She walked into my office with that look in her eye. The look that tells me I'm about to have a bad day. Sitting in the chair across from the desk, she said, "You need to handle this case."

There was no reason I had to handle the case but arguing with Connie is like banging your head against a wall; all you get from it is a headache. So instead, I took a different tack. I said I had to turn down the case because I wasn't qualified to handle it. Obviously, the case involved some technical matters with which I had no familiarity at all. Connie just rolled her eyes which meant she wasn't buying it, and I wasn't getting off that easily. She said that she'd help me with the technical stuff, and I could always call on Linda Chow if I needed more help. I hated to admit it, but she had me there.

I could have just ordered Connie to send the case back, and of course, she would have. But then my life in the office would be a living hell for a couple of weeks, and since I was unsure how things stood with Gracie, I wasn't about to open a battle on a second front. Battling with one woman is bad enough but battling with two at the same time is hell, and I wasn't about to go down that road. That's how Devon Matthews became a client.

While I read the Penal Law Code and the arrest report, Connie Googled HSMSE. It turned out to be the High School for Math, Science, and Engineering. Located on The City College of New York's campus on Covenant Avenue in Upper Manhattan, it's open to highly gifted students from across the city who are interested in math, science, or engineering. So how did a gifted student wind up being charged with fraud?

If my instincts about this kid, Devon Matthews, were right, I needed to see him right away. It was Friday morning, and he had been arrested earlier that day, so he was in The Tombs waiting to be arraigned. If he wasn't arraigned that afternoon, he'd spend the weekend in The Tombs or at Rikers Island Jail. If this kid was what he seemed to be on paper, he'd have a tough time surviving in jail, so I didn't want to see him locked up any longer than he had to be. I had Connie draw up my Notice of Appearance and headed to the Criminal Court Building to find Devon Matthews.

CHAPTER 20

After filing my Notice of Appearance, I called in a favor and had the calendar clerk put Devon's case on the afternoon arraignment sheet. Then I ventured down to The Tombs to find Devon. He wasn't hard to find. He was huddled in a corner, obviously terrified and apparently for good reason. He wasn't wearing a jacket or shoes which meant some asshole, or maybe a couple of assholes, had taken them from him. Stripped of anything of value by the animals in the holding cell, he was left alone, trembling in a corner. But his nightmare wasn't necessarily over. If the horde got bored, they might torment the poor kid just for fun.

I know a couple of the corrections officers at The Tombs from AA, and fortunately for Devon, one of them, my buddy, Dave, was working the desk that day. When he learned I was representing Devon, Dave got me an interview room, and he said I could keep Devon there until the calendar call. The corrections officers don't like seeing prisoners being abused, especially when the prisoner is some poor kid who can't defend himself, but unfortunately there's not much they can do about it. With The Tombs chronically overcrowded and undermanned, and nowhere else to put prisoners, all the corrections officers can do is try to keep things peaceful.

When Devon came into the interview room, he was shaking like a leaf. I had him take a seat, then I explained who I was and why I was there. Clearly, this kid wasn't the usual 18B Panel client. But he was still charged with a felony, and I needed to know the whole story before we went to the arraignment. Since Devon was an 18B Panel referral, I assumed he was indigent and couldn't post even minimal bail. So if I was going to keep him out of the system, he'd have to be released on his own recognizance. It was a tall order, but this kid wouldn't survive twenty minutes in Rikers.

Now that he had stopped shaking, I asked Devon what he had done to get arrested. He said that he had used someone's credit card to buy materials he and some of his classmates needed for a science fair competition. I asked him where he had gotten the credit card, and he said that he stole the number using a skimmer. He lost me on that one, so I asked him to explain. He said a skimmer was a device that fits over a legitimate credit or debit card reader and independently records the card's data. It doesn't interfere with the transaction, so the cardholder never knows his information has been compromised. The police found the skimmer in Devon's school locker that morning.

Devon said he placed a skimmer on an ATM on Broad Street in the Financial District, and in three days, he'd collected data on over fifty debit cards and more than twenty credit cards. I asked him where he got the skimmer, and he said that he built it himself. I didn't know whether to be impressed or scared. Was this kid a science whiz, or was it that easy to steal credit card information?

It turned out to be a little of both. Devon was a science whiz, but anyone with a computer could find instructions on the Internet for building a skimmer. He said building the skimmer was easy. The programming and mechanics were simple; the hard part was getting the shell to fit over the legitimate card slot. For that he had to go to the black market on the deep web.

I had no idea what the deep web was, but it didn't matter. All I needed to know was that he had purchased the shell on the black market. The charge for possessing the skimmer was a class A misdemeanor, although serious, paled in comparison to the felony charge, so I wasn't about to spend the little time I had with Devon talking about the skimmer. Devon could explain it all to me later; for now I just needed the basic facts.

My gut was telling me Devon was a good kid, so he must have had a good reason for stealing the credit card number. Not that it would make him any less guilty, but it might get him some sympathy at the arraignment. I assumed his actions had something to do with the science fair competition, so I asked him what that was all about.

Devon said it was a contest run by a trio of Silicon Valley tech companies. Scholarships and big cash prizes were awarded to the contestants who came up with the most innovative ways to increase the capability or efficiency of existing industrial, commercial, or financial systems, or invented new systems to address evolving problems. Contestants could enter as individuals or in teams of no more than five members.

Devon and two classmates had entered the contest as a team. Their idea was to create a drug management system for elderly patients that would help ensure the patient took his or her medications in the right dosages and at the right times. The system would automatically handle renewals and could notify caregivers if the medications were not taken. It was a great idea, and according to Devon, required little on the programming side, but a great deal on the mechanical side. He needed the money to buy the equipment that cost a little over twenty-six-hundred dollars.

The team had made numerous attempts to raise the cash. They did everything from begging to selling things on eBay, but all they were able to raise was five hundred dollars. That left them twenty-one-hundred dollars short. With time to complete the project running out, and certain that their project could win, Devon decided to "borrow" the money. Since no one seemed willing to lend him the money voluntarily, he decided to force the issue by using the skimmer. I asked how he figured that using someone else's credit card was "borrowing" money. He said that he planned on paying back the money from the cash prize, and if they didn't win, he'd pay it back somehow.

I must have looked skeptical because he said again, this time more insistently, that he intended to pay the money back. Then he said that he had been careful not to target a poor person. Having done his research, he knew that he could have captured more transactions from an ATM in a 7-Eleven store where the transactions average 3,000 a month. Instead, he had put the skimmer on the ATM in the Financial District where there would be less transactions, but hopefully they'd be conducted by wealthier people.

He chose an American Express card on the assumption that with the high annual fee and no balance requirement, the cardholder would be financially better off than a Visa cardholder. Again, he said that he planned on returning the stolen money with interest. It sounded nice, but I couldn't see how we could prove that he planned on returning the money. When I mentioned that, Devon said he had a file in his room containing all the pertinent information on the cardholder, together with an interest spreadsheet from a compound interest calculator. It certainly wasn't proof positive, but it was something.

I could understand to a point why winning the contest was so important to a kid like Devon. He was obviously a geek, a brilliant geek, but a geek nonetheless. But he was also a good kid. The kind that had obviously been raised with a strong conscience. So what would make him resort to larceny? When I asked him the question, he explained that he had been awarded a full academic scholarship to Stanford University, but it didn't include travel, books, and living expenses. He worked part-time jobs, but most of that money went for household expenses. What was left over wasn't enough to cover his expected expenses at Stanford, and his grandfather was hardly in a financial position to help. Even if he could help, Devon wasn't about to saddle him with that burden. But if his team won the contest, his share of the winning prize money would be enough to cover at least his first year's expenses. That was why the contest was so important to him.

When I asked Devon to name his teammates on the project, he refused to do so, claiming he acted alone, and his teammates had no knowledge of the theft. I didn't believe him, but at that point it didn't matter. Whether he was in court by himself or with company, he'd be facing the same issues.

We had a lot of ground to cover and not a lot of time to do it, so I switched gears and asked Devon about his home life. Devon lived in the Two Bridges housing project with his grandfather, a retired NYC transit worker. Devon had been born in South Carolina where his father, a Marine, was stationed in 1997. In 2002, his father was killed in Afghanistan, and Devon's mother moved them back to New York to live with his grandfather. His mother had died of cancer two years earlier, so now it was just him and his grandfather.

I asked Devon if his grandfather knew about his arrest. He said no, he had a friend call his grandfather and tell him he was staying at a friend's house for a couple of nights. With Devon's school being so far uptown, it wasn't unusual for him to bunk in with friends who lived closer to the school.

I asked for his grandfather's name and number, saying I'd call him and explain everything. But Devon insisted he didn't want his grandfather to know he'd been arrested. I asked if his grandfather could afford to post his bail if it came to that, and Devon said no. Then he added that his grandfather was sick, and he was afraid that the news of his arrest might kill him. It sounded overly dramatic, but I let it slide. At some point the old man had to be told, but it didn't have to be today. Unless, of course, Devon was put into the system and shipped off to Rikers. But I had Devon's address, so if it came to that, I could visit the old man and explain everything.

It was almost time for the arraignment calendar call, and I needed to head upstairs. As I was preparing to leave, Devon asked if he was going to jail. I could see that the thought of jail terrified him, and I wanted to say no, but I couldn't. I'd do my best to convince the assistant district attorney handling the arraignment and the judge that he should be released without bail, but it was a heavy lift. I answered the question the only way I could. I said, "I'll do my best."

I hated to leave Devon because once I left, he'd be sent back into the holding cells. I was about to prepare the kid for that when my friend, Dave, showed up. He was carrying a pair of sneakers and a jacket which he tossed on the table in front of Devon. They were Devon's. Dave had retrieved them from the scumbags who had taken them from Devon in the holding cells.

As Devon was putting on his sneakers, Dave motioned for me to join him by the door. Looking at Devon, he said, "If I put that kid back in the holding cells, they're going to eat him alive. I'll keep him in here until his case is called."

Donald L'Abbate

All I can say is, God was looking out for Devon that day, and He was smart enough to entrust him to two recovering alcoholics. Not that we're any smarter or better than anyone else, but maybe we're a little bit more understanding. You see, I lived a part of my life at the bottom of a deep, dark pit from which I couldn't escape on my own. Then I found a way out through AA and my higher power. It didn't mean I became religious or a born-again Christian; no, I just got back into contact with my conscience, or if you prefer, my moral compass. Believe it or not, AA has made me humbler and more willing to accept and forgive shortcomings in others. Okay, not with scumbag violent criminals or some asshole assistant district attorneys and judges, but with people like Devon. One last word, don't judge AA by me. I'm what you call a work in progress.

CHAPTER 21

In the Arraignment Part, the defense lawyers were milling about searching for the assistant district attorneys handling their clients' cases. I was looking for ADA Taylor Clark. Having learned the hard way that Taylor is a gender-neutral name, I called out for ADA Clark, instead of Mr. Clark or Ms. Clark. I'm not going to tell you how I learned that Taylor was a gender-neutral name; it's too embarrassing. Suffice it to say that it involved a very small men's toilet, a crowded restaurant, and a troublesome prostate. You can figure out the rest on your own.

Assistant District Attorney Clark turned out to be a guy, and a very big guy at that. I'd say he was six foot five or better. I introduced myself, told him who I represented and perhaps we could agree on some matters before the judge took the bench. It was an old tactic. If you needed a favor from a young ADA, one you'd never met before, you warmed him or her up a bit before asking for the favor.

If I simply asked Clark not to object to Devon being released on his own recognizance, he'd laugh and say no. No doubt about that. So instead of asking for a favor, I asked Clark if he had met Devon which, of course, I knew he hadn't. Then without waiting for an answer, I shook my head and said, "When you see him, I know you're going to feel sorry for him."

Clark's natural curiosity led him to ask why, and I launched into my spiel about Devon being this skinny kid, an honor student, never in trouble before, who had been thrown into the holding cells with all those violent criminals. Then I hit him with my best line. Looking up at him, I said, "He's not a big guy like you. He can't take care of himself like you can. I don't want to think about what's going to happen to him at Rikers."

Then hoping I had reached a soft spot in the big guy's heart, I asked if he'd agree to my request that Devon be released without bail. Clark scrunched up his face like he was in pain, but I knew it meant he was going to say no. I was right; he said that he felt sorry for Devon, but it was a felony, and Devon had to pay the price.

As if that wasn't stupid enough, he added an even more stupid comment saying, "If he can't do the time, he shouldn't have done the crime. My job is to see that he pays the price for his crime."

Why are so many of these young assistant district attorneys such assholes, or is it just my bad luck to run into the ones that are?

I wanted to yell at the behemoth that we weren't talking about the crime of the century. Instead, I politely pointed out that this was a class D non-violent felony, so even if Devon was convicted, he might not even do jail time. So why put him in jail before he was convicted? I got the scrunched-up face look again, so I just walked away disgusted.

I still had a shot at getting Devon released without bail even if Clark objected. The judge that day was Helen Rothman. She and I went back a long way, probably further back than either of us would like to remember. We get along well now, but our relationship had a rocky start. Helen was elected judge during my drinking days when I made a habit of quarreling with judges. As a result, we clashed a lot, mostly the result of my nasty tirades. I'm not proud of what I did, but I did it, and I take responsibility for doing it.

Most of the judges I harassed had no patience with my antics and fined me for contempt; one even put me in jail. But Helen was kind to me even when I wasn't kind to her.

Donald L'Abbate

When I got sober and was doing the ninth step, making amends to those I had harmed, I went to see Helen. She saw me in chambers, and I told her how sorry I was for the way I had behaved in her courtroom. There wasn't anything I could do about the past, but I promised that in the future I would treat her with the respect and dignity she deserved, not just as a judge but as a person. I kept my promise, and our relationship improved. I wouldn't say we're friends because we don't socialize, but we understand, and I believe, respect each other.

When Devon's case was called, and the court officers brought him into the courtroom, he looked much calmer than he had in the interview room. I had my friend Dave to thank for that. Now I needed to work a little magic and get Devon released.

The ID theft charge was a felony and would be sent to the Grand Jury for an indictment before Devon entered a plea. However, the charge of possessing a skimmer was a misdemeanor, and his plea on that charge was taken at the arraignment hearing. After Devon pleaded not guilty to the charge, Judge Rothman asked about bail. Assistant District Attorney Schmuck offered his two cents, stating that on the felony charge, bail of $5,000 was appropriate. It wasn't a particularly high amount, and under normal circumstances I'd have considered it reasonable, but these weren't normal circumstances.

It was my turn to address the judge, and my only chance to get Devon released without bail. It's in those moments when the adrenalin flows, and my heart beats faster that I know why I love being a lawyer. The anticipation, the fear, the excitement. As many times as I've had moments like that in my career, it never gets old.

It was also those moments that made me an alcoholic. The exhilaration of winning, the crushing impact of losing, the emptiness when the adrenalin drains; it's all tough to handle. Some lawyers handle it well; others like me don't. When I won a case, I celebrated by getting drunk. When I lost a case, I got drunk. I used booze to treat the pain and fill the emptiness. But booze wasn't a cure for what ailed me, and unfortunately, it took me almost a decade to figure it out. But enough on that topic.

I started my pitch by pointing out that Devon was only seventeen years old, an honor student at HSMSE, was headed to Stanford University on a scholarship, had no criminal record, didn't pose a threat to the community, and wasn't a flight risk. Before I could say anything more, the schmuck chimed in, saying that was why he had suggested such a low bail amount. As much as I hated to admit it, he had a point. I needed something more, but all I had was a Hail Mary, and it was time to throw it.

I said, "Judge, he can't make bail. But I ask you to look at this kid! He's no criminal; he's an honor student who did something stupid. Is he dumb, yes; is he a dangerous criminal? No! The only serious charge against him is a class D felony, and you can't get any lower than that. Even if convicted, he probably wouldn't get jail time. He's been accepted to Stanford University on a full academic scholarship, and he has a bright future ahead of him. But if you send him to Rikers, that bright future could be over in a minute. Look at him; he's a skinny little kid. What chance does he have of surviving in Rikers? If he isn't killed, who knows what psychological impact the experience would have on him and his future? Don't let a simple, stupid mistake turn into a death sentence, if not literally, then figuratively. Please, judge, release him on his own recognizance. It's the only humane thing to do."

As much as it pains me to do so, I must give the schmuck credit for keeping his mouth shut at that point.

Judge Rothman looked pensive which I took to mean she was at least considering my argument. I was feeling pretty good about our chances until the judge spoke. She said that she was moved by my argument, but a felony charge, no matter what class, warranted bail. My heart was sinking, but then she added, unless a responsible person could vouch for the defendant. It opened the door, but not much. I was mulling over the idea of vouching for Devon myself when someone in the gallery yelled out, "I'll vouch for the boy."

Everyone in the courtroom turned to the gallery. Standing in the second row was an elderly man, leaning on a cane. I looked back to Devon who mouthed that it was his grandfather. I breathed a sigh of relief.

Judge Rothman asked the man to step forward and identify himself. He said that he was Jerome Williams, and he was Devon's grandfather. The smile on the judge's face told me the tide had turned.

After asking Mr. Williams a couple of questions for the record, the judge ordered Devon released without bail.

While Devon was taken downstairs to complete some paperwork and retrieve his personal belongings, I spoke with Mr. Williams. I asked how he found out about Devon's arrest. He said the principal of the school had called him that morning and told him what had happened. The problem was that no one could tell him where Devon was, and he didn't know where to look. Finally, in desperation, he had walked to the Criminal Court Building. When he got there, he didn't know where to go or what to do. Having worked for the Transit Authority and knowing the camaraderie that existed between NYC employees, he approached a court officer and asked for help. The court officer was happy to help and ultimately brought him up to the Arraignment Part.

But Mr. Williams didn't want to talk about how he got there; he wanted to know how Devon got there. He wanted to know what Devon had done and how much trouble he might be in. I suggested we head downstairs, and while we waited for Devon to be released, I'd explain what was going on.

CHAPTER 22

While Mr. Williams and I waited outside the Criminal Court Building for Devon to emerge, he spoke about his grandson's life. He said the death of Devon's father in Afghanistan caused his daughter to go into a deep depression. Fearing that she might hurt herself or Devon, he had gone to South Carolina and brought the two back to New York to live with him. He'd hoped that with the change of scenery, his daughter would get better, but she didn't show signs of improving. He sought help from the Veterans Administration and was referred to a program in Brooklyn. But the facility was overcrowded, and the visits didn't seem to be helping. With his hands full caring for his daughter and Devon, he was forced to retire from the Transit Authority earlier than he planned. Money was tight, but between his veteran's benefits and his pension, they got by.

Eventually Devon's mother got better, thanks to help from the Wounded Warriors program, and for a while, life was good. But then she developed cancer and died after a two-year battle with the disease. Through it all, Devon seemed to take the tragedies in his stride. Mr. Williams said he'd done his best to protect and raise the boy, and he felt they had a very close relationship.

Devon, he said, was not just a good kid; he was a special kid. When Devon was in the first grade, he was classified as a gifted child and placed in a school for gifted students. By the time he was ready for high school, his IQ test score was 143, putting him just shy of genius status. Devon was an honor student from the first grade on and never had a disciplinary problem. With tears in his eyes, Mr. Williams said his grandson was a good kid and never got into trouble, so he was shocked when he learned that Devon had been arrested.

I was about to ask Mr. Williams if he had noticed any recent change in Devon's conduct when Devon emerged through the front door of the Criminal Court Building. I figured Devon hadn't eaten since his arrest early that morning, and he was probably hungry. He would have been given a cheese sandwich in The Tombs, but his chances of keeping the sandwich were less than his chances had been of keeping his sneakers. To save him the embarrassment of having to admit that he had his lunch taken away from him, I didn't ask if he'd had lunch, I just suggested we drop by the Worth Street Coffee Shop.

While Mr. Williams and I drank coffee, Devon devoured a hamburger and a plate of French fries, answering my questions about his little caper between bites.

The team had finished the project and submitted it to the contest headquarters. The winners would be announced in about two weeks. Devon was confident their entry would win, maybe not first prize but definitely second prize, at the worst. The first place prize was $75,000 to be used for higher education purposes. Devon, noticing the questioning look on my face, said the rules allowed the winning contestants to reimburse themselves for out-of-pocket costs of the project. That was how he planned on repaying whoever had suffered the loss, be it either the American Express Company or the cardholder whose number he had swiped.

Since the skimmer recorded account numbers, names, and expiration dates only, I was curious how he knew it was an American Express card. He said the credit card company can be identified by the first digit of the account number. All American Express accounts begin with the number three, while Visa cards begin with the number four, and MasterCard accounts begin with the number five. Also, the American Express accounts are always fifteen digits, while Visa accounts can be up to nineteen digits.

Again, I asked Devon for the names of his two teammates, but even under pressure from his grandfather, he wouldn't tell me. I assured him that I wasn't going to turn them in to the cops. But I needed to hear their stories in order to prepare a defense if we went to trial.

Devon was obviously struggling with his conscience, and since I didn't need the names immediately, I let it drop. The next time I asked for the names, I wouldn't let it drop, I'd press the issue until I got an answer. But that afternoon sitting in the Worth Street Coffee Shop wasn't the time to press it.

Devon suddenly looked very nervous and stopped eating. I think it may have been the mention of a possible trial that got him nervous. He said nothing, but his grandfather asked the question that was clearly on Devon's mind, *"What's going to happen now?"*

I explained that at the moment Devon faced a felony charge and a misdemeanor charge, neither of which automatically mandated jail time. However, the identity theft charge could lead to a further charge of larceny. Since the amount stolen was less than $3,000, the charge would be Larceny in the Fourth Degree, another class E felony. With two felony charges and a misdemeanor charge, I'd have to do some heavy negotiating to have Devon escape without a serious record. Not to be too negative, I added that it was possible, and Devon's history would certainly help. What would also help, and was probably necessary, was restitution of the $2,100.

Devon said that was no problem, and as soon as he received the prize money, he'd give me the $2,100. I didn't want to burst the kid's bubble, but I had to make sure he understood that if he expected to escape without a felony record, restitution wasn't optional. I appreciated his optimism, but I needed to know that the $2,100 was available right now and wasn't contingent on winning the contest. Devon looked crestfallen, but then his grandfather put his arm around Devon's shoulder and said, "You have my word. The money will be there when you need it."

I couldn't see Devon's face because he had his chin against his chest, but I heard him sob. He was a good kid, and I needed to get his ass out of this jam.

Seeing that both Devon and Mr. Williams were emotionally drained, I suggested we call it a day, and we meet again in my office on Monday afternoon when Devon was done in school. It was important that Devon return to his normal routine. The case would be hanging over his head for a while and returning to his normal routine would help to keep him from dwelling on it.

When I got back to the office, I found a message from Johnny McAvoy that the Grand Jury had returned an indictment against Little Tony, and he'd be arraigned in Supreme Court on the following Wednesday. That gave me plenty of time to prepare my Brady demand.

A Brady demand requires the district attorney to provide evidence it has collected which is material to guilt or punishment and tends to prove the defendant is not guilty. It included all the forensic reports that Sarah and I had previously discussed. It's called a Brady demand because the rule comes from the United States Supreme Court case, *Brady vs. Maryland.*

CHAPTER 23

It had been a long week, and I was beat. I was meeting Gracie for dinner at Pino's La Forchetta, after which I planned on catching a meeting. Between dealing with Joey Bats, trying to figure out the Savinos, arguing with Gracie, and now Devon's case, I needed a meeting. It wasn't that I wanted to drink; it was more that I needed to get my head straightened out.

Alcoholism is as much a mental and spiritual thing as it is a physical compulsion. For me, alcoholic thinking is as dangerous as a double scotch on the rocks, and alcoholic thinking can get into my head faster and easier than a drink can get into my hand. Most times I feel myself slipping into alcoholic thinking, but other times I don't feel it coming on, and that's when it's most dangerous. Of course, Doug, my sponsor, can sense it, as can Gracie. If Doug sees me in a bad way, he suggests I go to a meeting. Gracie, on the other hand, orders me to a meeting the moment I show any signs of slippage.

That night over dinner I told Gracie about Devon's case. On my way to the restaurant, I had begun formulating a plan for his defense, and I wanted Gracie's input. I didn't know who was out the $2,100, whether it was the cardholder or American Express, but either way, I was hoping that offering immediate restitution would convince either or both not to press charges. Gracie agreed that with the relatively small amount of money involved, if the victim chose not to press charges, her office was likely to drop the case.

As for the remaining charges, unlawful possession of identification and the unlawful possession of a skimmer, the evidence against Devon seemed solid, so all I could do was argue Devon's circumstances and beg for mercy. When I asked Gracie for her thoughts, she said it was a good strategy, but only so long as the larceny charge didn't materialize. If there was no larceny charge, a sympathetic assistant district attorney might be convinced to drop the identification theft felony charge down to a misdemeanor and even drop the skimmer possession charge altogether. It all hinged on having the potential larceny charge disappear. It was a plan, but I had my work cut out for me.

I felt better hearing Gracie's opinion, but there was still one lingering question I couldn't shake. How did the cops find Devon so quickly? The charge on the card was made less than a month and a half ago. Even if the cardholder reported the fraud immediately, it didn't leave much time for the cops to trace it to Devon. Clearly, a $2,100 credit card fraud case wasn't a high priority case, and under normal circumstances, I doubted it would have gotten much attention, if any, from the Detective Squad. So how come the cops were able to track down Devon so quickly? There was nothing in the arrest report that gave a clue, but my gut was telling me it was something I should look into. I made a mental note to ask Devon about it when we met on Monday.

With work talk out of the way, the conversation turned to a more intimate matter, namely the state of our relationship. Frankly, I didn't want to have the "relationship talk." I knew it was coming, and I had tried to forestall it by talking about work. Not that I didn't really want Gracie's opinion on Devon's case. I did, but if getting her opinion would put off the "relationship talk," all the better. But my plan didn't work out. When I asked Gracie about her day, she said it was fine, but it was time to clear the air.

For me, a clearing the air conversation is very much like a root canal. I don't get to say very much, and it involves a lot of pain. Every time we clear the air, I wind up apologizing, most times not knowing why or for what I'm apologizing. That's not to say an apology wasn't in order; it simply means that I was too dense to see why. Doug usually explains it all afterward, not that I always understand it even after he's explained it.

After Gracie and I have one of these "relationship talks," I go immediately to a meeting, and I share. Then I watch as the men shake their heads in bewilderment, and women give me the evil eye. But sharing works, and I go home happy, or at least not angry. One lesson I learned early on in AA is that life is a lot better when you're not angry all the time. Confused and baffled is okay and better than angry.

That night our "relationship conversation" went better than I expected. Gracie said she was sorry if she overreacted, but after her own experience with the Russian mob, she feared for my safety. As for taking the case against her wishes, she said it was my decision to make, and she shouldn't have been so demanding.

It almost sounded as if I was winning, but I knew there was another shoe to fall, and sure enough it fell. She said while she was sorry that she overreacted, I still behaved badly in the way I reacted. The way Gracie said it, I felt like a puppy who had peed on the carpet. But if that was the worst of it, I could live with it, so I kept my mouth shut.

My silence was rewarded when Gracie said she presumed I was going to a meeting, but if afterward I brought home some ice cream, we could have a little party. I wasn't certain what she meant by a party, but I was pretty sure it was code for having sex, so I was all in. When we finished dinner, we parted with a passionate kiss, and I left for my meeting a happy man.

CHAPTER 24

Monday morning I was at the courthouse filing some motion papers when Johnny McAvoy, the assistant district attorney handling Little Tony's case, approached me. We hadn't been formally introduced, but he recognized me, and knowing I was representing Little Tony Savino, he introduced himself. I didn't like him from the start. He was arrogant and condescending, but I had promised Sarah I'd play nice, so I gave him a chance. That was until he said Sarah Washington told him I was one of the good guys, but he didn't think so. So much for playing nice.

Apparently not satisfied at simply pissing me off with his last comment, he added gasoline to the fire. He said, as for Little Tony's case, it was a slam dunk, and I shouldn't expect any favors from him. There'd be no sweetheart deals; Little Tony was going to do hard time and lots of it. If I went crying to Sarah, he'd pile on more years.

I'm pretty thick skinned, or least I've become thick skinned since getting sober, so as pissed off as I was, I would have let his comments slide had he stopped there. But he didn't. He then made the mistake of asking if I understood what he was saying. That was it; he had gone too far.

Taking a step closer and locking my eyes on his, I said in a very calm voice that I understood he was an asshole, and now I knew why Sarah was considering firing him. Of course, that wasn't true, at least the part about Sarah firing him, but McAvoy didn't know that, and guys like him are usually insecure. I knew that I had hit the mark when the smirk on his face vanished. Then, with a smile on my face, I said if he didn't turn over the forensic reports in Little Tony's case immediately, I would complain to Sarah, and maybe that would speed up his firing. Then I turned and walked away.

I knew how to get to Johnny McAvoy because I had been just like him. He was me twenty years ago, an arrogant and brash personality, concealing an insecure ego. I knew from my own experience that the cockier someone like McAvoy acts, the more insecure he was. That knowledge gave me an edge in dealing with him and made it easy for me to zing him as I had. I didn't zing him just for the fun of it, but I'd be a liar if I said that I hadn't enjoyed it. I zinged him to let him know he couldn't mess with me. If he played fair and straight, we wouldn't have a problem, but if he tried to pull a fast one, he'd regret it. I hoped he got the message.

Until I saw the forensic reports, particularly the ballistic report, there wasn't much I could do on Little Tony's case. How good a defense we had depended upon what was in those reports. If the reports supported Little Tony's story, he'd have a damn good legal defense, but things would get dicey for me personally.

If the Ruccis wanted Little Tony convicted or wanted him to plead guilty to the murder charges, they'd be unhappy if I put on a strong defense. On the other hand, Big Tony would be unhappy if we didn't put on a strong defense. There was also the possibility that the Ruccis might be pressuring McAvoy to get a guilty plea or a conviction which might explain his arrogant attitude. It was a possibility, but I still believed McAvoy was simply an asshole, and that alone explained his attitude.

Then I had another thought. Gene Meyers was a damn good lawyer, but that didn't explain why the juries in his cases always seemed to acquit no matter how damning the evidence. The odds of so many legitimate jury acquittals were just too long to be ignored which was why it was rumored that Gene Meyers' winning streak had more to do with jury tampering than with his legal skill. How ironic would it be if the Ruccis wound up tampering with the jury to secure a conviction in Little Tony's case?

Just thinking about all of that gave me a headache. Fortunately, I didn't have to deal with any of it at the moment, and I knew better than to project. What I needed was a little time off to clear my head. With nothing on my schedule until my meeting with Devon and his grandfather later that afternoon, I had plenty of time to kill. Normally I would have gone to an AA meeting, but since it was a beautiful early September day, I opted for a long walk instead.

September is a great time of year to be in New York City. The temperatures generally hover around the 70s, and there's always something exciting happening. For me that year, the excitement was my Yankees, who were battling to make the playoffs for the first time in three years, and I was totally captivated by the drama. I couldn't remember being so excited about baseball since I was a kid. But excited I was, and I made it my business to catch all of the games. Most of the games I caught on television, but I did manage to get to Yankee Stadium a couple of times to see the games in person.

On the rare occasion where I missed a game, the next day I'd devour the newspaper articles, studying the box scores just as I had done when I was a kid. You can imagine my excitement the next month when, on October 1st, the team secured a wild card spot in the playoffs, notching the franchise's 10,000th victory, in a four to one win over the despised Boston Red Sox. But my heart would be broken five days later when they were eliminated in a one and done game, shut out by the Houston Astros. But that's baseball.

Leaving court that day, I didn't want to think about anything, not my cases, not even my Yankees. I just wanted to walk and enjoy the weather and clear my head.

My meandering took me over to Mulberry Street where crews were setting up for the San Gennaro Feast. If you've never been to the San Gennaro Feast, you're missing out on one of New York City's greatest events. The Feast honors San Gennaro, the patron saint of Naples, Italy. It takes place every year in early September and lasts for eleven days. It's billed as "The Feast of all Feasts," and believe me, it is.

Booths selling food, trinkets, or offering games of skill, line Mulberry Street from Canal Street to Houston Street, a nearly seven-block-long arcade decorated with lights and flowers and crowded with people.

The first Feast was held in 1926 when immigrants from Naples, who'd settled along Mulberry Street, followed their tradition of celebrating the day that Saint Gennaro was martyred. Over the years, the tradition grew into an eleven-day event, featuring food, fun, nightly entertainment, a meatball eating contest and, of course, a parade. It's not a parade as such, but a religious procession during which the Statue of San Gennaro is carried from the Church of the Most Precious Blood on Baxter Street through Little Italy. In the movie, *Godfather II,* the San Gennaro procession is the backdrop for the scene in which the young Vito Corleone settles the score with Don Fannuci.

There are many reasons to attend the Feast, but for me it's mostly about the food. I get hungry just thinking about the famed sausage and pepper heroes, the arancini or fried rice balls, and the still warm fresh mozzarella that melts gently on your tongue. Then there are the sweets, the zeppoles, deep fried dough topped with powdered sugar, not to mention the cannoli.

But it's not the food that makes the San Gennaro Feast something special. In Little Italy you can get the same food all year round. So why is it special when you eat the same food at the Feast? I don't know for sure, but I think it's the atmosphere. For some reason, buying the food from a booth on the street and eating it while walking through the crowds, makes it special. Maybe it's the Italian music playing in the background or maybe it's seeing everyone having fun.

I don't know, maybe I'm crazy, but if there is reincarnation, I want to come back as an Italian. Being Irish is okay, but let's face it, the Italians seem to have more fun and have better food than the Irish. After all, there's only so much you can do with a potato. You know what I mean?

In a few days, Gracie and I would be heading to the Feast's opening night, but just seeing the booths being set up and the lights being strung made me hungry. With my head now cleared, it was time to grab some lunch and head back to the office.

CHAPTER 25

That afternoon when Devon and his grandfather walked into my office, I could tell from the look on Devon's face that something was wrong. He looked as though his dog had just died, or at least how I thought someone whose dog had just died would look. As soon as he and his grandfather were seated, I asked what was up. He said that he had heard from the contest officials, and unless he cleared his name before the judging started in ten days, his project would be disqualified. Now Devon was afraid that his scholarship to Stanford might be in jeopardy as well.

It would take a miracle to have the case dismissed in ten days, but not wanting Devon to lose hope, I said that I'd handle it. I had no idea how I was going to do that, but I had ten days to figure it out. For now, we needed to talk about the case.

Someone had obviously reported Devon's arrest to the contest officials. Devon didn't know who, but I figured it was probably the same person who had turned him in to the cops. Then again, it was possible that nobody had turned him in; maybe Devon had done something stupid that made it easy for the cops to find him.

I thought it highly unlikely that our boy genius did something dumb, like having the materials delivered to his house or to the house of anyone connected with him. So maybe he used an easily traceable email address. Devon was smart, but he was probably book smart, not street smart, and criminals need to be street smart if they expect to survive.

When I questioned Devon about the scheme, he assured me there was no way the cops could have traced anything he did. I tended to believe Devon, but I wanted Linda Chow to check it out, so I needed to know the details.

Devon said he used a computer terminal in the New York Public Library, and set up a VPN, a virtual private network. Then he used something he called a Tor browser. It was all foreign to me, so I asked Devon to explain it in simple terms that a dummy like me could understand.

He said that the VPN and the Tor browser provided anonymity by making everything he did on the Internet run through so many servers that it was nearly impossible to trace his location. Even if someone could trace it, they'd wind up at the public library. Once he was anonymous, he opened a Google account under a false name, giving a phony location and date of birth. When Google required an identifying method of contact, he used an app called Burner. It all worked perfectly, and in less than two hours, Devon had a valid but untraceable G-mail account.

He then used his new G-mail account and the stolen American Express card number to purchase Bitcoin. Because the G-mail account was bogus, his identity was protected, and authorities tracing the American Express transaction would get nowhere. Any effort to trace the transaction would lead back to his fake G-mail account and a series of IP addresses, possibly ending at the public library, but more likely ending somewhere in Asia or in the Middle East.

As for the Bitcoin, it was like cash, but unlike cash it has no serial numbers that can be used to trace it. Using the Tor browser to add yet another layer of fog to the transaction, Devon bought the needed supplies using the Bitcoin. By using the untraceable Bitcoin, he effectively eliminated any possible link between the purchase of the materials and the stolen American Express card. The purchase was simply one of the 1.2 million dollars in sales conducted every thirty seconds on the Internet. But, more importantly, by making the purchase untraceable to the stolen American Express card, Devon was able to have the materials sent to his home address.

If Devon was right, the cops had to have been tipped off. It was the only way they could have gotten to him so quickly. But who would have known about the theft? Devon had been careful to conceal what he was doing, so other than his two teammates, no one should have known about the scheme. If it wasn't one of his teammates who turned him in, and that scenario seemed unlikely, it had to be someone Devon told about the plan.

Now we had a big problem, a live witness. Although the informant's testimony would be hearsay, which is normally excluded at trial, it would fall under an exception to the rule. Devon's statements would constitute a confession of guilt and, as such, would fall within the exception. That testimony, taken together with the skimmer, would likely be enough for a jury to convict Devon on the unlawful possession of identification charge, as well as the larceny charge, if and when it came.

However, if the informant heard the information from a third party and not from Devon, then it would be double hearsay and inadmissible at trial. Without the confession, the skimmer alone wasn't enough evidence to get the case past a reasonable doubt. The skimmer charge might stick, but it was only a misdemeanor. Of course, if the cops tracked down the original leaker, that would eliminate the double or triple hearsay, and we'd be back to an admission of guilt.

But my gut was telling me the person who contacted the cops was another contestant, and he or she wouldn't want their own identity known, so it was likely an anonymous tip. It was a small case, and normally it wouldn't have gotten much attention. But identity theft was one of the crimes the mayor had targeted in his war on crime, so the detectives had to act on all tips or risk getting a rip. A rip being cop slang for a disciplinary action.

After I explained that to Devon, he was still reluctant to reveal the names of his teammates. Finally pressured by his grandfather, Devon gave in, adding that the only other person besides his teammates who knew about the credit card theft was his friend, Margie McDonald. But he insisted that all of them could be trusted.

I admired his youthful confidence in his friends, but I didn't share it. Somebody had leaked the information, and it could only have been one of the three. But why? There was no apparent motive for any of them doing so. Devon's two teammates had nothing to gain and everything to lose by turning Devon in. That left Margie McDonald as the prime suspect, but Devon insisted she was a close friend and would never do anything to harm him.

It was possible that whoever did the leaking didn't give the information to the cops, but to someone else who did, or who passed it on to yet another person. That brought the two teammates squarely back into the picture along with Margie McDonald.

Assuming Devon was right, and his Internet transactions were untraceable, the case turned entirely on someone passing the information to the cops. If it had been an anonymous tip and the cops weren't running it down, we'd have a good defense, and I'd dare the assistant district attorney to convict Devon. But if it was one of the three who leaked the information, I'd be reduced to begging for mercy. Coming on too strong right away could hurt a mercy plea down the road but being too soft now would give an impression of weakness. I needed to know who leaked, and I needed to know now. I couldn't wait until the District Attorney's Office served its witness list to find out. When Devon and his grandfather left, I called Tommy and put him and Linda Chow on the case.

CHAPTER 26

Tuesday morning Tommy showed up at the office. He had been busy chasing leads in Little Tony's case and hadn't done much on Devon's case, but Linda Chow had and what she discovered confirmed Devon's story. His G-mail account and his online activities using that account were virtually untraceable, even for someone with Linda's talent. When she tried backtracking Devon's phony G-mail account, it routed through multiple local and foreign networks, eventually ending up somewhere in Pakistan. Even knowing the details of Devon's actions, she couldn't get a trace. So, clearly the cops hadn't found Devon through his online shenanigans and didn't have any hard evidence tying him to the fraudulent transaction.

If the cops hadn't found Devon by backtracking his accounts, they had to have been tipped off, but by whom? The most likely candidates were the American Express cardholder or the American Express Company. But according to Tommy, Linda confirmed that neither of them had filed a complaint with the police. That meant the police learned of the card theft from a third party.

As important as that information was, I really didn't want to know how Linda had gotten it. Still I needed to know the information was accurate, so I had to ask. As I suspected, the answer was exactly what I didn't want to hear. Linda had hacked her way into the American Express computer system.

Knowing that wasn't going to make me happy, Tommy made a dumb ass attempt to put a positive spin on it by assuring me that Linda had limited her search to the one account used by Devon. Like that made what she had done okay. I robbed the bank but only took a little cash, so it's okay. That's the type of reasoning I'm used to hearing from my 18B Panel clients, not from my investigator. Not that I'm much better.

I admit that I wanted to know what Linda had found. It was how she found it that I didn't want to hear. Maybe that makes me a hypocrite, but I've never claimed that I wasn't a hypocrite, at least not when it came to Linda's work. Or maybe it's a matter of situational ethics, deciding what's right and what's wrong based upon the circumstances and not some inflexible moral code. I'm not suggesting the ends justify the means; at least I hope that's not what I'm doing. I'm saying it's a question of where you draw the line, and drawing the line somewhere beats not drawing the line at all. My reason for not wanting to know how Linda gets her information is a practical one, not a moral one.

Anyway, Linda discovered that the unauthorized use of the card hadn't been reported by the cardholder, but the transaction had been flagged as fraudulent after a company-initiated records search. In other words, someone reported a fraudulent transaction on an unknown American Express account, and the company, using the date and nature of the transaction, had traced it to a specific account.

So, as suspected, the cops had been tipped off to the fraud and backtracked the transaction. By doing it that way, they still didn't have any hard evidence tying Devon to the transaction. Even with the transactional records, all the DA had was the skimmer and the informant's testimony. It might be enough for a Grand Jury indictment, but unless the informant had heard about the theft directly from Devon, it wasn't going to support a conviction. I needed Tommy to find out if it was one of Devon's teammates or Margie

McDonald who had tipped off the cops. But in the meantime, I wanted to hear what he had learned about Little Tony's situation.

Since I'd called him on Wednesday, Tommy had spent all his time tracking down information on the Ruccis and the Russians. As he'd promised when I gave him the assignment, he'd kept his distance from the Russians. He had made no direct contacts, or even indirect contacts, just surveillance and nothing more.

As for the Ruccis, there had been no direct contact either, but not for a lack of trying. Things were buttoned up tighter than a drum. No one on the inside was talking which meant there was serious shit going on. A couple of the street punks, non-connected wannabes, were talking, but it was all unreliable gossip, nothing worth listening to.

As for the Russians, from what Tommy could tell by driving around, it was business as usual. Tommy hadn't contacted anyone with Russian mob connections for two reasons. One, because he had promised me that he wouldn't, and two, because he didn't have a reliable informant when it came to the Russian mob. Most people were too frightened to talk about the mob, and those who weren't afraid to talk usually didn't live very long.

Tommy had just cruised around Brighton Beach and the neighborhoods where the Ruccis and the Russians were both operating, checking for signs of trouble. From what he could tell, the Russians were doing business with their usual arrogance.

The same couldn't be said for the Stagliano crew running the Mafia operations in the shared neighborhoods. To Tommy, the tension was obvious. The Stagliano guys were now working in pairs, sometimes groups of four or more taking book and selling drugs. Even then the guys seemed nervous, like they were expecting trouble.

There was no doubt in my mind that it had to do with the murder of the two Russians, but where was this leading? The fact that neither side had gone to war suggested something was in the works. Perhaps some sort of peace treaty. But it was an uneasy peace for sure.

I couldn't imagine what such an agreement might look like, but I was convinced that Little Tony fit into the terms somewhere and might even be at the center of the agreement. That would explain why the Russian goon had confronted me in the park the other day.

But my job wasn't to figure out how Little Tony fit into a possible mob war; my job was to defend him in a court of law. Of course, I had a lot more riding on the outcome of the case than simply another victory or defeat. Win or lose, somebody was going to be unhappy, and that wouldn't bode well for my life expectancy. It might come down to my being killed quickly by the Mafia or dying slowly at the hands of the Russians. And all of that for $100,000. This mob lawyer thing was really starting to suck. Maybe Gene Meyers was a lot smarter than I had given him credit for.

I told Tommy to keep his ear to the ground on the Mafia situation, but in the meantime to interview the three kids in Devon's case. Linda's confirmation that neither American Express, nor the cardholder, had tipped off the cops meant it was one of the three who had done it, either directly or indirectly, and I wanted to know which one it was. Had the culprit talked directly to the cops, or had he or she spilled the beans to someone else? The sooner I knew the answer to that question, the sooner I could work out a defense for Devon.

I still didn't know what to do about Devon's possible disqualification, but that would have to wait for another day. It wasn't a priority.

My priority at that moment was finding out what was going on with the Russians and the Ruccis. With nowhere else to turn, I called Detective Chen and invited him to lunch at Shoo's Restaurant. I wasn't sure he knew anything more now than when we last met, but I was coming up empty on all other fronts, so it was worth a try.

Chen showed up on time and with a healthy appetite. He loved eating at Shoo's; he said it reminded him of his grandmother's cooking. He must have really loved his grandmother's cooking because he always ordered multiple appetizers and entrees, most of which he took with him in carryout containers at the end of the meal. That was why I only took him to Shoo's when I needed something big, and Chen knew that.

Midway through our first four courses, I asked Chen what was going on with the Russian murder cases and why the Ruccis were in lockdown. He said the Russian murder cases were in the hands of the district attorney and his office was only holding the files open in case a follow-up was needed before trial. As for the Ruccis, all he knew was that there were some family issues, most likely having to do with old man Silvio's health. He said his confidential informants had clammed up which usually meant the problems were serious.

I asked if there were any signs of a war brewing between the brothers and the old man over control of the family business. Chen said not to quote him, but some of the guys in the Organized Crime Bureau thought that might be happening. There had been talk a while back that the old man had gotten senile and was acting crazy. But those rumors had quieted down, and some in the OCB thought the present situation had to do with the murder of the two Russians. In Chen's opinion, it could involve both an internal struggle for control and problems with the Russians. But as long as the streets were quiet, the cops were happy to let things be, or as Chen put it, there was no sense stirring the pot.

Maybe that approach worked for the NYPD, but it didn't do me any good. It was bad enough not knowing which team I was playing on, but I didn't even know what game we were playing. There were too many things I didn't know and maybe some things I didn't want to know. But I did know that sooner or later I stood a good chance of getting killed. However, until I saw the forensic reports there was nothing I could do, and as long as I was doing nothing, I figured I wasn't pissing anybody off, so nobody had a reason to kill me. That might have been wishful thinking, but I'm an optimist at heart.

CHAPTER 27

It was Wednesday, and Little Tony was being arraigned that morning on four counts of homicide. I had arranged for him and his old man to meet me at the Worth Street Coffee Shop before we went to court. I figured since both men had been through the process before, prepping Little Tony would be easy and it was. Over coffee and a bagel, I told Little Tony all he had to do was plead not guilty, and as long as the judge continued his bail, we'd walk out together in less than half an hour. I didn't think bail was going to be an issue, but with an asshole like Tommy McAvoy, I couldn't be sure. Better that Little Tony be prepared so if the issue came up, he wouldn't react. The last thing I needed was Little Tony copping an attitude in front of the judge. I mean, with his size, even frowning at someone is enough to be intimidating. I told him if things got tough, he shouldn't react; he should just try to look small.

As a regular in the Arraignment Part, I'm on a first name basis with most of the clerks. That, plus remembering them at Christmastime, helped to keep my cases at the top of the calendar.

So it wasn't surprising that Little Tony's case was the second one called that morning.

Things got off to a smooth start with my buddy, Tommy McAvoy, acting almost civilly. But that all changed when we got to the matter of bail. McAvoy asked that Little Tony's bail be revoked, and he be held at Rikers pending trial. I glanced over at Little Tony who wasn't showing any facial reactions, but he was slumping his shoulders with his head down in what I took to be an effort to look smaller. He was following my instructions, but frankly it wasn't helping. He didn't look any smaller; he just looked like a tired giant.

Turning my attention to the judge, I objected to McAvoy's request that bail be revoked, pointing out that nothing affecting Little Tony's bail status had changed since the last hearing when bail was set. McAvoy hadn't offered any proof that Little Tony had suddenly become a flight risk or a threat to the community. The only thing that changed since the last hearing was the Grand Jury handed down an indictment, which everyone expected, and that wasn't a reason to revoke Little Tony's bail.

McAvoy knew I had him, but he just couldn't give up. Obviously frustrated and rattled, he pointed to Little Tony, and he said, "Look at him; the man's mere existence is a threat to society."

I could tell from the look on the judge's face that I didn't have to reply, but I couldn't let it go. Addressing the judge, I said, "I hadn't realized that size was now a criterion for granting bail."

That brought a laugh from the gallery and a grin from the judge.

The judge ruled bail would stand, and we were done. McAvoy tried to get away quickly, but I managed to get into his face and sneer at him. It's one of the perks when you beat an asshole; you get to torment him. McAvoy didn't like it, but he knew he deserved it, and other than throwing a punch, there wasn't anything he could about it.

Gracie says when I act that way I just make things harder for myself. She reminds me that I must deal with these people, if not on the one case, then on others. She's right, but with a guy like McAvoy, we're never going to be on good terms. So why give up the pleasure of breaking his chops every chance I get? I'm not one to cut off my nose to spite my face, but I'm not above giving it a little nick here or there if it means I can torment an asshole now and then. Tormenting assholes is one of my pleasures in life. That and seeing scumbag violent felons put away for life is another one. Yes, I'm ranting, and no, I haven't forgotten about sex; that's why I said those other things were some of my pleasures in life.

Once outside the courthouse, a happy Big Tony offered to buy me lunch at his favorite restaurant in Little Italy. Even though it was still early for lunch, I was sorely tempted to accept. I knew lunch would definitely be a feast, but as tempting as his offer was, I had to decline. I needed to serve my Brady demand at the District Attorney's Office and then get back to my office to meet with Tommy who had information on Devon's case.

Tommy's a fast worker, so I wasn't surprised when he had called earlier that morning to tell me he had interviewed the three kids who knew about the credit card theft. He wouldn't give me the details over the phone, but he said it was all good. We agreed to meet at my office at one o'clock with Tommy bringing lunch from his grandfather's restaurant. Normally the idea of lunch from Shoo's would have me excited, but I kept thinking about the meal I could have had with Big Tony. Mafia lunches and dinners in Little Italy are legendary. I've never actually been to one, but I've heard a lot about them.

Hang out in Little Italy, and you'll discover there isn't a restaurant owner who doesn't bend over backwards when a mafioso like Big Tony comes into their place. It's a combination of fear, pride, and knowing these guys are huge tippers. The service is naturally impeccable, and no ordering is necessary. The restaurant's best dishes simply arrive and crowd the table. Antipasto, salads, pasta, fish and meat dishes. Generally, it's a three-hour affair, concluding with the espresso and dessert.

But duty called, so after serving the Brady demand, I walked back to my office to wait for Tommy, wonton soup, and egg rolls.

CHAPTER 28

By the time Tommy arrived, I was over my disappointment in missing out on lunch with Big Tony. The fact that I was starving hadn't helped, but it did make me more appreciative of the wonton soup and egg rolls.

Old man Shoo is a great chef and makes some of the best dishes in Chinatown. Not long ago he seemed to have lost interest in the restaurant. Tommy and I both noticed the change. I said that I thought it was because he's getting older and running the restaurant wasn't easy. Tommy said that was certainly part of it, but there might be more to it than that.

For the old man, the restaurant had served one purpose, to provide the means for his only son to escape the life of a cook and to become a professional. It had served that purpose, but when his son, Tommy's father, had died in the 9/11 attack on the World Trade Centers, things changed. The old man then had to raise his two grandsons, and with his wife gone, it wasn't easy. But he had the restaurant, and it enabled him to do for his grandsons what he had done for their father. Now with Tommy and his brother doing well on their own, he no longer needed the restaurant.

The old man could easily afford to retire. Not only had he been frugal with his money, he owned the building on Mott Street which was worth a couple of million dollars. As for the restaurant itself, he never intended for his son or his grandsons to take over the business. But he had four faithful waiters who had worked at the restaurant for decades, and Tommy always assumed the old man would turn over the business to them.

Neither Tommy nor his brother, Joey, had any interest in taking over the restaurant, and neither cared if their grandfather gave the business to the waiters. In fact, they favored the idea. The four had lived in the building on Mott Street for as long as either could remember. To Tommy and Joey, the four men were family, the only family they had besides their grandfather.

Tommy's concern wasn't about the restaurant; it was what would happen to his grandfather if he gave up the restaurant. Working in the restaurant was all the old man had known for sixty plus years. Without the discipline of that routine, Tommy feared his grandfather would become bored, and boredom was an elderly person's biggest enemy. When he said that, he was looking at me as though he expected some kind of confirmation. I didn't know whether to be honored that he was seeking my advice, or angry that he thought I was old enough to have firsthand experience, so I just shrugged my shoulders.

I was happy to leave it at that, but I could see Tommy was really troubled, so I reminded him that his grandfather had a pretty good group of friends. Tommy nodded in agreement but said most of his friends were other business owners, and their time together was spent discussing their businesses.

That's when Tommy came up with the idea of having an intervention. I didn't think he even knew what an intervention was, but apparently, he had seen one on some reality television show. Now he wanted to arrange for an intervention with his grandfather, and he wanted me to be part of it.

I owed a lot to old man Shoo, so if an intervention was going to help, then I was in. I had participated in a couple of interventions with people who had drinking problems, but I didn't think that would be helpful with old man Shoo. In the first place, he didn't speak much English, and I didn't speak any Chinese, so I wasn't exactly sure what my role would be. As it turned out, all I had to do was nod my head and bow. Tommy, his brother, Joey, and old man Shoo's friends did all the talking. I didn't know what they were saying, but afterward Tommy explained that the intervention had been a great success. His grandfather was turning over the restaurant to the four waiters, but he would stay on and manage the place. No more cooking, but he'd have a job that would keep him active.

It all seemed to work out fine. The old man regained his energy, and the quality of the food remained unchanged. But once again, I've digressed.

As we ate, Tommy related the details of his meetings with the three kids who knew about the credit card theft. He met first with Devon's two teammates, Marcus Thomas and Ernesto Alfaro. He had considered them the least likely of the three to have reported the matter to the cops because they had as much to lose as did Devon. He was concerned, however, that one of them might have told someone else what Devon had done, but after interviewing each one, he concluded neither had told the cops or anyone else.

Tommy is a human lie detector, so if he believed the two boys, so did I. Tommy did say both boys were devastated over possibly being disqualified from the contest, but neither one blamed Devon. They realized that if Devon hadn't done what he did, they wouldn't have had a project to submit.

When Tommy tried contacting the third kid, Margie McDonald, she wasn't as cooperative as had been Marcus and Ernesto. She wouldn't answer Tommy's calls, and she ignored his voice messages. Finally, with Ernesto's help, Tommy caught up with her outside the school. Even then she initially refused to talk to him, thinking he had something to do with Devon's arrest.

It wasn't until Ernesto assured her that Tommy was working for and not against Devon that she opened up. She first denied telling anyone what Devon had done, but Tommy didn't believe her. He didn't confront her about it, though; he simply did what he does when someone's not telling him the truth. No, he didn't beat her; he talked around the issue, circling in slowly toward the truth, drawing Margie in with him.

He told her that unless we could discover who had spoken with the cops, Devon was likely to be convicted and would go to jail. That wasn't exactly true, but strange as it may seem, sometimes deception is a way to arrive at the truth. The cops lie to suspects all the time, and it's perfectly legal.

Think of it what you will, but it worked with Margie. She said that she hadn't told the cops what Devon had done, but she admitted telling the story to her best friend, Cindy Morris, adding that she had sworn Cindy to secrecy. I don't know much about teenage girls and neither does Tommy, but one thing we did know was that teenage girls are not known for keeping secrets. So far Margie hadn't been contacted by the cops or anyone from the District Attorney's Office, and assuming Ernesto, Morris, and Margie were telling the truth, we were in good shape.

To avoid the hearsay problem, the district attorney needed testimony from the person to whom Devon had admitted the crime, and that was Margie. The fact that she hadn't been contacted yet by the DA or the cops suggested they didn't know her identity. From that I could reasonably assume it wasn't Cindy Morris who tipped off the cops. Had it been her, the cops would have asked how she came by the information and would have backtracked immediately to Margie. That meant there was at least another layer between Margie and the tipster and possibly more, or if we were really lucky, it had been an anonymous tip. If it hadn't been an anonymous tip, I could only hope there were enough layers to keep the cops from finding Margie before I was able to spring Devon.

Tommy was confident that none of the three kids would change their stories down the road, but he had taken sworn statements from them just to be safe. I asked Tommy to follow up with the Cindy Morris kid to find out who she told about Devon's little caper and if she had been contacted by the police.

Tommy asked what I planned on doing about the possible disqualification. I had no idea what I could do, or for that matter, if I should do anything. I was pissed about it, but since it didn't impact the criminal case, it wasn't a problem with which I was ethically required to deal. When I said that to Tommy, he just shrugged his shoulders and said, "Oh, well, if that's what you think."

Clearly Tommy didn't agree, but I wasn't in the mood to argue, so I didn't reply. After Tommy left, I thought more about it, and I began to wonder if there wasn't any I could do to help out Devon and his buddies. That night at dinner, I asked Gracie what she thought about the situation. She agreed that the disqualification wouldn't impact the criminal case, and so I was right; ethically it wasn't something I had to address. Then she added that I already knew that, so why ask her opinion unless I thought addressing the possible disqualification was something I should do. Sounding very much like Doug, she asked, "Putting technicalities aside, do you think it's the right thing to do?"

I admitted that I felt sorry for the kid, but I wasn't sure how I could help him. It was a civil matter, not a criminal one, and I wasn't a civil lawyer. Gracie said that didn't really matter because I was a clever lawyer, and I could figure it out easily enough. She was probably right about that. Truth be told, I was nervous about handling a matter outside of my area of expertise, and maybe I was looking for an excuse not to deal with the problem. If I did do something to prevent the disqualification, it had to be done pro bono, meaning I wasn't going to get paid for doing it. I couldn't bill the 18B Panel since it wouldn't be part of the criminal defense, and I wasn't going to bill Devon or his grandfather. But with the $100,000 fee I had just pocketed, that wasn't really a consideration.

CHAPTER 29

By the next morning, I had formulated a plan to help Devon, and with the deadline approaching, I had to act quickly. The first rule of combat is to *know your enemy*, so before I did anything, I wanted to find out as much as I could about the contest and the judges. Hoping to also enlist support from Devon's school, I figured the best place to start was with the school's principal, Mr. Taylor.

When I explained who I was and why I was calling, Mr. Taylor was initially reluctant to help. He said that he couldn't approve of Devon's conduct, adding that it had surprised him because it was totally out of line with the boy's character. Seeing that as an opening and hoping to soften Taylor's attitude, I explained Devon's motivation. Taylor listened patiently, then said he still couldn't condone what Devon had done. I admitted that I didn't condone it either, but I understood it, and all I asked of him was to do the same.

Taylor's silence told me his resistance was weakening, so I pushed on. I said Devon had suffered the humiliation of an arrest and might have a record for the rest of his life. However, if Devon made restitution as he promised that he would, the case was likely to be dismissed. Given that outcome, I asked Taylor if he thought disqualification from the contest was justified.

Again, when he didn't respond immediately, I took it as a good sign and continued. I said this wasn't a case of cheating or violation of the contest rules. Maybe the spirit of the rules frowned on stealing parts, but technically it wasn't a disqualifying event. Stealing ideas, yes, that would be grounds for disqualification, but stealing money to buy parts, no. The project deserved to be judged on its merits, not disqualified because it was funded in a questionable way.

Taylor still hadn't said anything, and I was beginning to wonder if he had hung up the phone. But then he finally spoke, asking what I planned on doing. I said that I planned to eliminate the threat of disqualification. I'd start by demanding that the judges reverse their decision, and if they refused, I'd take them to court. Taylor apparently liked the plan and agreed to help, so long as the school wasn't mentioned in the lawsuit.

I promised it wouldn't be and asked only that he send me all the information he had about the contest and the judges, together with a letter attesting to the good character of the three boys. Other than the letter, I needed nothing else suggesting in any way that the school was supporting the cause. With that understanding, Taylor promised to fax the letter and the contest materials right away.

An hour later I had everything I needed. Now I had to figure out what to do with it all. I might not know civil procedure, but I knew the best way to get someone's attention was to threaten a lawsuit.

Being a criminal defense lawyer, I'm not used to writing letters that threaten civil lawsuits. The threatening part was no problem, that I could do. But if the threats didn't work, and I had to start a civil lawsuit, that could be a problem. In my thirty-four years of practicing law, I'd never brought a civil lawsuit. I had learned how to do it in law school, but that was a lifetime ago, and I didn't remember much about it. Of course, Doug knew all about civil lawsuits, and he was damn good at handling them.

I called Doug, explained the situation, and I asked if he would give me a hand. He said that he would have liked to help, but he couldn't because he represented Tele-Data, one of the contest sponsors. As he explained it, threatening to sue your own client is never a good thing. To begin with, it's a conflict of interest, and it's likely to cause the client to fire you. I could see Doug's point; still I had to ask if Tele-Data was really that good a client. Doug hung up on me, so I guessed it was.

I spent the rest of the morning drafting a letter to the contest officials. When I was done, I thought I had written a very persuasive letter. It began with a well-reasoned and logical argument about why disqualification was unwarranted and constituted a wrongful act on the part of the officials. Then, in closing, I wrote that if they didn't reverse their decision within three days, they would receive a visit from Little Tony Savino who would make them an offer they couldn't refuse.

I told you that I wasn't good at civil litigation. Threats, yes, but civil litigation not so much. Of course, Connie said I needed to change the wording slightly. Instead of a visit from Little Tony, they could expect a lawsuit. I still think threatening a visit from Little Tony was the better option.

One thing was certain. I had gotten myself into something well outside my comfort zone, and by lunchtime I needed an AA meeting. I wasn't a mob lawyer, and I wasn't a civil litigator, so what the hell was I doing? Maybe if I was handling just one of the cases, it wouldn't have been as bad. But I was handling both, and I really didn't have a way out. If I tried turning back Little Tony's case, either Big Tony or one of the Ruccis would probably whack me, and if I turned Devon's case back to the 18B Panel, a new lawyer wasn't likely to follow up on the civil end.

It was one of those no-win situations I find myself in too often. So I went to an AA meeting and bitched. Sometimes that's what AA meetings are good for, and believe me, it helps to bitch. Technically it's called sharing, but I call it what it is, bitching.

CHAPTER 30

Going to meetings clears my head and helps me keep things in perspective. When I was drinking heavily, I couldn't do that because my overriding priority was getting drunk, and everything else in my life had to fit around that priority. When a court date got in the way of my drinking, I didn't go to court. The consequences didn't matter because I didn't care; all I cared about was getting drunk. The fact that my behavior could be putting someone else in jeopardy didn't bother me in the least.

When friends got in the way of my drinking, I got rid of my friends. Who needed a bunch of Goody Two-shoes telling me I needed to slow down on my drinking? I'd drink when I wanted to and as much as I wanted, and that was nobody's business but my own.

If you're getting the idea that I was a miserable bastard when I drank, you'd be spot on. A lonely miserable bastard, I should add. Was I that way before I started drinking alcoholically? Probably not, although I was never the easiest guy in the world to get along with. Still I had a lot of friends, and I took my professional responsibilities very seriously.

Do I blame my conduct on my drinking? That's a tough question to answer. I'd like to say yes, but I can't.

Much of what I did while drunk was driven by the booze. When I was drinking heavily, I did things I'd never done before, so to that extent my drinking drove my conduct. But that's not an excuse for what I did because while alcoholism is an addiction, it's also a choice. At any point in my drinking life, I could have chosen not to drink. I could have gone to AA before I was forced to go. It wouldn't have been easy, but it wasn't impossible. So, no, I don't blame my conduct on my drinking; I blame myself for my conduct.

Leaving the meeting that afternoon, I felt a lot better about everything. I had Devon's case under control, and while a successful outcome was far from guaranteed, I was doing the best I could. There wasn't anything more I could think of doing, short of sending Little Tony to threaten the contest officials. If it came down to a civil lawsuit, I'd figure out what had to be done, and I'd do it. How hard could it be to handle a civil lawsuit? If these ambulance chasers advertising on television can do it, I certainly can.

By the way, what is it with these television ads? Have you noticed how the guys in these ads all say, "I'm not an attorney; I'm an attorney spokesperson."

What is that supposed to mean? The fact that these lawyers can't speak for themselves should tell you something. I want to call one of their hotlines, you know, the ones like 1-800-Let's Sue, and say, "Hi, I'm not a client; I'm a client spokesperson," and see what they say.

In Devon's case, I might have been unsure of myself, but in Little Tony's case, I knew exactly what to do and how to do it. What made me uncomfortable handling Little Tony's case was the thought of getting killed. What made it worse was not knowing who would do the killing and why. Would it be the Ruccis if Little Tony wasn't convicted, or would it be Big Tony if he was convicted, or would it be the Russian mob who didn't need a reason? If I was going to die, I at least wanted to die a martyr, but you can't be a martyr if you don't know what you're dying for. The headline, *Lawyer Killed in Cause for Client*, sounds a hell of a lot better than, *Lawyer Killed in Random Shooting*. Or *"Beheaded"* if it was the Russian mob that killed me.

I admit that even after the AA meeting, I was still a little uneasy about Little Tony's case. Not enough to jump ship, if I could even do

116

that, but enough to be uneasy. In the past when I felt that way, I'd go for a drink. Just a short one to calm my nerves. Of course, that didn't work out so well because I never stopped at one short one, and after a while, I was so calm my bones went soft.

I don't think that I have to tell you that you don't make the best decisions when you're drunk, even though a booze-soaked brain will convince you that you are a genius, and everything you come up with is brilliant. Most times I got lucky and passed out before I acted on one of my brilliant ideas. But the couple of times I did act on them, when I sobered up, I discovered I was in deeper shit than I was before. That, of course, left me needing a short one to calm my nerves. Are you beginning to see a pattern here? That's alcoholism at work. At least that day after attending the meeting, I wasn't heading for the nearest bar.

That night Gracie suggested we grab a quick bite to eat at Shoo's before heading home. That was good news because it confirmed that I was completely out of the doghouse and wouldn't have to eat sushi for at least a week. Under the circumstances, I thought it best not to talk about Little Tony's case least I find myself back in the doghouse and eating sushi nightly.

Gracie knew if I didn't bring up work, it meant I didn't want to talk about it, and that night, like most nights, she followed my lead. She's good that way, and I love her for it. Of course, if she thinks I've gone off the deep end as I have done at times, she'll press the issue. Since she didn't press the issue, I took it to mean I was still in the shallow end of the pool. I was happy to leave it at that, ignoring the fact that the pool was full of sharks. After all, things could be worse; I could be eating sushi.

CHAPTER 31

The next morning as I sat reading the morning paper and enjoying my third cup of coffee, Connie brought in the mail. I noticed a thick Manila envelope with the seal of the District Attorney's Office. Suspecting it contained the forensic reports in Little Tony's case, I pulled it from the pile and ripped it open. It was the forensic reports, all the reports except the ballistic test reports.

When it comes to discovery in criminal cases, New York law is a bit behind the times, so even though I had served my Brady demand the day before, the district attorney wasn't required to comply with the demand until the eve of trial. But Sarah Washington had agreed to provide the reports which was her prerogative. If any were missing, it was McAvoy's doing and not Sarah's.

Why were ballistic test reports missing? Either they hadn't been completed yet, which was unlikely, or Assistant District Attorney Tommy McAvoy was withholding them. I was betting McAvoy withheld the reports because they probably supported Little Tony's story.

I was assuming the crime scene investigators, or the medical examiner, had recovered slugs from the scene or from the victims' bodies. If Little Tony was telling the truth that he hadn't killed the two Russians, but he had kneecapped one of them, the ballistic tests would show that two different guns had been used. One gun was used to shoot the victims in the head, killing them, and another gun was used to kneecap one of the victims. So, which slugs were matched to the gun Little Tony was carrying when arrested? Was it the slugs from the head shots or the slug from the kneecapping?

I had to consider the possibility that the slug from the kneecapping wasn't recovered. Shooting a kneecap would shatter it, but a bat or a tire iron to the kneecap would do the same. Unless the crime scene investigators had reason to believe the kneecap was shattered by a bullet, there was no reason to search for it.

Even without the slug from the kneecapping, the ballistic reports probably helped Little Tony's defense. They might not support my two-gun theory, but if the recovered slugs hadn't been fired from the gun Little Tony was carrying when he was arrested, that alone put a big ding in the district attorney's case. You could bet the ranch if the slugs had matched Little Tony's gun, the ballistic report would be setting on my desk. I made a note to call Tommy McAvoy and ask about the ballistic reports.

The first thing I did was to compare the arrest report to the crime scene reports, searching for any discrepancies between them. The arrest reports generally don't contain a lot of details, but the few they do contain usually overlap with details in the crime scene reports. Little seemingly meaningless discrepancies can often be used to create reasonable doubt. Trials, civil or criminal, are all about details, and when the details don't match up, jurors become skeptical and skeptical jurors are a defense attorney's best friends. That's why I look for discrepancies in the details. In Little Tony's case, there were no apparent discrepancies between the crime scene reports and the arrest report.

The Crime Scene Unit had conducted investigations at two locations. The first and primary location was under the Manhattan Bridge where the bodies had been discovered. The second location was the office where the two victims were presumably killed. I searched both crime scene reports looking for mention of either slugs or shell casings but found none. The Crime Scene Unit had recovered lots of fingerprints and taken dozens of photographs but found no additional physical evidence. Either the two Russians had been killed elsewhere, or the killer had picked up the shell casings, a common practice for hired guns.

It was the absence of any reference to the slugs that had my attention. If the two victims had been killed in the office, shot gangland style as Chen had said, the slugs had either gone right through their skulls or remained inside. The Crime Scene Unit would look for exit wounds, and if exit wounds were found, they would search the office for slugs. Since there was no mention of slugs in the report, I could safely assume none were found in the office, and so they had to be in the victims' skulls. The absence of any mention of a third slug from the kneecapping was understandable since the Crime Scene Unit would have no reason to search for a slug.

Next, I turned my attention to the medical examiner's reports, hoping the autopsy findings would detail where the slugs had come from. The medical examiner's reports, like the crime scene reports, were fairly straightforward. In each case, *"the cause of death"* was listed as "extreme brain trauma," with the *"mechanism of death"* being "a single gunshot to the skull." The "manner of death" was, of course, "homicide." Simply put, both Russians had died as the result of being shot in their heads.

The reports described the entry wounds at the back of each victim's head, but neither report mentioned an exit wound. That led me to conclude that the two had been shot with hollow point bullets. Hollow point bullets flatten on impact, reducing the slugs' penetrating power and increasing the damage they cause.

If there was no exit wound in either victim's skull, the slugs had to be in their brains and should have been recovered during the autopsy. But there was no mention of any slugs being recovered in either report. That didn't make sense.

In both reports, the medical examiner noted numerous injuries, including contusions, abrasions, ecchymosis, lacerations, and various fractures, which added up to them having had the shit beat out of them before they were killed. The report on Levka Baran noted a shattered right kneecap but offered no explanation as to how the injury was inflicted. There was no reference to a gunshot wound, nor any mention of a recovered slug.

There was no mention in either of the medical examiner's reports of a time gap between the beatings and the fatal gunshots to the victims' heads. Typically, the medical examiner would classify the beating injuries as being antemortem, meaning before death, or perimortem, meaning at or about the time of death, but in this case, he did neither. A time gap between the beatings and the shootings could support a claim that the beatings and the shootings had been done by two different people. Even if I could prove there was a significant time gap between the beatings and the killings, that alone wouldn't be fatal to the district attorney's case, but it would be another ding. You put enough dings in a case, and pretty soon you have a full-fledged dent.

I was beginning to suspect that the original reports might have been scrubbed, probably by Assistant District Attorney McAvoy. I'm not suggesting that the medical examiner would do anything overtly unethical, but I knew from personal experience that a friendly medical examiner could be convinced to leave out a non-substantive phrase or two if it helped the prosecution.

The only physical evidence recovered from the victims were skin cells found under the fingernails of victim number one. The cells had been sent to the DNA lab for analysis and comparison to the samples in the DNA database. It wouldn't be long before the lab matched the cells to Little Tony, but at least it wouldn't come as a surprise. Nor would it necessarily be fatal to Little Tony's defense. It only proved he had physical contact with the victim, but it didn't prove he had killed him. That made a time gap between the beatings and the killings significant and a reason why McAvoy might not want it mentioned in the reports.

I reread the two reports, hoping to find something that I could use in court. There is usually something in an autopsy report, or something missing from an autopsy report, that a good criminal defense lawyer can turn to his or her advantage. That's because the autopsy report is a standardized form, and the narrative is made to fit the form, rather than the narrative creating its own form. Sometimes that means squeezing round pegs into square holes, and when that happens, the doctor usually has some explaining to do.

There are other ways an autopsy report can be attacked. Occasionally a doctor will slip up and use the word "possibly" in stating his conclusions. That kind of mistake lays the groundwork for reasonable doubt because "possibly" is not close to the "reasonable degree of medical certainty" the law requires.

I look for any detail, no matter how small, in an autopsy report that I can turn to my advantage. A seemingly insignificant detail that I can use to raise a small question in a juror's mind. It's like a seed that if properly cultivated will bloom into reasonable doubt.

In this case, I found such a seed in both reports. The medical examiner noted "dried blood cells around the lacerations," meaning a scab was forming. If my memory from an old case served me well, not much scabbing occurs after death, so if there was some significant scabbing on the lacerations, that would prove there was a time interval between the beatings and kill shots to the heads. That was my seed, but I had to find out how long that interval might have been, and for that, I needed an expert.

When it came to expert medical examiners, there was only one that I wanted on this case and that was Dr. Theo Makris. He was a former New York City Medical Examiner and was now Professor of Pathology at SUNY Downstate Medical School in Brooklyn.

You know I love New York City, and l like to brag about it, so bear with me while I tell you something about Downstate Medical School. When Downstate Medical School opened in 1860, it was the first medical school in the country to be located in a hospital and to offer bedside training. It set the standard practice for all the teaching hospitals that followed. Today there are seven medical schools in New York City, but Downstate is the only one located in Brooklyn.

Enough trivia, back to Dr. Makris. We met when I was a young lawyer working in the District Attorney's Office, and he was a young doctor working in the Medical Examiner's Office. I hate to admit it, but that was over thirty years ago. Still, I remembered the first case we worked together like it was yesterday. It was my first murder trial, and it was Theo's first time testifying as an expert witness. A pair of rookies on our first big outings.

I wouldn't admit it then, but I was scared to death, brazen, but still scared. Theo, on the other hand, was so confident that he gave me confidence.

The case involved a husband who allegedly bludgeoned his wife to death in their bedroom. The husband, who had a record for domestic abuse, claimed he was with friends in a nearby bar when the murder occurred. It was a solid alibi but only if the time of death was before midnight. With very little forensic evidence tying the husband to the murder, the whole case hung on Theo convincing the jury that the wife was killed after midnight.

Theo was the second witness I called to the stand. The first was the investigating detective who set the scene. Then I called Theo who described the gruesome details of the murder, using the autopsy photos to illustrate his points. Then came the critical testimony, Theo's opinion that the victim had died after midnight. My final witnesses were the victim's neighbors who testified they heard someone screaming obscenities after midnight on the night of the murder. The only problem was they admitted on cross-examination that they couldn't be sure it was the victim who was screaming. The case was wobbly, and the defense knew it.

Hoping to create reasonable doubt as to the time of death, the defense called as its expert witness, Dr. Shaw, a well-known pathologist, and a frequent guest on television talk shows. Back then, there were far less so-called talking heads than there are today, but Shaw was a network favorite, and it was easy to see why.

To begin with, he was well-qualified, so attacking his credentials was not going to get me anywhere. But beyond his qualifications, he was handsome, well-spoken, and he was slick. Needless to say, the jury loved him.

Shaw testified that the physical evidence did not establish the time of death with a degree of reasonable certainty. He said, based on the victim's body temperature that had been measured by Theo at the crime scene, and applying the standard cooling rate of a body after death, something he called algor mortis, he concluded the victim died sometime between 11:30 PM and 1:00 AM.

It's never good when jurors nod their heads in agreement with a hostile witness, and there was a lot of head nodding during Shaw's testimony. Using Theo's own findings to support his opinion was brilliant. All I could do on cross-examination was to question whether he had taken into account the fact that it was a cold night, and as the crime scene photographs showed, the victim was close to an open window. Smiling condescendingly, he said that he had taken the temperature into consideration when he calculated the time of death.

If the jury believed Dr. Shaw, the half hour between 11:30 and midnight was grounds for reasonable doubt. The way that the jury had reacted to Dr. Shaw's testimony, I knew they believed him, and my already wobbly case had gotten even more wobbly.

Thankfully it was noon when Shaw finished testifying, and that gave me the luncheon break to come up with something to rebut his testimony. Theo and I ate together, and while I tried to think of a way to blunt Shaw's testimony, Theo spent his time studying the crime scene photos.

By the time lunch ended, I had come up with nothing and had no idea what to do next. But then Theo said I should recall him to the stand. He wouldn't tell me what he had in mind, but having no plan of my own, I agreed to do as he asked. Probably seeing the look of desperation on my face, Theo assured me that he had everything in hand. All I had to do was show him the crime scene photos, and ask him one question, which he had written out on a paper napkin, and he'd do the rest. Frankly, at the time it sounded a little over the top, but it worked.

After Theo looked at the crime scene photos, I asked him the question just as he had written it on the napkin.

"Dr. Makris, do the photographs show anything which causes you to question the accuracy of Dr. Shaw's opinion as to when the victim died?"

Holding up one of the crime scene photographs, Theo pointed to an open window not far from the body, noting that the curtains over the window were blowing into the apartment. He said Dr. Shaw's analysis had taken the temperature of the room into consideration when he calculated the time of death; however, he failed to take into consideration the effects of ventilation created by the wind blowing over the victim's body. Ventilation causes the body to cool more rapidly. Adjusting the rate of cooling to account for the wind blowing over the victim's body made the time of death between 12:30 AM to 2:30 AM.

Noticing the heads bobbing in the jury box, I smiled at Theo and announced I had no further questions for the witness.

Donald L'Abbate

The judge asked the defense attorney if he planned on calling Dr. Shaw back to the stand for rebuttal. After a hasty but animated conference between the two, Shaw left the courtroom. With no further rebuttal, we made our final arguments, and then the case went to the jury.

The jury returned with a conviction in less than an hour. Later that day as Theo and I sat having drinks and celebrating our victory, I told him it was his confidence that had given me confidence. That's when he confessed that he was scared to death but gained confidence from me. It seemed we were both good at putting on fronts to hide our insecurities. My insecurities eventually led me to drink alcoholically. Theo, on the other hand, dealt with his insecurities in a constructive way. He overcame them and rose quickly through the ranks of the Medical Examiner's Office, eventually becoming the city's Chief Medical Examiner before moving on to academia.

After I left the District Attorney's Office, we lost touch, but when I got sober, we reconnected. Now I needed to call him on Little Tony's case.

CHAPTER 32

My first call after reading the autopsy reports wasn't to Theo Makris, but to Assistant District Attorney McAvoy to ask when I could expect to receive the ballistic reports. If, as I suspected, he had the autopsy report scrubbed, he was probably doing the same with the ballistic reports, or at a minimum, he was holding on to them for as long as he could.

After ringing several times, my call was transferred to McAvoy's voice mail. Either he wasn't in his office, or he wasn't taking my call. Normally I have no patience with voice mail and simply hang up as soon as I'm connected. But I wanted the damn ballistic reports, so I left a message. It was a simple message: "It's Carney. I want the Savino case ballistic reports now! Don't make me go to Sarah, or I'll hand your pink slip to you personally. Have a nice day." See, I can be nice.

My next call was to Dr. Theo Makris. Knowing how busy he was between teaching and his consulting work; I hadn't expected to reach him on my first try. But I managed to catch him between lectures. Theo and I hadn't worked together in a while because he wasn't on the 18B Panel's list of approved witnesses. It wasn't that he didn't qualify; it was simply that his rates were too high.

With Theo's expertise and reputation, his services were in high demand which enabled him to be choosy when it came to accepting assignments. His rates were commensurate with his talents, but he was known to take on pro bono work now and then. I never used our friendship to pressure Theo into taking on any cases, but over the years I'd call him when I had a case I thought might intrigue him. If he found the case challenging, or if he thought justice wasn't being served, he'd take the case at the Panel's rates or even pro bono.

This time my retainer agreement with Little Tony gave me full authority to hire investigators and expert witnesses as I saw fit, so Theo's rates weren't an issue. But that didn't necessarily mean Theo would take the case. The last time we had spoken a few months earlier, Theo said he had reached a point in his life where he was only accepting cases that interested him, and then only if he had the time for them. I envied him that luxury and wished I could do the same. But I couldn't, which wasn't surprising when you considered how I wasted a decade of my life drinking. But it is what it is and crying over it won't change it.

After Theo heard the facts in Little Tony's case, he said the case sounded interesting. Not interesting enough for him to get involved, but he'd take the case as a favor to me. Theo asked me to send him a copy of the medical examiner's reports as quickly as possible, and of course, the ballistic reports as soon as they were available.

That's when it dawned on me that neither the crime scene investigation report, nor the autopsy report, mentioned any slugs being recovered. I specifically recalled Sarah Washington saying something about a ballistic report, and so I assumed slugs had been recovered.

When there hadn't been any mention of slugs in the Crime Scene Unit's report, I figured the slugs had been recovered from the victims' bodies. That seemed to be confirmed by the absence of a description of exit wounds in the medical examiner's autopsy report. If there were no exit wounds, the slugs had to have remained in the victims' skulls.

But there had been no mention in the autopsy report of the slugs having been recovered and logged into evidence. So, if they weren't recovered at the scene, and they weren't recovered during the autopsy, where had the slugs come from, and how could the absence of any mention of them be explained? I'd have to wait for the ballistic report to find out.

CHAPTER 33

It hadn't taken Tommy long to track down Cindy Morris, the girl Margie McDonald told about Devon's little crime spree. According to the report Tommy left on my desk, he caught up with Cindy just outside the school building, saying he was an investigator and that he needed to talk to her about a false report given to the police. When she asked if he was a cop, he said simply that he was undercover, never claiming to be a police officer but not actually denying he was. It was a little subterfuge that Tommy used from time to time.

At first, Cindy denied knowing anything about Devon, but when Tommy confronted her with Margie McDonald's sworn statement, she cracked. She admitted that Margie McDonald told her about Devon stealing the credit card number, but she denied telling anyone else about it.

Sensing she was lying, Tommy told her she could be facing serious charges for making a false report to the police. Now totally rattled, Cindy swore she hadn't told the police about Devon. Tommy believed that to be true, so he changed tactics. He told Cindy she could still be in trouble, but he'd be willing to overlook her involvement if she gave him the names of everyone she told about Devon. That's when she broke down and admitted that she had told only one person, George Braun. Tommy believed she was telling the truth.

Checking the contest materials I had received from Principal Taylor, I found George Braun's name on the list of contestants. My theory had been right. Devon was turned in by a fellow contestant probably fearing that Devon's project would win the contest.

I called Devon and asked him about George Braun. He said George was most likely his biggest challenger in the contest. He and George were constantly competing for number one in the class, and the contest could have a big impact on that competition. Devon explained that he was presently ranked number one in the class academically, and Braun was ranked number two, but he was behind by a very small margin. The winner of the contest would receive a bonus grade, and if Braun's project won, the bonus grade would move him into the number one spot. Why was the ranking so important? Because monetary prizes were awarded at graduation based on class ranking.

With all of that at stake, I had to believe Braun wouldn't want it known that he was responsible for the disqualification, so to protect himself, he probably tipped off the cops anonymously. That would explain why the tip hadn't been traced back to Cindy Morris or Margie. The tip had been good enough for the cops to check it out with American Express, but with so little money involved, it obviously didn't merit much of an investigation after that.

If nothing else, what I had told Silverman about another contestant being the snitch was true. But I was looking for something more.

After telling Devon that Braun had been the one who turned him in to the cops, I asked if he wanted me to try and have Braun disqualified. I figured I could call Silverman and demand that he honor his "sacred" obligation to protect the integrity of the contest and throw out Braun's project. Much to his credit, Devon said no, he'd rather lose to a better project than win by having a better project disqualified. He's a lot better person than I am; I'll tell you that.

Everything was beginning to fall into place, but before I approached Sarah Washington for a deal, I needed to convince American Express not to press the larceny charge against Devon. To do that, I turned to my friend and sponsor, Doug.

CHAPTER 34

I think that I mentioned in passing that Doug is a corporate lawyer and has never been much help to me on my cases. Don't get me wrong; he's a great AA sponsor and an excellent lawyer in his own right. However, he knows next to nothing about criminal law. Then it dawned on me that with all of Doug's corporate contacts, he might just know somebody at American Express who I could talk to, or even better, that the two of us could talk to.

As it turned out, Doug had several contacts at American Express, and he was more than happy to help. He made a couple of phone calls, and in short order we had an appointment with an executive who Doug believed had the authority to decide whether to press charges against Devon.

The morning of the meeting I met Doug at his office, and we took the fifteen-minute walk to 200 Vesey Street, American Express' headquarters. Just a block or so before reaching Vesey Street, we passed the World Trade Center site, and the 9/11 Memorial. Although it's been over seventeen years since that infamous day, I still remember it with the same anger and pain I felt on that day and hopefully will always feel. I owe that much to the three thousand innocent people murdered that day. I owe it to them to be angry over their senseless deaths. Angry that Tommy and his brother, Joey, were orphaned that day. Angry that first responders, brave men and women, died that day in the hopeless effort to save lives. Angry that twenty-six sniveling cowards murdered so many innocent people. And angry because I can't make sense of it and never will.

Neither Doug nor I said a word as we passed the site, but I knew he was equally emotional. Perhaps he didn't share my unrelenting anger because Doug isn't like me when it comes to not letting go. He's more understanding which is a good thing. Still, I don't think anyone who lived in New York on that day can pass the site and not feel something. Probably not the same anger I feel, but they feel something.

By the time we arrived at the American Express office, my anger had dissipated, and I was focusing on the task at hand. Fearing I might react badly if things weren't going my way, Doug had worked out a signal to stop me from talking. If he cleared his throat, I was to shut my mouth and let him pick up the conversation. As you might suspect, I didn't care for the plan when Doug first proposed it. Initially I told him to stuff it, but eventually Doug convinced me of the wisdom behind his plan.

I had one chance to persuade American Express not to press the larceny charge, and I couldn't afford to blow that chance. Knowing me as he does, Doug said my passion, which was good in many situations, might not be so good in this situation. It was Doug's kind way of saying if I lost my temper, I'd blow the deal for Devon. He was right, so I agreed to the muzzle signal, but I was determined not to make Doug use it.

Then Doug gave me a piece of advice that probably carried the day. He reminded me that I'd be appealing to a businessman, not a jury, and suggested I not make an emotional argument. American Express cared little or nothing about Devon's life; what concerned American Express was its own business interest. Doug said if I wanted to win, I had to explain why it was in American Express' business interest not to press charges. It was a tall order, but I had some ideas that I thought might work.

The Amex guy, Jack Dubinsky, came to the meeting well prepared, and after assuring me he was familiar with the facts, he got right to the point and asked why American Express shouldn't press charges. Following Doug's advice, I didn't go for sympathy. Instead, I said that given my client's circumstances, we'd have no choice but to take the case to trial which meant someone from American Express would have to testify.

Then I added, "I'm sure you're aware that would mean someone spending time with an ADA to prep for testifying at the Grand Jury hearing, then more prep time spent preparing for testifying at trial. You'd also need to have someone present at the trial to authenticate the charge records, so that would be more time spent on the case. It seems to me to be a lot of expense for a $2,100 loss which, if my client goes to jail, you probably won't recoup anyway. I'm here to offer you full restitution without any expenses attached and with no corporate loss of time."

Mr. Dubinsky thought about it, then asked what I meant by my client's circumstances. When I glanced at Doug for guidance, he gave me a slight nod, and I laid out Devon's story, but I did it in a very matter of fact way. When I finished, Mr. Dubinsky nodded and said if full restitution was made, the company wouldn't press charges. I explained that I had one or two small matters to clear up with the District Attorney's Office before we could issue a check, but I had a letter in which I personally guaranteed payment of $2,100 within forty-five days. After looking over the letter, Mr. Dubinsky extended his hand, and we had a deal.

It was nearly lunchtime when we left the American Express office, and since the famous P.J. Clark's was just down the block, I insisted on buying Doug lunch. P.J. Clark's might be better known as a saloon than a restaurant, but it's still a good place for burgers or a pub lunch.

As we ate our burgers, Doug said unless they added something new to the Code of Professional Responsibility, guaranteeing a payment on behalf of a client wasn't an attorney's obligation. Doug was right, and he knew damn well why I did it; it was just his way of letting me know that he knew why I did it.

When I first met Doug and asked him to be my sponsor, I had just stopped drinking, and I still had an edge to me. I tried to convince everyone, Doug included, that I was this tough guy. Of course, Doug saw right through my act, but he never really called me on it. Instead he'd poke at me a bit, like he was doing that day. But it was a good day, so I just laughed off his comment and enjoyed the moment.

Now that I had everything I needed to move on the case, it was time to go see Sarah Washington. Maybe Christmas would come early for Devon. I didn't share any of this with Devon or his grandfather because I didn't want to get their hopes up prematurely.

CHAPTER 35

On Monday morning, Assistant District Attorney McAvoy returned my call to tell me there were no ballistic reports because no slugs had been recovered. I knew from my earlier conversation with Sarah Washington that wasn't true. I figured McAvoy didn't know about our conversation because if he did, he'd know that he couldn't get away with the lie. But I didn't challenge him because his not knowing what I knew worked to my advantage. I simply thanked him for his call and let it go at that.

Sarah had said something about a ballistic report, so the slugs had to exist, or at least they did at some point. That meant they should have been recorded in a chain of custody log. A paper trail that listed chronologically the custody, control, transfer, and disposition of all physical evidence gathered during an investigation. Maintaining a detailed and accurate chain of custody log for every piece of evidence is a critical part of all investigations. Without such a record, the evidence's legitimacy becomes an issue, and a judge is likely to exclude it from the trial. That was why the log was so important, and why maintaining it was strict operating policy.

Sooner or later the log would turn up, and McAvoy would be forced to turn over the ballistic reports. Then his ass would be in a sling for lying to me in the first place. McAvoy was a jerk, but he wasn't stupid. He had to know how it would play out. So why lie when he knew damn good and well he'd get caught?

None of this was making any sense. Starting with the fact that none of the forensic reports mentioned the slugs. I figured the reports had been scrubbed, and I was probably right about that. But why? And why was McAvoy telling an obvious lie about the slugs? He had to know the chain of custody log would prove the slugs existed. Unless, of course, the log had disappeared along with the slugs.

The question was no longer where the slugs had come from, the crime scene or the victims' skulls. The question now was where had the slugs gone? Sometimes evidence gets lost, but it doesn't just disappear without a trace.

If the slugs had disappeared, so could the chain of custody log. But that wasn't something an assistant district attorney like McAvoy could have pulled off by himself. No, this would have required help from at least someone in the Medical Examiner's Office and possibly the Forensic Lab, as well as someone higher up in the District Attorney's Office than McAvoy, and possibly the NYPD's Property Clerk's Office. It would have to have been a very big conspiracy, with a lot of risk attached to it, so why would someone go through all that trouble?

I had to believe that the Ruccis had a hand in all of this, and I thought that I knew why. One possibility was the ballistic evidence proved the slugs that killed the two Russians came from Little Tony's gun, and the Ruccis made the evidence disappear to protect Little Tony. But I didn't think that was the case. Everything I knew so far told me the Ruccis wanted Little Tony convicted, not acquitted. That being so, the ballistic reports probably proved the slugs didn't come from Little Tony's gun, and that's why they needed them to disappear. I didn't know if they had the political pull to get it done, but if it only took money, they certainly had enough of that.

Sarah Washington was my friend, and I didn't want to believe she was involved in what I was now seeing as a widespread conspiracy. I took solace in thinking that Sarah would never have mentioned the ballistic report when we met the week before if she was involved in the conspiracy. Still, I couldn't be certain she wasn't involved, so I couldn't go to her directly. For the time being, I'd let McAvoy think I believed that there were no ballistic reports. I wasn't going to poke the bear until I was ready to kill the bear, and until I was sure there were no other bears around waiting to kill me.

I called Theo Makris. Theo, like me, had been born and raised in New York City and knew all about the city's politics and past corruption. So he wasn't shocked when I relayed the story of the missing slugs and the ballistic reports. He was, however, skeptical that it could involve so many people in so many different agencies without the plan being exposed. He said there had to be a simpler answer, but he needed time to think it through.

In the meantime, Theo had some good news for me. The x-ray taken of the Russian's shattered knee showed small sections with circular breaks inconsistent with a blunt force trauma, but consistent with a bullet passing through the kneecap. One of Theo's assistants was using Photoshop to piece together those fragments which might enable Theo to determine the caliber of the bullet. Theo said it was a long shot, but it might work.

Now I needed to talk to Big Tony. I called Joey Bats and asked him to set up a meeting as quickly as possible. I didn't tell him why, but I did say it was extremely important. Within half an hour I got a call from Big Tony. It was a funny conversation because neither of us wanted to say anything of substance over the phone.

I said simply, "We need to talk."

Big Tony replied, "Yeah, let's meet somewhere quiet."

I knew he meant somewhere we wouldn't be recognized, so meeting in Little Italy was out. But Chinatown wasn't, and I knew just the spot, the Nom Wah Tea Parlor on Doyers Street. We agreed to meet in an hour.

I was still trying to figure out what was going on with the ballistic reports when Connie announced that a Mr. Silverman was on the line and wanted to speak to me about Devon Matthews. At least my threatening letter had some affect, just how much of an affect I would soon find out.

After introducing himself as the chairman of the contest committee, Mr. Silverman said while he sympathized with Devon's situation, the committee had a sacred duty to protect the integrity of the contest. He sounded like a pompous ass, and this sacred duty sounded like a load of crap to me. But I didn't think calling him out on it was the way to go. I had something else in mind, something I hoped might change Mr. Silverman's mind.

I said that I understood protecting the contest's integrity was important. That's why I wondered how it was going to look when I held a press conference after the charges against Devon were dismissed, and I announced that the committee had disqualified his project based upon the slanderous and uncorroborated allegations of a jealous fellow contestant. I asked how that squared with the committee's sacred duty.

There was a moment of silence as Mr. Silverman processed the information and hopefully looked for an off ramp. Stammering only slightly, he said the committee hadn't looked at the situation quite that way, but now that I had called it to his attention, they would have to reconsider their position.

I hoped that was it, but unfortunately it wasn't. After apparently regaining his composure, Mr. Silverman asked quite pointedly how soon the charges would be dismissed, and if I was certain that the informant was a contestant. He said those were matters critical to the committee's consideration. In other words, he wanted to know if I was for real or if I was bluffing.

Silverman was slick, but I had played this game many times with prosecutors, and I played it much better than Silverman did. I said, "I don't know; maybe within a few days or possibly after the judging starts, but it'll happen. As for the identity of the informant, I have no doubt. If you don't believe me, then disqualify Devon. Did I mention that after the news conference, I plan on suing the pants off of you and all the other committee members?"

As I said earlier, I don't know much about civil lawsuits, so I'm not certain that "suing the pants off someone" is the correct technical term. I suspect not, but it had the desired effect on Mr. Silverman. He was clearly insulted by my threat, but he was smart enough to know that I had him cornered. All he could do was withdraw as quickly and as quietly as his ego would allow. But before I let him off the hook, I said that I'd appreciate a formal letter from the committee acknowledging it had no intention of disqualifying

Devon's project. After a few throat clearings, Mr. Silverman said he would see to it.

Now all I had to do was to get Devon's case dismissed, or Mr. Silverman and his committee might sue the pants off me.

CHAPTER 36

The Nom Wah Tea Parlor has been serving dim sum and dumplings since 1920. It opens every morning at ten thirty, and you can count on it being filled with customers, nearly all of whom are Chinatown locals. It was the perfect place to meet Big Tony. Not only did most of the patrons not speak English, but the noise level was so high it made eavesdropping on a conversation virtually impossible.

I arrived at Nom Wah early and asked for the booth in the back corner. I ordered a pot of Jasmine tea and two orders of steamed lotus buns. Then I waited for Big Tony to arrive.

I wasn't sure he and I were on the same page yet, but we would be after today. Either he was going to protect his son, and we'd work together, or I'd be off the case. I wasn't going to sell Little Tony down the river. I'd return the $100,000 and take my chances with the mob. But maybe I was getting ahead of myself again.

Big Tony showed up right on time. Taking his seat in the booth across from me and looking around, he said, "You done good, counselor."

He liked the place, but he was disappointed there was no espresso or cannoli. He didn't care for tea, but he liked the sweet steamed lotus buns. I said the important thing was nobody in the place knew who he was and if they did, they didn't care. It was either tea and anonymity or espresso and recognition. He got the point and sipped his tea.

I figured there was no sense beating around the bush, so I got right down to business. I told Big Tony everything I knew about the missing slugs and the missing ballistic reports, and how it affected Little Tony's case. When I finished, Big Tony just nodded his head and gave a simple, "Yeah."

It seemed nothing I had just told him came as a surprise. I didn't think he knew specifically about the missing slugs, but he had expected something, and now he knew what it was. Then he surprised me when he said that I shouldn't worry about it. I naturally asked why, and he said I'd find out soon enough. For the time being, I should just do the best I could and keep my mouth shut. It wasn't said in a threatening way, but it didn't have to be. Big Tony's eyes said what his mouth hadn't.

We finished our tea and buns in silence. Then when the check came, Big Tony grabbed it and said, "I got it, counselor. You just go do your job, and I'll make sure my son isn't railroaded."

I watched as Big Tony pulled a roll of bills the size of my fist out of his pocket, peeling a twenty-dollar bill off and dropping it on the table as a tip. Having seen the check, I knew it was just over eighteen dollars, but the twenty-dollar tip didn't surprise me. The old time Mafia guys were notorious for over-tipping. I don't know if they were being generous or just showing off, and I certainly wasn't going to ask Big Tony which it was.

Leaving the tea parlor, Big Tony shook my hand and said, "You'll hear from us soon," and then he walked off.

I was puzzled. Who the hell was "us," and what was I going to hear? Under other circumstances, I would have taken the comment as a threat. But as things stood, Big Tony and I were on the same team. So if "hearing from us soon" wasn't a threat, who was I going to hear from? As far as I knew, the only one on Little Tony's team besides Big Tony and I was Joey Bats, and I doubted he was anything more than a messenger. And how was Big Tony going to ensure that his son wasn't railroaded? Did he know something I didn't know?

I never thought when I took on Little Tony's case that I'd find myself in the middle of a Mafia family war, and quite possibly a war between the Mafia and the Russian mob, not to mention maybe having to expose high level governmental corruption. And all of that for $100,000. I was beginning to regret having taken the case, but I wouldn't admit that to Gracie or Tommy. There was no way I'd give either of them the satisfaction of saying, "I told you so."

No, better I should get killed. Did I actually just say that? I needed a meeting.

CHAPTER 37

After the meeting which, as usual, put my head back on straight, I had some good news for a change. There was a message on my cell phone from Mr. Silverman. The committee had reconsidered its position, and Devon's project was not being disqualified; however, there was a catch. If the charges against Devon weren't dismissed, he would be ineligible to receive the money. The message ended with Silverman saying a confirming letter would be forthcoming.

It certainly wasn't a total victory, but it was still a win. It did, however, raise the stakes because now I had to have the case dismissed and not just bargained down to a misdemeanor.

I called Devon's grandfather and gave him the good news. He said that he'd let Devon know as soon as he got home from school. Then he thanked me, saying he knew I had gone above and beyond what I was required to do, and he appreciated the effort. It's not often that a client thanks me, which is understandable since the last time most of my clients see me is when they're being hauled off to prison. At that point, the last thing on their mind is thanking their attorney.

Devon's felony charge was scheduled to go to the Grand Jury in a few days. Being a one-sided affair, the Grand Jury rarely fails to return an indictment. Once the indictment was returned, I could start taking steps to have the case dismissed. It would require motions and time which wouldn't play well with Mr. Silverman and his committee.

I felt more confident now that I knew Devon's project wouldn't be disqualified, but I still worried about the prize money if Devon's team won. What would happen if I couldn't get the case dismissed before the prize money was awarded? Could I force the committee to hold Devon's share in escrow pending the outcome of his case? I didn't know the answer to that question, so to be on the safe side, I had to assume I couldn't.

After the indictment, it would take at least a month, maybe two, before I could have the case dismissed, and that was if things went well. Any complication at all could delay the case for months. The only way to ensure Devon got his share of the prize money if his team's project won the contest was to have the case dismissed before it went to the Grand Jury.

I didn't know who at the District Attorney's Office was handling Devon's case. I just hoped it wasn't Assistant District Attorney Clark who handled the arraignment. Actually, it didn't matter which assistant district attorney was on the case; none of them had the authority to dismiss a case before a Grand Jury hearing. That decision could only come from on high. Hopefully Sarah Washington had reached that level, and I could convince her to drop Devon's case.

By cutting the deal with American Express, I eliminated the threat of a larceny charge, so the identity theft was the only remaining felony charge. If the cops hadn't yet identified the anonymous tipster, the district attorney didn't have much of a case, so now would be the best time to ask for a dismissal.

CHAPTER 38

That afternoon I paid a visit to Sarah Washington. I had all the information and arguments I needed, but I knew it wouldn't hurt to bring something more to the table. After all, I was looking for a favor and a big one at that.

Following my usual routine, I smiled sweetly at Sarah's young secretary and gave her a wink as I walked past her into Sarah's office before she had a chance to let Sarah know I was there.

From the look on Sarah's face, I got the impression she suspected my visit was something more than a social call. Her suspicion was probably confirmed when I placed a Starbucks Venti Caramel Macchiato and blueberry scone on her desk. Giving me one of her accusatory frowns, she asked if the coffee and scone were a bribe. I said that depended on whether I got what I came looking for. If I did, the coffee and scone weren't a bribe, merely a token of my affection. On the other hand, if I went away disappointed, I might have to report a bribe to her superiors.

Laughing, she said, "This tops everything even for you, Jake. Bribery and blackmail. What do you want?"

I gave her the case number, and she pulled up the file on her computer. After reviewing the file, she asked again why I was there. Smiling, I replied, "Because I want you to drop the case."

Sarah must have thought I was kidding because she started laughing and was about to close her computer screen. Then seeing the look on my face, she knew I wasn't joking. She stopped laughing and asked simply, "Why should I?"

I said her case began with an anonymous tip from someone who the cops had yet to identify. So, as of that moment she had no live witness tying Devon to the crime. Even if the cops found the informant as I had done, they would soon learn that his story was based on, at the least, three layers of hearsay. Unless there was other evidence to prove Devon guilty, the case crumbled.

I watched as Sarah tapped her keyboard, paging through the case file in what I presumed was a search for other evidence. Knowing there was none, I confidently challenged her to produce evidence from American Express or anyone else that proved Devon used the stolen account number.

Sarah went back to her computer, this time tapping the keyboard more aggressively. When she was done reading, she nodded and admitted the case looked bad. I said it looked bad because it was bad and should be dismissed now, not later. Why waste time going through with the Grand Jury proceedings only to have the case dismissed later? Actually I knew the answer to that question. If the Grand Jury indicted, as they were sure to do, the NYPD would be protected from a civil suit claiming false arrest. So to remove that obstacle, I assured Sarah that if all charges were dropped now, Devon would waive any civil claim for false arrest.

Sarah is a reasonable person, but she is limited in what she can do. She asked about the skimmer possession charge on which they had him dead to rights. There was no way to claim Devon was innocent on that charge, or we'd beat it in court. But it didn't mean the case shouldn't be dropped.

I said, speaking hypothetically, if Devon were to make restitution of the $2,100, he allegedly stole – which theft the prosecution couldn't prove – and if American Express refused to press charges, wouldn't that warrant a dismissal of the skimmer possession charge?

Before Sarah could respond, I threw in my final argument. It wasn't a legal argument; it was a plea for mercy. I told Sarah that Devon was a gifted kid with no criminal record whose life was in danger of being ruined by this one stupid mistake. I explained why Devon had done what he did and how his scholarship to Stanford could be in jeopardy. Finally, I told Sarah why Devon needed at least a chance to win the money from the contest and how the charges against him, if not dismissed, made that impossible.

I hoped that I had made my case because I was now out of arguments. If Sarah had any further objections, I'd be down to the old, "Oh yeah! Well I don't think so," response. Fortunately, Sarah had no immediate comeback. I'd dealt with Sarah enough to know that didn't mean she'd have the charges dropped; it just meant she was considering doing so.

I knew enough not to push the matter any further. If Sarah was considering dropping the charges, I was grateful. I would understand if she didn't because she'd be going out on a limb to do so. Dropping charges before a Grand Jury hearing is rarely done and often smacks of impropriety.

After what seemed like a long time, but probably wasn't more than half a minute, Sarah said she couldn't drop the charges; it was just too much of a reach. But then she added that she'd personally handle the Grand Jury proceeding, and given the nature of the evidence, she wouldn't be surprised if the Grand Jury failed to indict.

That didn't mean she'd throw the case. She'd simply present the evidence much as I had presented it to her. Knowing she didn't have testimony from the anonymous informant at trial, she wouldn't use it during the Grand Jury proceedings, and without the testimony, there wasn't a case.

I owed Sarah big time, but I couldn't say that because it would sound as though she was doing me a favor that I didn't deserve. She wasn't really doing that because the case was a loser for her, but she was shortcutting the process.

As I was getting ready to leave, Sarah asked how I was getting along with Tommy McAvoy. Not certain where the conversation was headed, I said simply that she needed to talk to him about manners. Sarah laughed and said McAvoy was no longer her problem. He had been reassigned to another bureau chief, along with the Savino case.

I can't tell you how happy I was to hear that news. As much as I knew in my heart that Sarah wouldn't have anything to do with hiding evidence, I admit that somewhere in a deep dark corner of my mind, there may have been the tiniest bit of doubt. Why, I don't know. Maybe it's just a part of being a criminal defense lawyer, where you question everything, most of all, your own client's story. Or maybe it was my cynicism from years of dealing with lying scumbag clients. Whatever it was, Sarah didn't deserve my doubting her.

Now that I knew for certain that Sarah wasn't involved, I considered telling her the story, but I didn't want to involve her in what was looking like a very messy political scandal. She was on the outside, and there was nothing to be gained by bringing her inside at that point. Maybe later when I knew more about the scheme, I could bring her in but not until then. I just thanked her and left.

CHAPTER 39

As I usually do when I'm in the DA's Office, I dropped in on Gracie after leaving Sarah. Unlike most times, though, this visit wasn't going to be strictly social. I was there to tell her about the widening conspiracy I had discovered in the Savino case.

Gracie was on the phone when I entered her office, but when I closed the door, which I rarely did, she knew something was up, and she cut her call short. I started the conversation with the tantalizing words, "We have a big problem."

Then I laid out the situation in detail. When I finished, Gracie looked stunned which wasn't surprising. The existence of such a widespread conspiracy that included her own office was nearly inconceivable. But there was no other way to explain what was happening.

Gracie suggested we go see her boss, but I nixed the idea, saying that until I knew more about the scheme, I wasn't trusting anybody. Naturally, Gracie didn't concur, but since it was my case, she agreed to do it my way.

Donald L'Abbate

Everyone in the office knew that Gracie and I lived together, and I was handling Little Tony's case, so any inquiry she made into it would raise ethical questions. If anyone involved in the conspiracy found out Gracie knew about it, they'd be looking to end her career instantly.

I wouldn't want Gracie doing anything that could jeopardize her career. Not knowing who we could trust meant there was very little she could do. If the wrong person found out she was mucking about in the Savino case, she could find herself suspended in an instant. Until we knew who the players were, I had to assume that everyone in the office, including Gracie's boss, was under suspicion.

Naturally Gracie didn't agree. The mere thought of corruption in her office pissed her off royally, and she wanted to root it out herself. I understood her feelings, so I let her vent before forcing her to face reality. The only way this scheme worked was if somebody high up in the office was in on it. If that person, whoever he or she was, suspected Gracie knew about the scheme, Gracie would be in a world of trouble, and she'd be no help to me at all. It was better if Gracie played it low key and did nothing overt, at least for the time being. If she could find out who had taken over the Savino case without attracting attention, that would be enough.

Gracie is thick headed, not as thick headed as I am, but to her credit she listens to reason, so in the end she agreed to lay low. Not happily, mind you, and not without notice that if by chance she came across any evidence of corruption, she wouldn't keep it to herself. I knew Gracie was blowing off steam and arguing with her would do no good. If push came to shove, I trusted Gracie to do the right thing, and I'd back her to the hilt.

At that point, I wanted Gracie to calm down, so I tried changing the subject to a less contentious topic, like dinner. I was under pressure to come up with something fast, and given how much Gracie loves sushi, I suggested we meet for dinner at the new sushi restaurant on Houston Street. The problem was that I didn't know of a new sushi restaurant on Houston Street.

Under pressure I couldn't remember the names of any of the sushi restaurants Gracie drags me to, so I had improvised. I figured the way these restaurants were popping up all over the city, there had to be a new sushi restaurant somewhere on Houston Street. Luckily

Gracie said she wasn't in the mood for sushi, and she'd rather eat at Ecco. I quickly and happily agreed.

Once outside the building, I called Theo Makris and got his voice mail. I left a message that we needed to meet and asked him when he'd be available. I was hoping that Theo had some insights into what was happening, plus I wanted his thoughts on the autopsy report. Not wanting to discuss any of this over the phone, I was prepared to meet Theo in Brooklyn.

With everything happening in Little Tony's case, I nearly forgot the good news about Devon's case. I was about to call his grandfather to tell him that the charges were going to be dropped, but then I thought better of it. It wasn't that I doubted Sarah, but things can go wrong. So why set Devon and his grandfather up for a big disappointment? Better to wait a couple of days and deliver good news, not promises.

I was heading back to the office when my cell phone rang. It was Theo. His classes were over for the day, and he was about to head home, but when I explained why I had called, he agreed to meet me in his office that evening.

So much for dinner at Ecco.

CHAPTER 40

SUNY Downstate Medical Center is located on Clarkson Avenue in the Prospect Lefferts Gardens section of Brooklyn. From Lower Manhattan, it's not a long taxicab ride over the Brooklyn Bridge and down Flatbush Avenue. But it was rush hour, and I don't like riding in taxicabs. To be honest, I hate riding in any motor vehicle.

Gracie always thought I was just plain weird, but then I discovered that I suffer from a condition called amaxophobia; a fear of being a passenger in a motor vehicle. It's a very real condition recognized by mental health professionals.

Since learning that I suffer from amaxophobia, Gracie still thinks I'm weird because the fear is irrational, and I refuse to do anything about it. Why should I? I live in Manhattan where I can get almost anywhere without ever getting into a car, and I have no intention of going anywhere that would require otherwise.

Gracie offered to get me a medical bracelet, saying I suffer from amaxophobia, so in case I was in an accident, they'd know not to put me in an ambulance but to take me to the hospital on the subway. I told her making fun of someone with a serious medical condition wasn't nice and probably violated some federal law. She didn't seem to care. But I'm carrying on for no reason, aren't I?

I don't have to tell you that I didn't take a taxicab to Downstate. I took the IRT Number 5 subway train from the Brooklyn Bridge–City Hall Station to Winthrop Street and walked the three and a half blocks from there to the medical school on Clarkson Avenue. The whole trip, not including the four minutes I had to wait for the train to arrive, took forty minutes. That was only eight more minutes than it would have taken in a taxicab if there was no traffic, and it cost me a hell of a lot less money.

Arriving at the medical school, I found Theo waiting for me at the reception desk. He said his new office wasn't easy to find, and he didn't want me wandering the halls for hours looking for him. As we walked to his office, I asked if he had found anything helpful in the autopsy reports and he said sadly no. But he had found the reports somewhat odd. Having done hundreds of these reports himself and having read hundreds of reports prepared by others, he said there was always a flow to them. These reports lacked that flow. I asked what that meant, and Theo said it meant we needed to reexamine my conspiracy theory.

By that point, we had reached Theo's office and had taken seats around a small conference table. On the table were the autopsy reports, the autopsy photographs, and some copies of x-rays, along with a pot of coffee and some sandwiches. Apparently, I was in for a long night. I called Gracie and told her not to wait up for me, then I took off my jacket and tie and bit into an egg salad sandwich.

CHAPTER 41

Theo said my theory about the missing evidence was too complicated. For it to be true, there had to be a conspiracy involving the Medical Examiner's Office, the NYPD Property Clerk's Office, the District Attorney's Office, and quite possibly the city's Forensic Laboratory. That was too many people and too many hands through which the evidence would have passed for there not to have been a leak. I had to admit when he put it that way, my theory did sound a bit outlandish, but how else could you explain what happened?

Theo said there was something called Occam's razor, a problem-solving principle, that says the simplest explanation is usually the right one. Theo believed my explanation was too complicated to be right. He said that I was looking at the problem from the wrong direction, and in doing so, I made it a lot more complicated than it was. I had started with the missing ballistic reports and worked backward. Theo suggested that instead of working backward, we start from the recovery of the slugs and work forward.

Having been New York City's Chief Medical Examiner for almost ten years before becoming a professor at Downstate, Theo knew how the system worked. The doctor performing the autopsy would have put the slugs into plastic evidence bags, marked each bag with the time, the date, and identification information. After the autopsy report was completed, a clerk would prepare a transmittal form and send the slugs to the Forensic Laboratory for ballistic testing. But what if the slugs were never sent to the Forensic Laboratory? What if the slugs were discarded at that point in the process?

Theo had a point, but Sarah had told me she was expecting a ballistic report. At least that was my thinking until Theo asked if she had actually said she was waiting for a report. Perhaps she mentioned a ballistic report because she was assuming there'd be one. I tried but couldn't remember her exact words. But Theo was right. If Sarah was under the impression that slugs had been recovered, she'd naturally expect a ballistic report because that was standard operating procedure. But that didn't mean there was an actual ballistic report, or that the Forensic Laboratory had received the slugs and was doing any testing.

If a clerk in the Medical Examiner's Office had tossed the slugs, then the Forensic Laboratory and the NYPD's Property Clerk's Office were out of the loop, making the conspiracy a lot smaller. It would also mean that I'd never find a chain of custody log sheet for the slugs. But could a clerk do it all by himself? Theo said it could be done, but only if someone in the District Attorney's Office was involved.

Again, Theo's reasoning was simple. Who else besides the doctor who performed the autopsy would actually know if the slugs were recovered? No one. Who would ask if the slugs had been recovered? Most likely only the assistant district attorney handling the case. The cops had no reason to ask, and no one at the Forensic Lab would even know about the case if the evidence was never sent to them. The way that the system worked, making the evidence disappear wouldn't be that difficult.

The doctor performing the autopsy dictated his findings into a microphone hanging over the body. The taped findings were then transcribed by a clerk and formatted into a draft report. Once the draft report was reviewed and approved by the doctor, the clerk filed the report electronically and sent a copy to the District Attorney's Office. The same clerk would collect any evidence bagged by the doctor during the autopsy, prepare a chain of custody log for each item, then pack and ship them, or store them as the situation required.

Theo said the doctors working in the Medical Examiner' s Office were so busy that they had no time and no reason to look at their reports once they had been electronically filed. Only if a doctor was called to testify would he review his report, and by that time, he'd probably have no independent recollection of the case.

In reviewing the autopsy reports, Theo noticed that they lacked the typical flow, which led him to conclude that they had been altered from their original format. Someone had omitted words or whole sections of the reports and had not done so accidentally. The reports had been intentionally altered to probably hide the existence of the slugs.

In Theo's opinion, it all could have been done by the clerk. Once the doctor approved the draft versions of the reports, the clerk would make any necessary changes, then file the reports, and send copies to the District Attorney's Office. In the process, the clerk could have scrubbed all mention of the slugs from the two reports. By not preparing a chain of custody log sheet, then disposing of the slugs, it was as though they never existed. The only persons who would know about the disappearing slugs would be the clerk in the Medical Examiner's Office and one or maybe two lawyers in the District Attorney's Office.

If Theo's theory was right, the two lawyers in the District Attorney's Office would be Tommy McAvoy and the bureau chief who had taken over Little Tony's case. It made sense, and it was a hell of a lot less complicated than the scenario I had created. I guess old Occam's razor made sense.

But what about Sarah Washington? She had mentioned the slugs being tested, so did she know they existed, or was she simply assuming the slugs would be recovered and tested? Either way, she was a loose end in the scheme. I wasn't one-hundred-percent certain who was behind this whole thing, but I was still betting the ranch it was the Ruccis.

My first thought was to tell Sarah what I knew and what I suspected. But until I was certain that the scheme went no higher up in the District Attorney's Office than McAvoy and his new boss, I needed to be careful. At the moment, Sarah knowing or suspecting there had been slugs recovered made her a loose end. A loose end that wasn't necessarily fatal to the scheme's success.

But if Sarah let on that she knew about the scheme, she'd be more than a loose end. She'd become a threat, and that wasn't good. One thing I've learned about the Mafia over the years is they don't like loose ends, but what they dislike even more are threats to their plots. If the Ruccis found out that Sarah knew the truth about the slugs, they might arrange for her death, so at that point, I had to keep her in the dark.

My priority was finding out the name of the clerk who had transcribed the autopsy tapes and getting my hands on the original reports dictated by the doctor. According to Theo, that wouldn't be an easy task, not if I went about it legally, but I had something else in mind. Or I should say someone else in mind?

CHAPTER 42

It was late when I finally left Theo's office, and I was reluctant to call Linda Chow. But the more I thought about this new conspiracy theory, the more excited I became. By the time I reached the subway entrance, my excitement had gotten the better of me, and I called Linda's cell phone. After apologizing for calling so late, I asked if she'd be able to access the files on the computer system at the Medical Examiner's Office. Apparently, Linda found my question insulting as evidenced by her response, "Do pigeons shit on statues?" It's a New York City thing, so if you don't know what Linda meant by that, it's okay.

Standing at the Winthrop Street entrance to the IRT subway, I gave Linda a quick rundown of the system's operating procedures as they had been explained to me by Theo. Then I told her that I needed the name of the clerk who handled the files, copies of the original recordings that the doctor made while he performed the two autopsies, and copies of the original transcriptions of those recordings. Linda didn't see that as a problem, and she promised to work on it first thing in the morning.

Assuming Linda was able to get me the evidence that the conspiracy existed, I wasn't sure what I'd do with it. One thing was certain. If the slugs that killed the two Russians had been fired from the gun Little Tony was carrying when arrested, it was most likely game over. On the other hand, if they hadn't come from Little Tony's gun, we'd be looking at a damn good defense. But I wouldn't know either way unless the slugs were tested, and now it seemed like the slugs were gone.

By the time I got back to Gracie's place, it was nearly eleven thirty, and I expected Gracie to be sleeping. On my way up in the elevator, I debated about waking her with the latest news. As it turned out, she wasn't asleep; she was sitting on the couch waiting for me.

Gracie was anxious to hear what I had learned, but first I had a couple of questions for her. Knowing how worked up she had gotten earlier that day when I told her about the conspiracy, I wanted to be certain she hadn't done anything to tip off our hand.

Fortunately, Gracie didn't take offense at my questioning. I think she understood why I was concerned. She said that after I left her office, she calmed down and realized I was right about keeping things under wraps until we knew more. She did, however, find out that Jim Hannah was now in charge of Little Tony's case.

As much as Gracie was anxious to hear my news, I was more anxious to hear about Hannah.

Gracie didn't like Hannah. He was a recent transferee from the Maryland State Attorney's Office, a move considered by most to be a demotion. No one knew for sure what was behind the move, but everyone agreed it couldn't have been a good thing. Some thought it involved corruption, while others put it down to nothing more than his inability to get along with others. It couldn't have involved any criminal conviction because his license hadn't been lifted. That didn't mean criminal charges hadn't been brought, only that there had been no conviction.

From what Gracie knew, Hannah was an arrogant son of a bitch and had very few friends in the office. If his abrasive personality weren't enough, the fact that he had been brought in from outside to fill a senior slot when there were people in the office equally as qualified, or more qualified, to be promoted to the position made him even more unpopular.

Gracie said Hannah and McAvoy were peas in a pod, and she didn't put it past either one of them to bury evidence. Then Gracie said Hannah and McAvoy reminded her of me during my drinking days, kindly adding that unlike them I was at least ethical. It was a kind of backhanded compliment, and I didn't know whether to say thanks or be insulted. To be honest I agreed with Gracie's assessment; I just didn't like being reminded of my past ways. Not that I try to forget them because that's just a way of denying them. I own what I did when I drank and denying the things I did or trying to mitigate the harm I did could lead me back to the bottle. That's what the fifth step is all about. I admitted to God, to myself, and to Doug the exact nature of my wrongs. It wasn't easy, but it was necessary because it was the step that brought me back to the truth and started me on recovering my self-esteem.

When Gracie finished her story, I filled her in on my meeting with Theo. Gracie agreed that Theo's take on the case made sense, more sense than my original conspiracy theory. In either case, people in the District Attorney's Office had to be involved. Gracie hoped it was limited to Hannah and McAvoy, and so did I. But until I was sure, I had no intentions of talking with anyone in the District Attorney's Office about it. That is, other than Gracie.

There were a number of questions I needed answered before going public with the conspiracy. It was still complicated, but thanks to Theo, the conspiracy had been whittled down to two offices which made it a lot less complicated. Like all conspiracies, this one was a chain, and I was thinking that the weak link in this chain was the clerk at the Medical Examiner's Office. Once I learned his or her identity, the next step would be determining who was pulling the strings and why. I was still betting that the Ruccis were the ones pulling the strings. I just couldn't figure out why they wanted the slugs to go missing. Was it to exonerate Little Tony or to ensure his conviction?

CHAPTER 43

The next morning Linda Chow called and said she was working on my project, but it was taking longer than she expected. I asked her why, but her explanation went way over my head, so I just let it go. I still had some homework of my own to do, and I had just gotten a new case assignment that required my immediate attention.

I usually have anywhere from thirty to forty active cases at any time. It sounds like a lot of cases but it's not. Most cases get resolved quickly through plea bargaining because most of my clients are guilty. We go through the initial arraignment, then wait for the inevitable Grand Jury indictment, after which it's simply a matter of negotiating a reasonable charge and prison term.

There are times when the assistant district attorney offers unreasonable terms, forcing me to make a motion challenging the evidence or the charge. When that happens, the case is delayed for a couple of months. If my motions are successful, which they usually are, the assistant district attorney is forced to offer more reasonable terms. I'm not bragging when I say my motions are usually successful; I'm just stating a fact. I'm successful because I don't make frivolous motions.

After nearly thirty years in the business, I know when to fight and when to deal, and with my clientele, it's mostly deal making. Very few of my cases go to trial. Unless an assistant district attorney is totally unreasonable or an asshole, plea bargaining is the only way to go when a client's guilty. Most of the clients assigned to me by the 18B Panel are repeat offenders who know they don't have a shot at beating the charge. All they want to do is get the whole thing over with so they can do their time and get out. Some cooperate and get a good deal; others insist on being jerks and wind up serving longer prison sentences.

I don't mean to sound callous, but I've gotten to the point that I can tell in ten minutes if a client is guilty. It's an easy call with most hardened criminals because they make no effort to hide their guilt. They wear it on their faces with pride and show absolutely no remorse for what they've done.

Those newer to the criminal justice system often claim innocence, but their stories are generally ridiculous beyond belief. To give you some idea of how ridiculous the stories can be, one of my clients claimed he had stabbed the victim by accident. A claim that might be credible but not when the victim has been stabbed ten times. When I finally convinced this idiot that nobody with a working brain would believe the stabbing was accidental, he changed his story, claiming that he only did it because the victim deserved it. Mind you, he wasn't claiming self-defense; he was claiming he was justified in stabbing the victim ten times because the victim laughed at him. I didn't see that as a winning defense, and obviously neither would a jury.

Anyway, that morning, just before I heard from Linda Chow, I had a call from Joe Benjamin, the 18B Panel Administrator. He had a new case he wanted me to handle. Usually it's a clerk who calls in the assignments, so when it was Joe on the line, I knew something was up. All Joe would say about the case was that the client's name was Albert Briggs, and the charges against him were Arson in the first degree, violation of Section 485.05 of the Penal Law Code, hate crimes and possibly homicide. He said news of the case was breaking shortly, and I should get to The Tombs as quickly as possible.

I guess if I had thought about it, I might have put it all together sooner, but I didn't. It wasn't until I got to the courthouse to file my Notice of Appearance that I learned Briggs had firebombed a synagogue, critically injuring two worshipers. He was arrested at the scene where, after a scuffle with the cops, he bragged about killing Jews.

When I arrived at The Tombs, I wasn't surprised that Albert Briggs was a skinhead with a swastika tattooed on his forehead. That alone made him easy to identify. That and the fact that he was sprawled out on a bench in the overcrowded holding cell with no one around him. The other prisoners were keeping their distance from Briggs because they were afraid of him. When I called out Briggs' name, everyone cleared a path for him as he made his way to the bars.

Watching Briggs approach, I understood why everyone was afraid of him. He stood a full head and shoulders taller than me, and his neck and heavily tattooed arms bulged with muscles. His hands were huge with prison tattoos on each of his fingers.

As he approached the bars, he asked in a very deliberate and threatening tone what I wanted. I told him that I was his lawyer, and I was there to hear his side of the story. He pressed his chest against the bars and gave me a long stare trying to intimidate me, and frankly, it worked. I've looked into the eyes of evil men many times, and I've gotten used to it. But when I looked into Briggs' eyes, I got chills. Most psychotic killers have dead eyes, but Briggs' eyes were burning with hatred. I'd never seen eyes like that before, and they scared me. Not out of fear for myself, I was safely on the other side of the bars, but fear for what a man so possessed with hate could do. I figured this firebombing couldn't be his first crime, and quite possibly not his worst.

Without backing away and staring directly into his hateful eyes, I asked again, "What's the story?"

Then, with a smirk on his face, he said, "It's not a crime to kill a Jew or one of the mud people; it's a public service."

Of all the monsters I'd come across in my years of practice, none compared to this one. His words brought me back to my childhood, sitting on the stoop in front of Lenny Goldberg's apartment, listening to his Grandmother tell stories about the Nazis and the prison camps. Thinking as I listened, how glad I was to live in a country where things like that couldn't happen. Yet here I was face-to-face with that very same evil.

Without saying a word, I turned and walked out of the holding cell. Once outside the courthouse, I called Joe Benjamin and told him I wouldn't take the case. I've known Joe for a long time, and I owe him a lot. It was at his insistence that I went to AA and got sober. In truth, he probably saved my life, and I would do almost anything for him. But this I couldn't do. Joe reminded me that everyone is entitled to a defense, and as a lawyer, I had an obligation to represent clients, even though I disliked them or thought they were guilty.

I said that wasn't the point. I knew Briggs was guilty; there was no doubt about it. I mean, he admitted it to the cops and to me. That didn't bother me; I represented clients that I knew were guilty all the time. What worried me was that Briggs was crazy and might even be legally insane. If he was legally insane, he might be found not guilty by reason of insanity, and instead of being sent to prison, he'd be put in a mental institution. I couldn't live with myself if I did anything that kept that monster from going to prison.

Joe admitted I had a point, but it didn't change the fact that I had an ethical obligation to defend a client. He was right to a point, but not if I couldn't do my best for the client. With the way I felt about Briggs, I might very well ignore the insanity defense in order to see him imprisoned. Joe agreed if that was the case, I shouldn't represent Briggs, and he'd assign someone else to represent him. But given the time constraints, he asked that I handle the arraignment, and I agreed to do so.

Later that afternoon, I appeared in Arraignment Part with Briggs, saying only the minimum required of me to get through the proceedings. When it was done, Briggs was hauled off to Rikers Island.

Sometimes justice takes different forms. In the case of Albert Briggs, it took the form of a clerical error made by one of the corrections officers at the jail. It seems that Officer Milken missed the note that Briggs, a professed racist, was to be kept segregated from the general population. As a result of Milken's oversight, Briggs was put into the unit reserved for the most violent inmates, including members of the infamous MS-13 gang. Briggs lasted less than five hours. When his body was discovered, his throat had been cut, and he had been stabbed more than thirty times.

An investigation into the incident found no evidence to support charges against any of the inmates. As for Officer Milken, he was told to be more careful in the future.

When no one claimed Briggs' body, it was buried on Hart Island, New York City's Potter's Field.

I can understand if you don't think what happened to Briggs was right. I mean, it pretty much goes against everything the law stands for. But maybe there are times when the law is inadequate at protecting us from evil, and when that happens, what do we do? Do we do nothing, or do we look to extraordinary measures to deal with evil? Do we stand on principle and let evil reign, or do we turn to practicality and rid society of the evil?

I'm not talking about your run of the mill criminals; I'm talking about true evil, that rare kind of evil, the kind that makes the bravest among us shudder. There are no easy answers, but I can tell you that in the case of Albert Briggs, I shed no tears, and I don't see any harm having been done to our legal system.

The same day Briggs was killed, the Grand Jury refused to return an indictment in Devon Matthews' case. That was because Sarah Washington chose to do the right thing and not the technically correct thing. Justice is blind, so sometimes she needs to be pointed in the right direction.

CHAPTER 44

Leaving the courthouse after the Briggs arraignment, and heading back to the office, I was thinking how Little Tony's case couldn't get any stranger when I found out how wrong I was. Walking my usual route up Mulberry Street, I intended to turn onto Mosco Street and cut over to Mott Street. Before I got to the corner, two men stepped from a big car parked at the curb and stood directly in front of me. I didn't need an introduction to know they were mafioso. They didn't touch me; they just blocked my path and said, "Mr. Rucci wants to talk to you."

I knew it was one of those offers I couldn't refuse. I'd be going with them willingly or unwillingly; the choice was mine. The back door of the car was open and seeing no sense in resisting, I climbed in. One of the goons climbed in and sat beside me, and the car pulled away from the curb and headed up Mulberry Street.

I didn't know where they were taking me, or for that matter, which Mr. Rucci wanted to see me. I was pretty sure my back seat companion wasn't about to enlighten me, so I kept my mouth shut. In the past, I'd been known to offer a wisecrack or two in such situations, but that never worked out too well for me. Maybe I was starting to get smart.

I wasn't blindfolded, so apparently it didn't matter if I knew where we were going. Either our destination wasn't a secret, or maybe I was going to be killed after the meeting. I hoped not because I didn't want to give Gracie and Tommy the satisfaction of telling each other they told me not to take the case. Of course, if I had to beg for my life, I couldn't envision that argument carrying much weight. Can you see it?

"Please, Mr. Rucci, don't kill me because if you do, my girlfriend and my best friend will gloat."

"Oh, I'm sorry, Jake, I didn't realize that. I won't kill you."

No, that wasn't going to happen. Besides, if Gracie found out that I called her my girlfriend, she'd probably kill me if Rucci didn't.

North of Houston Street, we turned right and headed into the East Village. On East 10th Street, the car pulled up in front of a small bar and grill. Two goons who had been standing in the doorway walked to the car as we pulled up to the curb. One of the goons opened the back door and motioned for me to get out.

Grabbing me by the arm, he nudged me toward the front door. It was a gentle nudge, nothing too rough, just enough of a push to let me know where we were going. The second goon led the way, opening the door, then standing aside to let me and the other goon enter.

Standing in the doorway, I told the two goons I was an alcoholic and going into a bar could put my sobriety in jeopardy. I guess they didn't care because the one behind me pushed me through the door.

The place was dimly lighted, and it took a moment or two for my eyes to adjust. The place was laid out in typical fashion for a bar and grill. To the right was the bar. Long and lined with stools. Across from the bar against the opposite wall were several tables. Other than me and the two goons, the place was empty. No customers or even a bartender. Either business was bad, or the place had been emptied in my honor. Whatever it was, I didn't like the look of things.

Once inside, goon number two stopped and frisked me. After taking away my cell phone, and apparently satisfied that I wasn't carrying any concealed weapons, he nudged me forward toward a door in the back wall. I don't think that I have to tell you my palms were getting a little sweaty.

Goon number one knocked on the door, and without waiting for a reply, opened it. He reached back, grabbed my shoulder, and pushed me inside. Following me into the room, he closed the door, then he nudged me toward a table where an old man sat waiting.

The old man stood, smiled, and said, "Good day, counselor. Please have a seat."

There was only one other chair in the room, so I assumed it was for me. As I approached the table, the old man extended his hand and introduced himself; he was Silvio Rucci.

He looked to be in his late seventies, maybe early eighties. He was well-dressed in an expensive looking suit that fit him like a glove. He had a full head of gray hair and a matching gray mustache. When he had stood up, I guessed his height to be slightly less than six feet tall. He was thin, old-man-type thin. But his frame and his hands were those of a once powerful man. His grip when we shook hands was strong.

He asked if I wanted a drink, an espresso, or perhaps some mineral water. His voice was deep and strong with a trace of an Italian accent. I politely declined the offer, hoping we'd soon get down to business. I had no idea why I had been brought there or what Rucci wanted, but I was anxious to find out. Actually, I was anxious to learn if I'd be walking out the front door, or if my body was going to be carried out the back door.

It seemed that rumors of Silvio Rucci's mental deterioration were highly exaggerated. He certainly wasn't the drooling fool some were making him out to be. It made me wonder what the hell was going on, and who was calling the shots. I didn't have to wait long to find out.

Silvio Rucci said his three sons had been trying to replace him as the head of the family and might have succeeded had they not started fighting amongst themselves. The battle between the brothers had caused friction in the family, friction which Silvio was able to parlay into support from some of the older capos. Although Silvio's support came from only a few of the capos, with the brothers battling each other, no side was able to muster a majority force. It was basically a standoff.

I wondered why the old man was telling me this, and what, if anything, he expected me to do. Those answers would soon be coming. But first came a warning. Mr. Rucci said he believed I was an honorable man, a man with a checkered history, but still a man who could be trusted. What he was about to tell me, I was to tell no one. To quote Mr. Rucci as nearly as I can recall, he said, "If you tell anyone, the consequences for you will be swift and severe." It was a really nice way of saying, "If you blab, I'll kill you." However it was said, the message was clear.

After threatening my life, Mr. Rucci announced we should have a cup of espresso and pastry before continuing with business. He was definitely old school Mafia.

As if on cue, a door opened, and a man, wearing an apron, entered and put a tray with two demitasse cups, a small coffee pot, and a plate of sfogliatella on the table. Sfogliatella are clam shaped pastries made up of thin layers of pastry dough over a light filling of ricotta and almond paste. They resemble the American lobster claw pastry but are generally smaller and have less filling.

Smiling amiably, Mr. Rucci filled a demitasse cup and passed it in my direction. I noticed the traditional bottle of anisette, an Italian liquor used as a coffee sweetener, was missing. Instead, there was a small sugar bowl. Mr. Rucci had done his homework.

Pushing the dish of pastries across the table, Mr. Rucci suggested that I try one, saying they were fresh from Ferrara's oven. The man may have been a vicious killer, but he had style. I mean, what could be better at a meeting than a warm sfogliatella from Ferrara's Bakery and a good cup of espresso? Maybe leaving the meeting alive would be better, but if I died, at least I wouldn't die on an empty stomach.

Mr. Rucci didn't have much to say while we drank our coffee and ate our pastries. When we were done, he waved his arm, and the man in the apron, who had been standing nearby, cleared the table. With the room once again empty, Mr. Rucci said, "Now I'll tell you the rest of the story. But remember, counselor, not a word of this is to pass your lips. Capisce?"

He was looking me in the eye, his own eyes hard and cold. I knew the look; I'd seen it in the eyes of some of my most vicious clients. Mr. Gracious Host was gone, and Mr. Ruthless Gangster was back. I nodded my head to let Rucci know I understood what he was saying. Then I sat back and waited. He'd either trust me and tell me his story or send me away. At that point, I figured he hadn't told me anything that warranted killing me, but I wasn't sure.

CHAPTER 45

Apparently satisfied that I could be trusted, Rucci told me the rest of the story. When the Russians got wind of a possible coupe in the Rucci family, they saw it as an opportunity to move in on the family's territory. The Russians thought that with the family divided and distracted, it wouldn't be able to fend off a territorial invasion. The old man said that was a miscalculation on the part of the Russians. When the Russians made their first move in Brooklyn, he had a sit-down with his three sons, and he convinced them that they had to set aside their differences and deal with the Russians, or the Russians would eventually take over the entire family.

At Silvio's suggestion, his oldest son, Junior, sent two men to deal with the interlopers. When that didn't go so well, he, Silvio, sent Little Tony to deliver a stronger message. Little Tony was told to beat the crap out of the two Russians but not to kill either of them. Why? Because the Rucci family couldn't afford an all-out war with the Russians and killing two of their soldiers was likely to start a war. Beating the crap out of the two would necessitate a sit-down which could lead to a negotiated settlement. Even if the Ruccis had to surrender a little territory while they sorted out their internal issues, it was better than an all-out war.

Everything would have been fine if the youngest son, Willie, hadn't decided to take matters into his own hands. According to Silvio, Willie, a hothead, decided that simply beating up the two Russians wasn't enough, so he killed them.

Faced with a possible calamity, Silvio and his oldest son, Junior, had a sit-down with the head of the Russian mob. Having no real leverage and needing to avoid a war, he was forced to give the Russians the bookmaking territory that was at the heart of the matter. But that wasn't enough to appease the Russians who demanded the death of the person who had killed the two Russian mobsters. It wasn't a matter of sentimentality; it was simply that one of the dead Russians was the nephew of the boss' wife. Unless the Ruccis turned over the murderer, there'd be a war. Apparently, domestic tranquility came with a large price tag.

That obviously created a big problem for the Ruccis. There was no way Silvio would turn over his youngest son to the Russians, but unless he turned over someone, there'd be a war, and his family was likely to lose. Silvio was turning all of this over in his mind when Junior unexpectedly agreed to the Russians' demand.

Junior would later explain to his father that they'd simply turn over some dead body to the Russians, and that would be the end of it. But the Russians were smarter than that, and Silvio knew it. It was a lesson Junior soon learned when the Russians demanded proof of guilt accompany any person or body that the Ruccis turned over as the murderer.

If nothing else, Junior proved to be deviously creative when he asked if a criminal investigation leading to a conviction would be enough proof of guilt. The Russians agreed, provided the murderer wound up dead. Junior assured them that once the murderer was convicted, the Ruccis would arrange for him to be killed in prison. Accounts would be settled, and a bloody gang war avoided. It sounded great, but was Junior willing to turn over his younger brother to the Russians?

When asked that very question by Silvio, Junior said no, and it seemed he had a plan. A plan Junior wouldn't share with his father, but which he said would save Willie's life. A few days earlier, Silvio learned the plan was to frame Little Tony for the murder of the two Russians.

Things were starting to make sense. The Ruccis needed Little Tony to be convicted of murdering the two Russians. They couldn't risk his being acquitted, and Gene Meyers probably balked at throwing the case. Gene may have done some questionable things for the Ruccis, but I had to believe he'd draw the line at putting an innocent man away for life.

As I had suspected all along, the Rucci brothers were looking for a lousy lawyer, and along came Joey Bats with a recommendation. That's how I came into the picture. But when I started talking about a plea deal, or worse, a successful defense, everyone got nervous. I was expecting Silvio Rucci to explain how my well-being was tied directly to Little Tony's future. But I was wrong. Really wrong.

To my utter surprise and confusion, Silvio Rucci said he didn't want Little Tony convicted. At that point, I didn't know what to think. Did he want to save his son or not? Seeing the confused look on my face, Rucci explained. It wasn't that he didn't want to protect his youngest son, but he didn't believe the Russians would fall for the deception. And there was more to it.

Leaning toward me as though to emphasize the importance of what he was about to say, he whispered that he couldn't afford to lose the loyalty of Big Tony, who was on his side in the fight for control of the family. When a mafioso whispers, it means that it's a private conversation, and it had better stay that way. I knew if I uttered one word of what I had just heard, I'd be dead.

My head was spinning, and I had quite a few questions. Such as, what about Sally Boy Stagliano? Since Silvio hadn't mentioned him as being an ally, I had to figure he wasn't. It made sense. Big Tony was old school like Silvio, but Sally Boy wasn't. He was one of the new crops of Mafia gangsters who didn't hold to the old ways.

I understood all of that, but I still didn't know what Mr. Rucci expected me to do. Figuring I was on safe ground, I asked why I was there. Mr. Rucci said he'd explain, but first he wanted to know if I could get Little Tony off. I said that I had thought so, but recent developments were changing my view.

He said that he understood there were problems with the case which made me wonder if he knew about the missing slugs and might be the one behind the scheme. Or maybe it was Junior who was behind it, and the old man didn't like it, but he wasn't in a position to do anything about it. I suspected that was the case, but I wasn't about to ask. Instead I asked what he wanted me to do. Not that I would necessarily do what the old man wanted, but at least I needed to hear him out. If I was going to die, I wanted to know why.

Mr. Rucci nodded and said I should do everything necessary to get Little Tony off, but I shouldn't seem too confident. I wasn't sure if he meant I shouldn't seem too confident or too competent. Then he added, "I find you to be a smart man, so I suspect you know why you were hired. Remember that, don't rock the boat, and everything will be okay."

Mr. Rucci was reminding me that I was hired because no one thought I was competent enough to get Little Tony acquitted or smart enough to figure out he was being framed. It was also a warning.

At that point, after listening to the old man, everything pointed to Junior as the one behind the whole setup. If Junior began thinking I wasn't as dumb as he thought I was, he might just take me off the case, and it probably wouldn't be by way of a letter. So playing stupid would be the way to go while I kept my cards close to my vest.

We were apparently done because Mr. Rucci waved his hand, and the goon at the door opened it and motioned for me to follow him out. I stood up, smiled at Mr. Rucci who smiled back, then I made for the door, moving as quickly as I could without running.

When we got to the sidewalk, the goon handed me my cell phone and asked if I wanted a ride back to my office. I declined the offer, wanting to be away from him and his buddies as quickly as possible.

CHAPTER 46

Walking quickly down 10th Street, I glanced at my watch. It was nearly five o'clock, and I had been with Mr. Rucci for almost three hours. I still wasn't sure what it had been all about, but I was alive, so I figured that I was ahead of the game.

I was supposed to meet Gracie for dinner at this little sushi joint in Tribeca at six o'clock. For those of you not familiar with New York City neighborhoods, let me explain how they get their names. Tribeca, for example, is the *triangle below Canal Street*. Soho is another neighborhood, defined as the area *south of Houston*. Houston being a street in Lower Manhattan as well as a city in Texas. But our Houston is pronounced *"house-ton."* Nolita is the neighborhood *north of Little Italy*. You get the idea? Me, I like the old traditional names like Hell's Kitchen, the Upper East Side, Harlem, and Murray Hill. But what do I know? I still call Avenue of the Americas Sixth Avenue.

But back to the story. I couldn't figure out what old man Rucci meant when he said that he knew about problems with the case. Did he know about the missing slugs, and if he did, was he the one who had arranged for them to disappear? But that didn't make sense if he wanted Little Tony acquitted.

That meant Junior had likely arranged for the disappearance of the slugs and had either told the old man about it, or the old man had a source inside Junior's circle. Obviously, Junior had a clear motive for framing Little Tony for the murder of the two Russians, but was he getting help in the process?

Junior would know that the slugs recovered from the victims weren't going to match Little Tony's gun because Little Tony hadn't killed the victims. But I didn't think Junior was smart enough to realize it would be a problem for the prosecution. Someone who understood it was a problem, and a big one, had to be giving Junior advice. I had no proof as to who that someone was, but I'd bet the ranch it was Gene Meyers.

Gene Meyers was working behind the scenes for Junior to make sure Little Tony was convicted of murdering the two Russians. He was acting as a shadow prosecutor, alerting Junior to any shortcomings in the prosecution's case so Junior could eliminate them. When he counseled Junior that the slugs would give Little Tony a strong defense, Junior made them disappear. Then, fearing a plea deal that might not satisfy the Russians' lust for revenge, Junior kept a plea deal off the table by buying off the assistant district attorney. With no plea deal in the offering and the slugs gone, I'd be forced to trial without any exculpatory evidence to support a defense, and a conviction seemed inevitable. The more I thought about it, the more I was convinced that Junior couldn't have figured that out on his own, and Gene Meyers was the brains behind the operation.

I was still trying to process it all when I arrived at the sushi restaurant and found Gracie was already there. I apologized for being late, then explained what had kept me. Naturally Gracie was upset, and even more so when I told her that if old man Rucci found out we were having this conversation, he'd kill me. But I trusted Gracie not to squeal, so I told her the whole story, even what the old man had whispered. I was living life on the edge.

Gracie was still very angry that her office had been compromised, and she again suggested that we go the district attorney and report Hannah and McAvoy. The district attorney was Jerome Vitter, and while Gracie didn't have a close relationship with the man, she believed that she could go to him directly. Alternatively, she suggested we go through her boss, Senior Deputy District Attorney Joe Sebert.

I reminded Gracie we had no proof yet, and if we went to Vitter too soon, we'd risk Hannah and McAvoy learning they were under investigation. They could then cover their tracks, making it almost impossible to prove a case against them. We had to wait until we had proof of the conspiracy before we moved against Hannah and McAvoy.

We decided not to ruin dinner by talking any further about the case, and instead, we discussed the weather and the newest fashion trends, none of which interested me in the least. There's nothing you can do about the weather, so other than complaining about it, what's there to talk about? As for fashion, I have no interest in the subject whatsoever because as a trial lawyer, I have a steadfast rule to never make my appearance an issue, and appearance starts with your clothes. That's why I wear simple dark suits, white or blue shirts, and solid color or classic striped ties. No jewelry, just a class ring and a watch, and not a Rolex. Of course, I could never afford a Rolex, but I could have gotten a good knockoff from Tommy back when he was in the business.

In case you're wondering why no jewelry and no overly fashionable attire, it's because they attract the jury's attention, and a good lawyer always wants to keep the jury's attention focused on the case. Never make yourself an issue in the case because you never know how a jury's going to react to you. If they wind up hating you or the way you dress, they could take it out on your client.

It was a lesson I learned very early in my career and have never forgotten. I was prosecuting a murder case; it was my first big case; and I was dressed to the nines. Back then I was a flashy dresser. Double breasted suit, dark shirt, with a bright paisley tie. The defense counsel on the case was a legendary old lawyer who had more wins to his credit than I could even dream of having. Two days into what was expected to be a two- to three-week trial, the old guy says to me, "Junior, you're going to lose this case."

I figured it was just trash talk, the old guy trying to get my goat, so I said, "Why? Because you think that you're a better lawyer than I am? Well, you're wrong; I'm better than you are."

The old guy laughed and said, "No, Junior, you're not going to lose because you're a worse lawyer; you're going to lose because the jury hates the way you're dressed."

I didn't believe him, but I started to notice that when I questioned witnesses, the jurors were staring at me and not looking at the witnesses. So just to be on the safe side, I went to a different suit, wore a white shirt, and a dark blue tie. Sure enough, the jurors who had been staring at me stopped, and instead, looked at the witness. The old guy was right, and he had taught me a valuable lesson.

By the way, I lost the case, but at least it wasn't because of how I was dressed; it was because the old guy was a better lawyer than I was. Another lesson learned.

But back to Gracie and me and our dinner conversation. We don't normally have detailed discussions about our cases. At most, we'll just mention an interesting case, but we never talk strategy or anything like that. But with Little Tony's case, it was different. Gracie had an interest because of the conspiracy in her office, not to mention that both our lives could be in danger. So, after dinner we headed home for a little strategy session.

CHAPTER 47

Gracie put up a pot of coffee while I laid out on the breakfast table what little information I had about the case. When the coffee was brewed, Gracie fired up her laptop computer, and fueled with caffeine, we talked strategy. Little Tony's best defense was the two-gun theory, but without the slugs to prove two guns had been used in the attack, it would be nearly impossible to prove. Theo could offer supporting testimony, but it would be theoretical at best, and theory falls short of hard evidence.

No, without the slugs, the next best way to raise reasonable doubt would be to expose the conspiracy. By showing that the prosecutors had tampered with the evidence, I hoped to cast doubt on the integrity of the whole process. But again I needed proof; I couldn't rely merely on speculation. Even at that, I had to be careful that the plan didn't backfire with the prosecution arguing that Little Tony had the slugs disappear because they came from his gun and proved him guilty. It was a tightrope but worth the walk if I could prove the conspiracy existed.

How was I going to prove Hannah and McAvoy were both in on the scheme? Gracie suggested we start by looking at anomalies, such as why the case had been transferred from Sarah Washington to Hannah. What was there to be gained from the transfer?

Gracie said that assuming what old man Rucci told me was true, anything short of Little Tony being convicted of murder wouldn't solve the Ruccis' problem with the Russians. That meant a plea deal had to be out of the question. Making the slugs disappear weakened the defense, but not to the point that the prosecutor would refuse to plea bargain.

There was only one way to ensure Little Tony wasn't offered a plea deal, and that was by controlling the assistant district attorney handling the case. Only someone familiar with the system would understand it, so Gracie said I was probably right in thinking that Gene Meyers was helping out behind the scenes.

It was all starting to come together. Then Gracie said that everyone, including Gene Meyers, knew Sarah Washington was incorruptible. Junior, knowing he couldn't buy off Sarah Washington, needed to find a new assistant district attorney he could buy off.

No one ever claimed that Meyers himself bought jurors or prosecutors, but most of us in the business believed someone bought the jurors on many of his cases. He might not have been the one who actually made the payoffs; he was too smart for that, but he certainly knew they were being made. I felt certain that if there were corrupt lawyers in the District Attorney's Office Gene Meyers knew who they were.

Gracie recalled Hannah being the prosecutor on at least two of Meyers' mob cases where the defendants were acquitted. After the trials, there had been talk in the office about Hannah dropping the ball when he examined some of the key prosecution witnesses, but nothing ever came of it. That just about clinched it for me. As for Gracie, she had been convinced that Hannah and McAvoy were both in on the scheme from the start.

Gracie wanted to turn Hannah and McAvoy in first thing in the morning. I appreciated Gracie's enthusiasm, but I reminded her that we still had no proof and turning them in wouldn't help my case. To start, we had no evidence that either of them had done anything wrong. All we could show was that Hannah had the case transferred to himself for no apparent reason, and that wasn't going to get us anywhere.

Even if Gracie succeeded in convincing District Attorney Vitter that something wasn't right, the best we could expect would be a switch of assistant district attorneys, and that wouldn't get me the slugs. Not that it mattered because, at that point, I had given up any hope of getting my hands on the slugs. I had to assume the clerk at the Medical Examiner's Office had thrown them away, and even if they were somehow recovered, the chain of custody would have been lost, and no judge was likely to admit them into evidence.

The more Gracie and I discussed the case, the more I began to think that even if I proved the conspiracy existed, it was going to be more difficult getting Little Tony acquitted than I first thought. If I exposed the scheme too early, the district attorney might simply replace Hannah and McAvoy and blame the whole thing on a couple of overzealous prosecutors. I needed a way of turning the scheme into an anchor that would sink the prosecution's case.

We seemed to be going in circles and getting nowhere until Gracie came up with a brilliant thought. I had just mentioned the missing slugs for the umpteenth time when Gracie, who was busy tapping away at her laptop, yelled out, "spoliation" which in a legal context means destroying evidence. It was a brilliant idea, and I didn't know why I hadn't come up with it myself.

Technically destroying evidence wasn't a defense to the charge of murder because it had little to do with actual innocence or guilt. It was an issue of fairness and whether the prosecution had done something that kept the defendant from receiving a fair trial.

If we could prove the prosecutor had destroyed evidence helpful to Little Tony's defense, we'd likely be entitled to what's called an adverse inference charge. I could argue that the missing evidence, if presented to the jury, would have proved Little Tony's gun hadn't killed the two victims. Then at the end of the case, the judge would instruct the jurors that they could assume if the evidence had been preserved, it would not support the prosecution's theory of the case. It didn't guarantee an acquittal, but it was at least the start of a defense.

It would be the base I needed for Theo's testimony and evidence that the two-gun theory was probable. Of course, there were a few other problems to deal with, but unless I solved this one, the rest didn't matter.

It was late, and I was about to suggest we knock off for the night when Gracie said we might be able to do better than simply an adverse inference charge. Under a US Supreme Court case, we might be entitled to a dismissal of the indictment if we could prove that Hannah and McAvoy went along with disposing of the slugs, believing they could form a basis for exonerating Little Tony. In other words, if I could show that Hannah and McAvoy participated in the scheme to destroy evidence, knowing that the slugs would prove Little Tony was not guilty, the judge might have to dismiss the case. It was a tall order, but it wasn't out of the question.

Even if the judge wouldn't dismiss the case, he'd still have to instruct the jury that they could assume the evidence was favorable to the defendant. I had nothing to lose by going for the dismissal.

For any of it to work, several things had to fall into place, starting with the clerk at the Medical Examiner's Office. First and foremost, we had to prove he had changed the autopsy reports and disposed of the slugs. I didn't see that as a problem. I was confident Linda Chow could hack her way into the medical examiner's computer system and not only identify the clerk, but she could retrieve the missing files as well. After all, Linda was a world-class master hacker. I made a note to give her a call the next morning to see how she was progressing.

Once I had the records in hand, I intended to confront the clerk and get him to confess to disposing of the slugs. After that, the next step would be showing they were material to the issue of guilt. That was easy and would come from Theo, who'd testify that ballistic testing of the slugs would confirm his findings based on the x-rays that the slugs didn't come from the gun confiscated when Little Tony was arrested. Not only would that mean the slugs were material to the issue of guilt, but more likely exculpatory.

We were on a roll, but then we hit a roadblock. I asked Gracie if we needed to prove that the clerk had acted on instructions from Hannah or McAvoy. For all we knew, he could have been bought off by one of the Ruccis without Hannah or McAvoy knowing anything about it.

Gracie said overall it didn't matter because the clerk was an agent of the State, but it would affect what the judge could do about it. If the District Attorney's Office didn't know about the evidence tampering, a judge wasn't likely to dismiss the case but only give the jury an adverse inference charge. That meant I needed to prove Hannah and McAvoy were either the initiators of the tampering or at least knew about it and did nothing to stop it.

Everything came back to the clerk and the need for his cooperation. Without it, I couldn't tie the Ruccis to the scheme, and I had no proof that Hannah and McAvoy even knew about it. The clerk was likely the one who actually destroyed the evidence, and that made him the weak link in the chain. Breaking him down was critical because he was the one person who I was relying on to testify that Hannah and McAvoy were in on the scheme. Without that testimony, Hannah and McAvoy could claim they knew nothing about the slugs or what the clerk had done. I was hoping that offering the clerk a deal on the felony charge of tampering with evidence would be incentive enough to have him testify, but that remained to be seen.

By that time, it was three thirty in the morning, and despite the caffeine or perhaps as a result of too much of it, we were getting punchy, so we called it a night.

CHAPTER 48

Despite having gone to bed at three thirty that morning, we were both up and alert when the alarm went off at seven fifteen. It had been twenty-five years since Gracie and I worked on a case together, and I had forgotten what a good team we made. I think we both enjoyed the experience, but with the start of the new day, our teamwork ended. Gracie was once more the prosecutor, and I was again the defense attorney.

Strategizing on a common issue had been fun, but in the end, Gracie was still on one side of the fence, and I was on the other side. Maybe down the road we'd wind up on the same side again, but not that morning.

On my way to the office, I called Theo and left a message for him to call me. Then I called Tommy's office and spoke with Linda Chow. Being as carefully cryptic as I could, I asked if she had gotten the information I needed from the Medical Examiner's Office. I was careful not to use the word "hacking," fearing that our phones might be tapped. Perhaps I was taking this mob lawyer role too seriously.

Linda said she had run into a problem and suggested I drop by the office rather than discussing it on the phone. Figuring that meant trouble, I said that I'd be by in half an hour. I called Connie, told her I wouldn't be in the office until later, and I headed to Tommy's office on Elizabeth Street.

Motivated by my curiosity, I made it to Tommy's office in less than twenty minutes. The look on Linda's face when she greeted me suggested I wasn't going to be happy with what she had to say. At first the news was good; Linda had no trouble hacking into the system and locating the final autopsy reports. But that's where the good news ended. The original taped commentaries and the original autopsy reports were not on the system. They were gone, apparently erased. And the bad news didn't end there. Whoever had erased the files knew what they were doing because Linda had been unable to recover them. The only way these files could have been erased so completely was by using a highly sophisticated erasure program.

Linda was able to identify the clerk who posted the final autopsy reports. His name was Vijay Shankar, and from what she could tell, he was the only one who had handled the autopsy files. She couldn't be certain he was the one who erased the files, but Shankar's ID and password were the only ones associated with the files, making him the prime suspect. Linda was now digging further into Shankar's life, looking for anything that tied him to the erased files.

If Linda couldn't recover the original tapes and reports, I was hoping she might find something else in the files that would prove the slugs once existed. I could try talking to the doctor who performed the autopsies, but the doctors in the Medical Examiner's Office never spoke voluntarily to defense lawyers. I'd have to subpoena him at trial, and if he didn't remember the case or had no recollection of having found any slugs in the victims, his testimony would be a disaster. No, I wanted solid proof that the slugs had once existed and had been intentionally destroyed or discarded.

Without the files from the Medical Examiner's Office to back up my claims, I was left with the clerk Shankar as my only source of evidence. But Linda wasn't certain that he was the one who had changed the reports and erased the files. He was likely the one to have done it but likely wasn't going to cut it.

I wanted to confront Shankar but doing so too early I risked alerting Hannah and McAvoy that they were next. Given such a warning, they'd be able to clean things up and possibly come up with cover stories.

Whatever I did, it had to be coordinated, and it had to take everyone by surprise. The problem was that I had no idea how to do that. I wasn't even sure who was behind the scheme, and that was important. I was assuming that it was Junior Rucci, based on what Silvio Rucci had told me at the meeting. But what if the meeting with Silvio Rucci was just a ruse to keep better tabs on me? And what about Big Tony? After our meeting at the tea parlor, I believed he was on Little Tony's side, but I still wasn't convinced he and Silvio Rucci were working together.

There were lots of questions and very few answers. Most of the questions would be answered if I knew who was behind the frame-up. Was it Silvio Rucci, or was it Junior Rucci? As they say in poker, think long, think wrong, so I went with my gut. My gut was saying old man Rucci was telling me the truth, and Junior was behind the frame-up.

I'd play it that way, and if I was wrong, the whole case would blow up in my face. Not to mention that Little Tony would go to prison, and Big Tony would probably kill me. Gracie was right; I'm not cut out to be a mob lawyer. I liked it better when I was simply an 18B Panel lawyer. That way, all of my violent criminal clients who had reason to kill me were behind bars, not in bars sipping espresso coffees and plotting my death.

I was about to leave when Tommy arrived and suggested we talk a little more about the case. Linda had a couple of more things to run by me, and Tommy had some thoughts. Having nowhere else to be and out of ideas of my own, I thought it a good idea.

Tommy suggested that I grab a coffee and join him in the conference room. I hate early morning meetings in Tommy's office because his coffee is lousy. The tea is great, but the coffee stinks. That's because Tommy is Chinese. Some of you may think that my last comment is politically incorrect, and some may even claim it's a racist comment. But my comment simply recites facts; Tommy is Chinese; he has lousy instant coffee in his office; and he has a great selection of teas. So, you tell me why simply stating facts is politically incorrect or makes me a racist. And if that's not enough to change your thinking, try this one on for size. I once asked Tommy why he had such a large selection of teas, but only lousy instant coffee, and he said it was because he was Chinese.

As I sipped my lousy instant coffee, Linda explained that she was totally frustrated in her attempt to retrieve the voice files and the original autopsy report files. She had easily accessed the network servers where the case files were stored and found that the typical case file contained voice files, a draft autopsy report, at least one corrected report, and a final report. But the case files on the two dead Russians contained only the final autopsy report which made them unique. But being unique was not proof that the files had been scrubbed.

That wasn't the only anomaly Linda found. The system had an auditing component that monitored all activity on the network. Whenever a network file is accessed, the identity of the person accessing the file, along with the time, date, and the action taken is recorded to a secured file called an event log. It was a security feature that enabled the administrators to track activity on the system.

When Linda examined the event log, the only activity recorded for the files on the two Russians was the posting of the final reports by Vijay Shankar and nothing else. There were no event log entries for the posting of the autopsy audio files, nor for the original draft reports. So, not only had those items been deleted, the log record that would have shown when and who had done the deletions, was scrubbed.

I asked if any of the deletions could have occurred accidentally, but Linda assured me that wasn't the case. The system was programmed to automatically send all deleted files to a "trash holding bin" where they were stored and could be recovered if they had been accidentally deleted. None of the files I needed were in the "trash holding bin."

When a clerk deletes a file and sends it to the "trash holding bin," the action is recorded in the event log. But as Linda had pointed out earlier, the event log had been scrubbed. Linda said that meant the system's safeguards had been overridden three times, once when the files were first deleted, again when the files were removed from the "trash holding bin" and erased from the server's hard drives, and finally when the event log had been scrubbed. That could have only been done by a highly skilled computer technician using a very sophisticated override and erasure program.

I asked Linda if there was any way to recapture the missing files. She said perhaps she could if she could examine the servers themselves, but it was doubtful. The files were likely lost forever.

The files were the best evidence for proving the slugs existed, and that evidence had been destroyed and discarded. But the files were gone, and I couldn't easily prove they ever existed. If I couldn't prove that they existed, I certainly couldn't prove that they had been intentionally destroyed. More importantly, without those files I had no physical evidence proving that the slugs ever existed.

Testimony from the doctor who performed the autopsies was too risky because I had to subpoena him not knowing what he would say. Besides, if Theo was right about how busy the doctors in the Medical Examiner's Office were, the doctor might not recall recovering the slugs. Even if I got lucky and the doctor recalled recovering the slugs during the autopsies, it would only prove they once existed, but it wouldn't prove they had been intentionally disposed of.

I could argue the reason they disappeared was because they were material to Little Tony's defense, but the best that would get us was adverse inference charge and not a dismissal. If I hoped for a dismissal of the charges, I'd need Shankar to testify that he intentionally destroyed the files and disposed of the slugs, then he'd have to implicate Hannah and McAvoy in the scheme. When I put it that way, it sounded simple enough, but I knew it was far from simple.

Tommy, who had been sitting in on the meeting, asked what I needed him to do. That was an easy question to answer. I needed to know everything about Vijay Shankar there was to know. I wanted his work history, his bank records, his marital history, his criminal record if he had one, who he hung out with, and what he did for fun. In other words, everything from his background to the brand of toothpaste he used.

I still had no idea how I'd approach Shankar, but before I tried, I wanted to know everything there was to know about him. Threat of a felony conviction alone might not be enough to turn him, so it would be good to have something else to pressure him with. Tommy knew what I needed and said he'd get right on it. I told him to pull out all stops and to hire as much help as he needed.

In the meantime, I asked Linda to go back into the medical examiner's computer system and look for other irregularities in Shankar's files. Maybe he had done something like this before, and if Linda could find it, I'd have something else to threaten him with.

With so much going on in Little Tony's case, I had nearly forgotten I had a conference that afternoon in Devon's case. The Grand Jury had failed to return an indictment in the felony case, so the felony charge had been dismissed. But misdemeanor charges aren't sent to the Grand Jury, so the charge of possessing a skimmer was still pending. The conference in Criminal Court was to discuss resolving the case. The assistant district attorney would be looking for a plea deal, but I wanted the case dismissed.

CHAPTER 49

Judge Mahon held the pretrial conference in the robing room behind his courtroom. Mahon had been recently appointed by the mayor to the Criminal Court bench in what was considered by most to be a surprising appointment. With his background as a criminal defense attorney, everyone figured Mahon wouldn't be one of those tough on crime jurists that the mayor favored. I was hoping that was true because I needed all the help I could get with Devon's case.

The assistant district attorney handling the conference was Taylor Clark, the same assistant district attorney who had handled the arraignment. We hadn't gotten along particularly well back then, and as much as I would have enjoyed busting his balls this time around, I knew it was best if I didn't. So rather than making some snide remark, I gave Clark a big smile and a warm hello. But I couldn't leave it at that, so I moved closer to give him a man hug, but he moved away.

Maybe I overdid the friendly thing because I had clearly frightened Clark who was staring at me as though I was crazy. I didn't appreciate his attitude and was sorely tempted to give him the finger, but for Devon's sake I didn't.

Judge Mahon's robing room, like nearly all the robing rooms in the Criminal Courts Building, was small, with barely enough space for the desk, a few chairs, and two filing cabinets. With the judge, his law clerk, the court reporter, Clark and I in the room, it was a tight squeeze. It was what I like to call intimate with me sitting shoulder to shoulder with Clark much to his discomfort. Had I known we would be sitting in each other's laps that afternoon, I would have eaten a head of garlic at lunch.

If you think I'm very childish, you'd be right. AA is trying to make me a better person, but as I tell my sponsor, Doug, I'm a work in progress. Doug and Gracie believe the pace of my progress leaves a lot to be desired, but as I tell them, progress is progress. Besides, I think maturity is highly overrated.

Getting down to business, the judge asked about the case. Before I could open my mouth, Clark jumped in, and puffing up his chest, he said it was a serious class A misdemeanor, possession of a skimmer. Of all the ways to present the case, that was the most ridiculous. So much so that I couldn't help but snicker. My reaction didn't seem to bother Clark who continued explaining how serious the charge was.

I would have interrupted with a smart-ass comment just to break Clark's rhythm, but I noticed a skeptical look on the judge's face and decided to keep my mouth shut. When opposing counsel is losing on his own, it's best not to interrupt. If the judge wasn't buying Clark's bullshit, I wasn't going to risk opening my mouth and changing his mind.

When Clark finished his little tirade, the judge asked if there were any other charges pending against the defendant arising from the use of the skimmer. Judge Mahon knew exactly what was at issue and was getting right to the point. If the skimmer had been used in a larceny, then the possession charge would be treated more seriously. But absent a larceny charge, it was a simple and easily disposed of misdemeanor.

The question was a simple one. Were there other presently pending charges? Since the Grand Jury had failed to return an indictment on the felony charge, the answer was "no." Had the judge asked if there had been other charges brought against Devon, then the answer would be "yes," and we'd need to explain they were dismissed. That would have been a minor complication which I wanted to avoid, so rather than chance how Clark would answer, I jumped in and said there were no other pending charges against the defendant.

Clark was about to say something, but fortunately the judge was ready to move on and asked for my thoughts on a disposition of the case. I said, off the record, Devon did possess the skimmer, but it was never proved that he had used it in a crime. I explained that Devon was a good kid, a genius, slated to go to Stanford University on a scholarship, and a conviction on even a misdemeanor could jeopardize his future. The judge nodded, then looked to Clark and asked what he thought. As I expected, Clark was unsympathetic, saying there was no way he could agree to a dismissal, not when the defendant had been caught red-handed.

The judge looked to me for a reply, and I said, "This is nuts. We're in a city where the District Attorney's Office refuses to prosecute misdemeanor marijuana possession, but they'll ruin a kid's life for possession of a skimmer? Where's the justice in that?"

The judge agreed and suggested an adjournment in contemplation of dismissal or an ACD as it' commonly called. What happens with an ACD is that the case is adjourned for a given period, after which, if the defendant hasn't gotten into more trouble, the case is dismissed. It was a reasonable suggestion but not one I could live with. We needed an immediate dismissal, or Devon might not be able to collect the prize money if his project won first prize. Of course, that wasn't a reason likely to persuade the judge to dismiss the case. I needed something else.

Somehow Devon's case keeps me coming back to situational ethics. Do I tell a little white lie, hoping to get the kid off, or do I play it straight and let his life go down the tubes? Okay, that's a bit of an exaggeration, but it sounds better put that way. In other words, I'm waffling on my belief that the ends don't justify the means, and I'm hoping you don't call me on being a hypocrite.

Anyway, I told the judge that holding the indictment open could jeopardize Devon's acceptance to Stanford and ruin his life. I didn't know that to be a fact, the part about the admission to Stanford, but it seemed reasonable. As for it ruining his life, that was a matter of opinion, and I'm entitled to my own opinion.

Whatever you think about the tactic, it worked. Judge Mahon looked at Clark and asked, "Do you really want to ruin this boy's life over a case you don't have an ice cube's chance in hell of winning?"

That pretty much ended the arguing. Clark could have held his ground, but he was smart enough not to. He had to appear regularly before Judge Mahon who could make his life hell, so rather than argue and piss off the judge, he simply said, "Well, judge, when you put that way, we don't oppose an immediate dismissal of the charges." It was the first and only smart thing Clark said that day.

The judge smiled, said he'd issue the order that afternoon, and we were done. Devon's case was finally over; all that remained was for me to fulfill a promise I had made earlier to Devon's grandfather. With that in mind, I called Mr. Williams and asked him to meet me at my office in an hour and to bring Devon along.

Of course, both Devon and his grandfather were thrilled when I told them that all charges against Devon had been dropped, and he was no longer involved in any criminal matters. I didn't mention anything about the promised restitution, but Mr. Williams wasn't one to overlook an obligation and asked when it needed to be paid. I told a little white lie and said the matter had been resolved without a payment needed from Devon.

The truth was that I had sent my own check to American Express. I felt sorry for Devon and his grandfather, knowing Mr. Williams would be hard pressed to come up with the money, and Devon would need all the prize money for his education. I figured the fee I earned from the 18B Panel on the case would just about cover the twenty-one-hundred dollars, so I'd consider Devon's case to be my pro bono good deed for the year. Besides, I had just scored the big fee on Little Tony's case, and I was feeling flush.

But that wasn't the end of it with Devon. I had made a promise to Mr. Williams, and it was time for me to keep it. Turning my attention to Devon, I laced into him, saying that for a supposedly smart kid he was pretty stupid, and he was damn lucky not to be sitting in prison. He had gotten a couple of big breaks, breaks he wasn't likely to get again, so if he had any smarts at all, he wouldn't do anything so stupid again.

Donald L'Abbate

The kid was close to tears, and I felt badly talking to him like that, but his grandfather and I had agreed it needed to be done. Once I was convinced Devon had gotten the message, I gave him a hug, and he hugged me back, while his grandfather nodded and smiled.

I'm not much of a hugger, but at that moment it seemed like the right thing to do. For an instant, I felt like a father talking to his son which was something totally foreign to me. With my own father having abandoned me and my mother when I was a little kid, I don't have any great father-son memories, and I don't know what a father is supposed to do.

Maybe being a father is instinctive, and that's why I was comfortable dealing with Devon on a personal level. At my age, chances are I'm never going to be a father, and I'm okay with that. But at that moment with Devon, I felt like a father, and it felt good.

In my line of work, cases that end as happily as Devon's case are rare and far between. I can't recall the last time a client hugged me, which is understandable. I mean, when your client is being dragged off to start serving a long prison term, hugging his lawyer probably isn't high on his priority list. Besides, there haven't been many clients I'd want touching me, no less hugging me.

CHAPTER 50

Now that Devon's case was finished, I could turn my full attention to Little Tony's case. The first item on the agenda was figuring out what to do about Vijay Shankar. My plan was to learn as much as I could about the man, then confront him and force him to admit to the conspiracy. It was a good plan, but as with most of my plans, it was easier said than done.

Assuming Tommy and Linda turned up enough evidence to send Shankar to jail, which seemed certain, it wouldn't help unless I could offer him a plea deal and I couldn't. It was the old carrot and the stick routine, and while I'd have the stick, I'd be lacking the carrot. The carrot for the deal could only come from the district attorney, and I couldn't go to him until I knew Shankar would cooperate.

It was a problem I had to work out, and I was counting on Tommy and Linda for help. I figured once I knew everything there was to know about Vijay Shankar, I'd find some way of turning him.

I was considering my next move when Big Tony called, saying we needed to meet and asked if I could arrange a private room at Shoo's for lunch. I said that wouldn't be a problem, but I needed to know how many we'd be. Big Tony said it would be just the two of us, and it needed to be private.

I had no idea what Big Tony wanted to discuss, but a private meeting between just the two of us gave me a bad feeling, and I figured whatever he had to say wasn't going to make me happy. Not that I was afraid Big Tony intended to kill me. If he was going to kill me, it wouldn't be at Shoo's.

There were too many things about this case that I didn't know, the first of which was who I could trust. My client, Little Tony, had become a non-entity, with all the shots being called by his father. My gut told me Big Tony was working to save his son so him calling the shots was okay. But what about Silvio Rucci? Where did he fit into the picture? Were Big Tony and Silvio Rucci working together as they claimed, or was either one of them planning to double-cross the other? Of more immediate interest was how Big Tony would react when he found out I knew about Vijay Shankar and his role in the evidence tampering. Would it come as a surprise, or had he known about Shankar and the scheme all along?

CHAPTER 51

As always, old man Shoo was very accommodating, and Big Tony and I were seated in an alcove room just off the main dining room. With the heavy curtain drawn closed, we had complete privacy, totally isolated from the hustle and bustle of the busy restaurant. After we ordered our lunches, Big Tony got down to business. He and old man Rucci wanted a status report. Where did Little Tony's defense stand, and what was I doing to earn my fee?

It wasn't a particularly friendly question, but it was asked politely enough. I figured if Big Tony had any real qualms about my handling of his son's case, we'd be having this meeting in an alley and not in Shoo's restaurant.

I said there were problems with the evidence, but I was dealing with them. I left it at that, waiting to see if Big Tony would open the door and he did. He demanded to know about the problems. Now I was in a quandary. I suspected he was fishing to find out what I knew, but I didn't know why. Should I mention Shankar and the missing slugs or not? I had the sense the missing slugs weren't a surprise to anyone except me but my knowing about Shankar would be.

I decided it was time for me to go on the offensive.

Answering Big Tony's question, I said, "You already know about the missing slugs. So let me ask you, was it old man Rucci who had them disappear?"

Big Tony shook his head and said it was Junior, not the old man. Junior had tried to keep it a secret, but the old man found out about it. He didn't know all the details, but he knew it involved some Indian guy, a clerk in the Medical Examiner's Office and a couple of assistant district attorneys. It had cost Junior a small fortune, and now there was a problem.

I didn't know how much money Shankar had gotten, but I had to believe Hannah and McAvoy wouldn't risk their careers unless there was a lot of money involved. Big Tony said he didn't know how much money had been paid, but the money was only a small part of the problem.

For the moment, things were looking up. Big Tony and I were on the same page, and Silvio Rucci was there with us. Unless, of course, there was a double-cross in the works, I now knew who was on the team and what I would do about Shankar. But things have a funny way of turning quickly as they did in this instance.

The problem Big Tony had mentioned changed things. Junior, in his rush to frame Little Tony and save his brother, had done things stupidly, and now his ass was on the line as well. Unsure who he could trust in the family and not wanting his old man to find out he was framing Little Tony, Junior had cut the deals with the clerk and the assistant district attorney himself. If any of them got caught, they were likely to take Junior down with them.

Old man Rucci had consulted with Gene Meyers who, as I suspected, was acting as shadow counsel. Meyers said Junior could be looking at a conspiracy charge in the two murder cases. It was a stretch but knowing how much District Attorney Vitter lusted for Rucci blood, he was likely to pursue the charge. That would put Junior in the Russian murder cases up to his eyeballs.

Now I knew why we were having this meeting. If I blew the whistle on Shankar, and he turned on Hannah and McAvoy, old man Rucci would lose two sons. Willie would go away for the murder of the two Russians, and Junior would, at a minimum, do time for bribery and possibly murder. It wasn't a good picture.

Big Tony must have seen the look in my eyes because he said, "Yeah, counselor, we ain't going with Shankar. So, what else have you got up your sleeve, and it better be good."

I didn't particularly care what the Ruccis wanted, and I wouldn't abandon the spoliation issue just because the Ruccis didn't want me raising it. My obligation was to Little Tony and that didn't change because the Ruccis were paying the bills. But none of that really mattered because the Ruccis held all the cards, and I held none. If I tried to implicate Shankar, the Ruccis would buy him off or kill him. Buying him off was risky, but killing him guaranteed his silence, so I was pretty sure which option the Ruccis would take. Either way it spelled the end of the spoliation issue.

Shankar, being the one who did the actual tampering, was the keystone linking everyone else to the conspiracy. Without Shankar's testimony, the district attorney had no case against Hannah or McAvoy which meant there'd be no reason for them to roll on Junior. So if I insisted on using Shankar as a witness, I'd be signing Shankar's death warrant.

Technically, spoliation wasn't a defense to the charge of murder, but even if I couldn't get a judge to throw out the case because of it, it could still bolster our two-gun defense. I explained that the district attorney's case rested on circumstantial evidence, but it was strong circumstantial evidence. The two-gun theory, the different slugs used in the killing, and the kneecapping was the best evidence we had for raising reasonable doubt. But without proving the conspiracy to explain the absence of the slugs, I'd be hard pressed to do that. I'd try making the case with Theo giving his expert opinion as to the size of the bullets based on entry wounds. But without having the slugs as evidence, McAvoy could easily punch holes in Theo's testimony, claiming it was speculative at best. Without the slugs, or proof that the slugs had been intentionally destroyed, the two-gun defense was on life support.

I knew Big Tony probably didn't want to hear that, but I needed to say it because what I was about to say next was a bit touchy, to say the least. Without proving the evidence tampering, the only other defense I had left was to offer up an alternative suspect. I didn't have to explain to Big Tony that meant going after Willie the Worm and going after him hard.

If convicted, Willie would face twenty-five years to life in prison, but the Russians were likely to kill him before he served a year of his sentence. Even if Willie wasn't charged, the Russians might figure I was right about Willie being the murderer and kill him anyway. Old man Rucci was sure to know the consequences if I went after Willie, so how was he going to respond if I did?

Since it was Big Tony and not Silvio Rucci seated across the table from me, I was more concerned with his reaction than I was of old man Rucci's. Luckily for me, Big Tony didn't seem bothered by my assessment. Then he surprised me by saying that nailing Willie for the murders wasn't a problem for anyone. I took that to include old man Rucci, but I was smart enough not to ask the question directly. Instead, I asked if I'd be getting any help along those lines. Big Tony said not to worry about it, which I took as a yes. Then he added that for the time being, I shouldn't let on that anything had changed, but I shouldn't go after Shankar or the assistant district attorneys. That was a problem and a big problem.

First, I wasn't going to abandon a defense to save Willie's ass, and then there was Gracie. There was no way Gracie was going to turn a blind eye on this corruption. Of course, I couldn't let Big Tony know there was a problem for fear he'd solve it by whacking both of us.

Why, oh, why, did I take this case? I knew the answer to that question. I took it for the money. Maybe I should have listened to my mother when she said money was the root of all evil. But then again that was easy for her to say because we didn't have any money.

CHAPTER 52

After lunch with Big Tony, I dropped in on Tommy for an update on Vijay Shankar.

Tommy's office is one big room. In total square footage it's probably not much bigger than my office, but my office is divided into two rooms, the reception area and my private office. Tommy's office has no interior partitions which makes it seem bigger.

There are two large windows looking out onto Elizabeth Street. Tommy's desk is against one of the windows, and Linda's desk is against the other window. Next to Linda's desk is a long table cluttered with what I take to be computer equipment or a NASA launch station. File cabinets along the back wall, a small kitchen area, a couch, and a large conference table and chairs complete the office's furnishings.

We sat around the conference room table. Both Tommy and Linda had files in front of them, so I figured they each had something to report. Tommy asked if I wanted a coffee or a tea, but I wasn't in a tea drinking mood, and I certainly didn't want any of his lousy coffee. Working together as long as we had, Tommy can tell when I'm growing impatient, so without further ado, he nodded for Linda to begin the briefing.

Linda had combed through several of Vijay Shankar's files on the medical examiner's computer system, searching for any sign he had tampered with files in the past. Having found nothing suspicious in any of those files, we assumed that tampering with evidence wasn't something Shankar did on a regular basis.

If that was true, Shankar might react like most first time criminals when they're caught and fold like a cheap suit. I'd never met the man, so I couldn't say that for certain, but I know the pattern, and it rarely varies. First timers aren't smart enough to ask for a lawyer right away. They think asking for a lawyer makes them look guilty, so they figure they'll just talk to the nice detective. Once they waive their rights, the nice detective isn't so nice anymore. At first, they all deny knowing anything, then they start to sweat, and soon after that, they break down and confess.

Even though I still hadn't decided the best way to approach Shankar, I wanted all the information I could get on the man. If I didn't use it myself, I'd need it to convince either the district attorney or the cops that Shankar was guilty of evidence tampering.

Tommy's investigation was thorough. Shankar was forty-seven years old and had immigrated from India nineteen years earlier on an H1 visa. He had a degree in computer science from the University of Delhi, in New Delhi, was single, lived in a basement apartment in the Fort Greene section of Brooklyn, and had no criminal record. Prior to working at the Chief Medical Examiner's Office, he had been employed by AT&T as a technical engineer. His job as a clerk at the Medical Examiner's Office was definitely a step down from his last position and well below his qualifications.

Linda searched his personnel file at AT&T but found nothing to suggest he had been sacked for cause. Even though Shankar was clearly overqualified for the clerk's job at the Medical Examiner's Office, there was no evidence that he was searching for a better position. He hadn't filed his resume on any of the job sites, nor was there any record of his having applied for a better job with the city. With nothing unusual in Shankar's work history, there was nothing to leverage his cooperation except possibly his immigration status.

Having found nothing out of the ordinary, they were about to call it quits when Linda located two bank accounts in Shankar's name, one at Citibank and the other at the Bank of India in Mumbai. The Bank of India account was a joint account in the names of Vijay Shankar and Indira Shankar. Logging onto Facebook, Linda learned that Indira Shankar was Vijay's mother.

Linda confided she could have hacked into both bank accounts but hacking into the Bank of India account was an international crime, and she didn't want to run afoul of Interpol. She didn't care as much about running afoul of the FBI, so she did hack into the Citibank account.

What she found was a $100,000 deposit ten days earlier, followed by a wire transfer to the Bank of India account in the same amount. While wire transfers to the Bank of India account occurred regularly, no prior transfers had exceeded $1,000, nor had the balance in the Citibank account exceeded $3,000. It didn't take a genius to figure out why Shankar was suddenly so flush, and I knew who paid him.

It was great information; I just wasn't sure how I was going to use it or if I even could. If word leaked out that Shankar was cooperating, or even being investigated, Junior would kill him. I could try approaching Shankar on my own to keep things on the lowdown, but if I did and he refused to cooperate, there wasn't much I'd be able to do after that. I still didn't have the carrot. I couldn't lock him up or offer him a plea deal. Not to mention that if he panicked, he might run back to India, and I'd probably never see him again.

The alternative was going to the cops. They had both the stick and the carrot, and theoretically, they could protect Shankar from Junior. But witnesses in protective custody had been killed before, so there were no guarantees that Shankar wouldn't wind up dead. Besides, going to the cops posed another problem. With the cops involved, word of Shankar's arrest would get back to the District Attorney's Office before I was ready to move on Hannah and McAvoy, and they might be able to cover their tracks.

No matter how I tried to work things out, it came down to the same problem; sooner or later word would get out that Shankar was cooperating with the cops, and he'd wind up dead. Obviously, a dead witness did me no good, so unless I figured out how to keep Shankar safe, I'd have to cook up some other defense.

CHAPTER 53

I spent the rest of the afternoon trying to come up with a defense not premised on the evidence tampering, but I wasn't having much luck. Without the missing slugs and with no explanation as to why we didn't have them, my options were limited. Pointing to Willie the Worm as the killer was a good tactic, but I needed evidence to make it work.

I could still cobble together the two-gun theory, using Theo as an expert witness. He could testify that, based on his experience, he could determine bullet calibers by examining entry wounds. But there were two problems with that. First, he'd have to admit on cross-examination that his conclusions were estimates at best, and the only way to know for certain the caliber of the bullet was to examine the slug.

Then there was the problem with the kneecapping wound. Theo's opinion as to the caliber of the bullet that shattered the Russian's kneecap was based on pieced together portions of the x-ray. I could already envision the cross-examination on that point. Theo was a great witness, but even a great witness would have problems with that one.

I was stymied. The two-gun scenario was the best defense Little Tony had. It wasn't perfect, and it didn't guarantee an acquittal, but to have any real chance of an acquittal, I needed to account for the slugs. But I couldn't figure out how to do that without exposing Shankar. I was going in circles, so naturally I kept coming back to square one. That was the square where Shankar was dead.

As if the situation wasn't bad enough, it was going to get a lot worse. I still had to explain to Gracie why exposing the corruption in her office wasn't going to happen. I didn't need a fortune teller to know dinner that night wasn't going to be a happy time.

I expected Gracie to be upset when I told her what had transpired earlier that day at Shoo's restaurant, but I hadn't expected her to go ballistic. But ballistic she went. She said there was no way in hell that Hannah and McAvoy would go uncharged and ranted on from there. Knowing better than to argue with Gracie when she was so worked up, I kept my mouth shut and let her rant on for a while.

When she finally calmed down, I pointed out that I wanted Hannah and McAvoy put away as much as she did, but Vijay Shankar's life hung in the balance. Gracie agreed that Shankar was needed to prove the conspiracy, and if he was killed, there'd be no case against Hannah and McAvoy. As eager as she was to nail the two, she wouldn't put Shankar's life in danger, but she insisted there had to be a way to protect Shankar. I didn't necessarily share her conviction, but I knew our conversation wasn't about to end anytime soon.

Later that night at home over coffee, we began tossing around ideas. We quickly dropped any plan that involved approaching Shankar directly, agreeing it was the surest way to get him killed. What we needed was a plan that offered Shankar witness protection and preferably didn't give him the option to decline. If you think that sounds like having him arrested, you'd be right. But who was going to arrest him?

The District Attorney's Office employs its own staff of detectives, but Gracie wasn't sure who in the office could be trusted. If it turned out that someone on the Detective Squad was on the take, or even accidentally spilled the beans, Shankar would be dead before the detectives got to him.

NYPD detectives were the next most likely candidates for the job. But the detectives would probably apply to the District Attorney's Office for an arrest warrant, so we dropped that idea and considered using the FBI. The FBI wouldn't need a warrant from the District Attorney's Office, but unfortunately the FBI didn't have jurisdiction over the case, and we couldn't come up with a scenario in which they did.

Then I had an idea. What if I got Detective Chen to arrest Shankar without a warrant, and to hold him at an NYPD safe house while the detectives from the District Attorney's Office grabbed up Hannah and McAvoy?

I admit the plan had its shortcomings. It required bending the law, and it probably put Chen's career at risk, not to mention we might all get arrested. But other than that, it was a good plan. Gracie thought so, too, questioning only how I'd get Chen to go along with it.

It was going to be a hard sell, and I'd probably have to offer to buy Chen the special Emperor's Banquet at Shoo's before he'd even consider doing it. Even at that, I wouldn't blame Chen if he turned me down. But I was running out of options. Of course, neither Big Tony nor old man Rucci could find out what I was up to, or Shankar might wind up dead, and I might wind up in the morgue next to him.

CHAPTER 54

The next morning, I called Detective Chen and invited him to dinner that night at Shoo's. Chen knew that I only bought him food when I wanted something from him, and if I was offering dinner, it was probably something big. If I offered coffee and a Danish, it was small talk and a little information. Lunch meant I needed a lot of information or a small favor. But dinner, that was the biggie; it meant I needed a big favor.

What I wanted from Chen this time was more than a big favor; it was a possible career ending stunt that could land us both in jail. That was why I was ordering Shoo's special gourmet dinner, a multi-course feast Shoo called the Emperor's Banquet. I didn't mention it to Chen, fearing he would turn down the invitation based on the size of the bribe alone. When he asked what was up, I said simply that it was important, and I couldn't talk about it over the phone. I told him to meet me at Shoo's at eight o'clock, and I'd explain it all then.

The Emperor's Banquet isn't simply a special dinner or even just a feast. It is a celebration of food in the style of the famous Han Quan Xi banquet thrown by Kangxi, the fourth emperor of the Qing

Dynasty. As Tommy explained it to me, Xi threw the banquet in celebration of his sixty-sixth birthday and in the hope of settling disputes between the Han and Manchu people. One-hundred-eight courses were served over three days, and the banquet became known as one of the greatest Chinese meals of all time.

Old man Shoo's recreation of the banquet doesn't come with one hundred eight courses, only seven, but there are choices for each course. As you probably suspect, it isn't served over three days either, more like three hours. But much like the original Emperor's Banquet, Shoo's recreation costs a fortune. It was a big investment but not when measured against the favor I was asking.

Chen arrived at Shoo's right on time. Whenever there was a meal involved, I could count on Chen being punctual. If he wasn't at the restaurant by five minutes past eight, I would have known he wasn't coming.

We were in the private alcove, the same one where the day before I had lunch with Big Tony. It was quiet, private, and made Chen nervous because he sensed we'd be getting into something he'd rather not get into. When the waiter arrived with the special menu for the Emperor's Banquet, Chen knew for sure he was in for a rough night.

After the waiter left with our appetizer and first course orders, Chen got right to the point, asking, "Okay, Jake, what the hell do you want?"

I said before I could tell him anything, I needed his assurance that he'd keep what I was about to tell him to himself until we worked out a mutually acceptable plan. Naturally Chen was reluctant to make any promises. He reminded me that he was a cop, and if anything I told him conflicted with his duty as a cop, he couldn't keep it quiet. I knew he'd say that, and I also knew I had no choice but to tell him everything. I only hoped that once he heard the story, he'd understand there was a good reason to keep things quiet until we could move safely.

For the next ten minutes Chen said nothing as I laid out the details of the conspiracy. When I was done, Chen said, "Holy shit, that's incredible."

His comment surprised me, and I said, "Really, is that all you can come up with? You're a detective and all you come up with is the old 'holy shit' thing? That's a comment you use when the New York Mets are in first place in September, not when you hear about evidence tampering and corruption."

Chen gave me a funny look and asked if Sarah Washington was involved. Chen had worked closely with Sarah, and I knew he liked her as much as I did. I could see the relief in his eyes when I said she wasn't.

By that time our appetizers had arrived, and we sat quietly enjoying the Emperor's Banquet. If the story I had just told him shocked Chen, it hadn't spoiled his appetite.

Now came the hard part, convincing Chen to arrest Shankar and hold him in a safe house, all without authorization. How do you convince a cop to do something that's possibly illegal and potentially career ending? By convincing him that what I was proposing was good for the NYPD. To do that, I needed to take him through a series of steps.

The first step was highlighting the political implications involved in the conspiracy. While Chen munched away on the fried dumplings, I said that the mayor's war on crime made it necessary to keep the conspiracy quiet for the time being. Chen kept eating but gave me a skeptical look. He was obviously wondering how the mayor's war on crime figured into this whole conspiracy mess. I had anticipated his reaction and was prepared to explain.

I said we both knew the war was dragging on far too long and not producing the victories that the mayor was looking for. Recently, one newspaper editorial described the mayor's war on crime as New York City's Viet Nam. That made the mayor unhappy, and he took out his frustration on the police commissioner. As we've all learned at some point in our lives, shit floats downhill, and recently the rank and file cops had felt the mayor's frustration.

Chen didn't stop eating, but this time he nodded his head, acknowledging that the rank and file had been the target of the mayor's displeasure, and they didn't like it. Having gotten Chen to that point, I said the Shankar situation could make matters a lot worse for everyone, including the rank and file. Chen put down his chopsticks; I now had his full attention.

I asked, what was the last thing the mayor needed at this point? Chen knew it was a rhetorical question, so he said nothing. Nodding my head for emphasis, I said the last thing the mayor needed was a scandal related to the war on crime, but that was exactly what he would have if word of the evidence tampering got out prematurely. Think of the headlines, *JUSTICE FOR SALE IN NYC - ADAs AND MED EXAMINER CLERK ON THE TAKE.*

It would be a disaster for the mayor, the district attorney, and the police commissioner. Chen didn't need me to tell him what that meant for the rank and file.

It was time to set the hook. If, instead of the story coming out prematurely, it came out in connection with the arrest of the corrupt ADAs and clerk, it would no longer be a scandal; it might even turn out to be a feather in the mayor's cap. The headline would be, *COPS UNCOVER BRIBERY SCHEME - WAR ON CRIME TAKES DOWN MAFIA PLOT.*

When Chen nodded and picked up his chopsticks, I knew that I had him. Then it was just a matter of laying out the specifics. With five more courses still to be served, I figured that I could go about it slowly so as not to spook Chen.

By the end of the meal, Chen agreed to work with me and to keep it all under wraps for the time being. But we needed a specific plan of action. Whatever we did, it would have to be done on a very tight schedule, and everything would have to fall into place at once. If it didn't, the whole plan would come undone, and we'd be up the creek without the proverbial paddle.

I gave Chen a quick rundown on what Tommy had learned about Shankar and suggested we meet the next day at Tommy's office to work on a plan. I chose Tommy's office because it was neutral territory, private, and gave us access to all the information we had on Shankar. Chen agreed and said he'd meet me there at nine o'clock.

CHAPTER 55

The meeting at Tommy's office the next morning confirmed what I had known from the start; the plan to turn Shankar wasn't going to be easy to pull off. The key to the operation was keeping Shankar alive which meant getting him into protective custody and hidden before anyone, especially Junior Rucci, knew about it.

At that point, I had no reason to believe Big Tony and Silvio Rucci were working against Little Tony, but until I was one-hundred-percent certain, I wasn't taking any chances. No one outside of our little group would be told about the plan.

The plan called for Chen to make the arrest which seemed simple enough, but of course, it wasn't. To start with, Chen needed grounds for making the arrest. Unless he had probable cause to believe a crime had been committed, he'd need a court issued arrest warrant. Typically he'd go through the District Attorney's Office to secure the warrant, but obviously he couldn't do that.

He could use the irregularities Linda Chow had uncovered in the medical examiner's records as a basis to charge Shankar with conspiracy, but that would expose Linda to several federal hacking charges. Besides, it was all secondhand information and didn't amount to probable cause for Chen to make the arrest without a warrant. Unless we came up with something better, it wouldn't be a legal arrest; it would be simple kidnapping.

It was Tommy who came up with a solution. He'd be a confidential informant, telling Chen what he had learned from another unidentified source about a conspiracy to destroy evidence. Tommy wouldn't identify the source but would provide Chen with enough details for Chen to have probable cause to make an arrest. It was, of course, all trumped up and only marginally adequate at best, but it would be enough to give Chen cover, so long as we were successful in exposing the conspiracy. If we weren't successful, nothing in the world was going to save any of our asses.

We still had the problem of jurisdiction. Chen operated out of the Fifth Precinct, and the actual destruction of the evidence had occurred in Brooklyn which wasn't in the Fifth Precinct. However, the Fifth Precinct might have jurisdiction if the conspiracy was hatched by the Ruccis at the Bocci Club which was in the Fifth Precinct.

That's when I would come in as a confidential informant, relaying to Chen what I had learned from unidentified sources, namely Joey Bats, Big Tony, and Silvio Rucci. As long as I didn't include any information I had gotten from Little Tony, I was okay ethically, at least when it came to client confidentiality. As for my duty as an officer of the court, well, we were at the edge of the envelope on that.

Now we were down to deciding where to pick Shankar up and where to keep him. On those issues, we deferred to Chen who called the operation an off-books or under the radar job. In reality, it was kidnapping, but of course, we weren't looking at it that way.

To begin with, Chen said he needed help, and he'd recruit some of the guys from his precinct to work off the books. Of course, we'd have to pay them which I said wasn't a problem. Fortunately, my retainer agreement with Little Tony didn't require his approval before I hired expert witnesses or investigators. I figured Chen and his guys fell into the category of investigators.

With the manpower issue settled, I asked Chen when and where he intended to pick up Shankar. He said that he'd like to do it Friday after Shankar left work. Since Shankar lived alone and seemingly never went out socially, no one was likely to miss him until he didn't show up for work on Monday morning.

As for where Shankar would be picked up, Chen said that was obvious. Chen may have thought so, but I didn't think it was obvious. As I saw it, there were three options, pick him up near his job, near his home, or somewhere in between.

Chen said I was right about there being three options, but only one was viable. Why? Because the goal was to snatch him quickly and without a commotion. If Shankar chose to make a scene, Chen didn't want a bunch of witnesses with cell phone cameras around. That's why arresting him on a Manhattan street near his job or on a subway weren't options. So the arrest would occur in Brooklyn, close to Shankar's apartment.

Chen was familiar with the area and said Shankar's street was the best place to grab him. It would be done by him and one other cop using an unmarked car borrowed from the traffic pool. He'd muddy the license plates, so if someone happened to be watching and became suspicious, all they could report was a description of the car. Without any further identification, the car was essentially untraceable.

Shankar would be taken to a safe house in Nassau County. I knew the place because it was the same safe house Chen had used to keep one of my clients out of harm's way a couple of years earlier. Chen warned me he could only keep Shankar there for twenty-four hours, after which he'd either have to book him or turn him loose.

So long as Shankar confessed, Chen wasn't in jeopardy. He'd simply claim Shankar had been kept in protective custody to protect him from being killed by the mob. I didn't want to think of what would happen if things fell apart, and we had to turn Shankar loose.

I would have one day to work things out.

CHAPTER 56

Later that night at dinner when I told Gracie what we were doing, she wasn't very enthusiastic about the plan. She liked the idea that we were doing something, but she wasn't crazy that it involved kidnapping. I kept saying it wasn't kidnapping; it was a legitimate arrest, but she insisted on calling it kidnapping.

I wasn't going to spend the night arguing over it, so I told her to call it whatever she wanted, but if it worked, we needed a plan for approaching District Attorney Vitter. Gracie, being Gracie, asked if there was a plan in case the kidnapping didn't work. I said yes, it was called disgrace and disbarment, and it involved me living out the remainder of my life in my micro-apartment, lonely and miserable. Gracie laughed and told me not to worry; she'd take me in like a stray, but of course, I'd have to earn my keep. If we didn't have more important things to talk about, I would have pushed back, but we had more important things to talk about.

We were working on the assumption that Shankar had contact with Hannah and McAvoy, and he could implicate them in the scheme. Gracie had assured me early on that it was inconceivable that one of the two, or both, wouldn't have asked about the slugs. All we needed from Shankar was a confession that he had tampered with the evidence, and Hannah and McAvoy knew about it. That would be enough to charge them with corruption.

In the meantime, Linda Chow was investigating Hannah's and McAvoy's bank records, looking for any unusual activity. I had to assume they were both smart enough to have hidden the payoffs, but you never know. For my purposes it didn't matter; I didn't need to prove the bribery, just their involvement with the evidence tampering. Once under pressure from that charge, one of them would likely crack and turn on the other in exchange for a lighter sentence, and that's when the bribery would come to light.

Gracie suggested she should be the one to go directly to Vitter. That would trigger an internal investigation, which would run concurrently with any investigation by the NYPD. While the internal investigation was in progress, Hannah and McAvoy would be suspended and their cases transferred to other ADAs in the office.

Once the news about Hannah and McAvoy broke, I'd make a motion to dismiss the murder charges against Little Tony. Even though Hannah and McAvoy were likely to deny any wrongdoing, it didn't matter. It would be Shankar's admission that he had tampered with the evidence that counted. With such an admission, I was almost assured of getting an adverse inference charge.

Hannah and McAvoy were the icing on the cake, the key to having Little Tony's case dismissed entirely. Fortunately, I didn't have to prove Hannah's and McAvoy's involvement beyond a reasonable doubt, only that it was more likely than not. Everything was starting to fall into place. The only thing that could go wrong was Shankar getting killed, but I had confidence in Chen keeping him safe.

CHAPTER 57

Friday night Gracie and I had just returned from dinner when Chen called. Shankar had been picked up earlier and was now in the safe house in Freeport, Long Island. The pickup had gone smoothly and without incident. When Chen approached Shankar and identified himself as a cop, Shankar knew he was caught and went along quietly.

Once at the safe house, Chen read Shankar his Miranda rights, and although Shankar never demanded a lawyer, he refused to talk. That was until Chen produced copies of his bank records and threatened to involve his mother. At that point, Shankar broke down, and after signing a Miranda waiver, he told Chen everything.

Shankar confirmed that he had prepared the draft reports from the audio files recorded by the doctor while performing the autopsies on the two dead Russians. After the doctor approved the draft reports, Shankar had deleted references to the slugs recovered by the doctor during the autopsies. Then after he deleted the audio files and the original draft reports, he posted the altered final report onto the system. Finally, he disposed of the slugs, throwing them into a trash can on 44th Street.

Much of that I knew or at least suspected. I knew from Shankar's bank transactions that he had been paid $100,000 to change the autopsy reports and dispose of the slugs, but I wasn't sure who had paid him. I knew from what Big Tony had told me that Junior had been the one who paid off Hannah and McAvoy, but Big Tony hadn't mentioned anything about Shankar. So, who paid off Shankar? Had it been Junior, someone on Junior's behalf, or one of the two assailant district attorneys? Fortunately, Chen had come up with the answer.

Once Shankar cracked under Chen's questioning, he readily admitted that he had accepted the $100,000 bribe. He said that he was paid the money personally, but he didn't know the name of the man who made the payment. He was, however, able to pick Junior Rucci out of an array of photographs of possible suspects.

All the pieces were starting to fall into place. But there was one last connection I was praying Shankar would make, and he did. When Chen asked him who gave him his instructions, Shankar said it was Hannah and McAvoy. He'd met with them twice, and they told him exactly what to remove from the autopsy reports and what evidence to get rid of. As for the technical end, that was all Shankar.

Chen had recorded the interview on his cell phone, and while we spoke, Shankar was writing out his story on a legal pad. The question was, what do we do next? Chen wanted to take Shankar to Central Booking, but I didn't think that was a good idea.

To begin with, Gracie wanted Shankar in front of Vitter before he went into the system and for a good reason. Once Shankar was in the system, Hannah and McAvoy would know they were in trouble and were likely to do something to protect themselves. Maybe fabricate some cover story or run for their lives. Linda hadn't been able to trace the money, but I assumed the bribe had been somewhere in the high six figure range. I couldn't see these two guys throwing away their lives for anything less than that.

I agreed with Gracie about getting Shankar in front of the district attorney, but for me, the bigger problem was Junior Rucci and what he would do when he learned Shankar was in lockup. It wasn't unheard of for a Mafia hitman to get himself locked up in Rikers

Island in order to kill another inmate. Nor was it uncommon for one prisoner in Rikers Island to kill another prisoner. Unless Shankar was put in protective custody, his life expectancy could be measured in days, not years. Even in protective custody, his odds of surviving were only slightly better.

If Shankar was killed, I could use the tape recording and his written statement when I made the motion to dismiss the charges against Little Tony, but live testimony from Shankar would be a hell of a lot more persuasive. There was little doubt that Shankar was worth more to me alive than dead. That may sound cold, but my job requires me to deal with reality.

I asked Chen to hold Shankar at the safe house until he heard back from me. I promised it wouldn't be more than a day, but if it turned out to be longer, I'd buy him another Emperor's Banquet at Shoo's. Chen was naturally uneasy and reminded me that we were on thin ice, and the sooner we got back on solid ground, the better. I knew Chen was right, but with all that was riding on this, I saw no choice but to hold Shankar in the safe house.

When I finished talking with Chen, I brought Gracie up to date, and we tried to figure out what to do next. Gracie suggested we get Shankar to tell his story directly to the district attorney in private. That way Vitter could open an investigation into Hannah and McAvoy, and he could order Shankar held at the safe house. In theory, it was a brilliant idea that solved both our problems and got Chen off the hook. But there were some practical problems.

It was nearly eleven o'clock on a Friday, so how were we going to get Shankar in front of Vitter? We couldn't wait until Monday morning, besides which we needed the meeting to be private, so we couldn't simply march Shankar into Vitter's office. I suggested she call Vitter at home and tell him the story.

At first Gracie agreed, but after thinking it over, she changed her mind. She was afraid that Vitter might not take her seriously, and if he didn't, we'd have nowhere to turn. On the other hand, she knew her boss, Joe Sebert, would believe her, and he had a close relationship with Vitter. Rather than call Vitter directly, she suggested that she call Sebert. I agreed, but looking at the time, Gracie said it was too late to call him, and she'd do it first thing in the morning.

The timing was good. It would be Saturday, so both Sebert and Vitter were likely to be at home and not in the office. That would cut down on the possibility of a leak and word about Shankar getting out prematurely. We wanted the meeting to be away from the office, again for security reasons, and the weekend made that less of a problem.

There was still a possible problem with the plan. What if Joe Sebert or Vitter was in on the scheme? Once Gracie told the story to Sebert, we'd be exposed. It was a risk, not a great one, but one I still wanted to minimize. We had one advantage, and that was our control over Shankar. As long as we held him, we called the shots.

I explained to Gracie why she couldn't tell Sebert where we had Shankar hidden. Of course, she argued, saying there was no way her boss was in on the scheme. But eventually she conceded that we had to minimize all potential risks, no matter how small, and she agreed not to tell Sebert where Shankar was being held.

I figured if Sebert gave Gracie a hard time, it would tell us he was in on the scheme, and we'd have to go around him directly to the DA ourselves. Then if Vitter showed any signs that he was in on the scheme, we'd back off and go to the police commissioner or the mayor instead. As long as we had Shankar hidden away, we called the shots. It was just a matter of how long we could keep Shankar hidden away.

CHAPTER 58

Saturday morning before Gracie called her boss, I called Chen to tell him the plan. Needless to say, he was a little nervous since his career was on the line, and he reminded me we were on the clock. I assured him the idea was to move as quickly as possible but not to get too far ahead of ourselves.

Chen was okay with the idea of going through Sebert to get to Vitter if I trusted Sebert. I said that I relied on Gracie's assessment that Sebert was a straight shooter, and I had no reason not to trust him. Chen said that was good enough for him, but he added if there were any doubts at all about Sebert or Vitter, we do videoconferencing rather than producing Shankar in person.

With no one besides Chen and his buddies knowing where Shankar was being held, we controlled the situation. Chen didn't want to give up that advantage until we were sure everything was tied up tight. I told Chen we were on the same page with that, and I promised I wouldn't commit to producing Shankar unless I was sure everything was solid. Chen said he'd go to the safe house and wait for me to call.

Gracie, who had been sitting next to me listening in while I spoke with Chen, reminded me that she trusted Joe Sebert but understood both Chen's and my concerns. Now that we all agreed to the plan, it was time to move on it.

Gracie called Sebert and told him the whole story. She began with the missing medical examiner's files. As she was laying out the facts, Sebert interrupted her, often asking pointed questions and challenging her comments. But once she told him about Shankar's confession, he stopped interrupting and just listened. I'm sure he didn't want to believe the story was true, just as Gracie hadn't wanted to believe it when she first heard it. Who wants to think that people you've worked with, people you've socialized with, people you think that you know, are corrupt? But Shankar's confession implicating Hannah and McAvoy made it undeniable.

Sebert wanted Shankar brought to his office, but Gracie said she couldn't do that. She said Shankar had demanded a meeting with Vitter off premises, or he'd deny everything. It was the first time I ever heard Gracie tell a lie, and I gave her a shocked look. Apparently, Gracie didn't find it humorous, and she elbowed me in the ribs, letting me know how she felt.

Sebert said he'd call Vitter, and if Vitter agreed, they'd arrange a meeting somewhere away from the office. He said that he'd call back as soon as he could.

When Gracie hung up, I told her that I noticed her nose had grown a bit, and I started to laugh. It was definitely a mistake because Gracie was not in the mood for kidding. I should have realized that, but as you know, I'm not a particularly sensitive guy. So we sat in icy silence, waiting for Gracie's phone to ring and for her nose to return to normal size.

CHAPTER 59

Sebert called back in half an hour, but it seemed much longer, especially with Gracie busting my chops over my Pinocchio comment. In fairness to Gracie, I should mention that I kept staring at her nose and making faces. When I'm bored, I do things that get me into trouble. I don't know why I do that, but I've been doing it since I was a kid. You'd think by now I would have learned my lesson, but I haven't. I do it less often since getting sober, but I have no intention of stopping. Doug says it's the last remnants of my immaturity, but I say it's therapy. Gracie says it's just plain rude. When she says that, I laugh, and she hits me.

But back to the phone call. Sebert said Vitter initially refused to believe the story, and it took a while to convince him otherwise. He was still skeptical, but he agreed to meet away from the office and insisted on bringing one of his investigators. Gracie wisely said she'd have to check with Shankar before she could agree to the investigator being present, and it would help if she knew who Vitter had in mind. Sebert said Jack Cooper had been mentioned, but Vitter didn't know if he was available.

Gracie looked at me, and I shrugged my shoulders. Cooper started working at the DA's office long after I was gone, and I only had a few minor dealings with him, not enough to form an opinion on whether he could be trusted. Looking at Gracie, I could tell she had her own doubts about Cooper. My suspicion was more or less confirmed when Gracie said she'd get back to Sebert and ended the conversation.

Gracie said as far as she knew Cooper was a straight shooter, but then again, she had thought the same about Hannah and McAvoy. When I asked Gracie if Cooper had given her any reason to suspect he might be crooked, she said no, and I got the feeling maybe she was simply getting a little gun shy.

I didn't think it was unreasonable for Vitter to want one of his investigators at the meeting, and I didn't see any harm coming of it. As things stood, nothing short of Cooper killing Shankar was going to save Hannah and McAvoy, or for that matter, Junior Rucci. If Cooper did kill Shankar, he'd have to kill the rest of us as well, and I just didn't see that as a winning strategy for Cooper.

It was my turn to make a call, and I dialed Chen's number. When I told him Vitter was willing to meet with us away from his office, but was insisting that Jack Cooper be present, Chen didn't balk at the idea. He said that he had worked closely with Cooper on several cases, and he trusted him. He would have preferred limiting the meeting to just us and Vitter and Sebert, but he was okay if Cooper was there. In fact, he said if Vitter had any doubts about the scheme, Cooper being at the meeting might be helpful. It was obvious Vitter had confidence in Cooper.

Chen then said something which got me thinking that maybe this meeting was a big mistake. He said once Vitter heard what Shankar had to say, he might have Cooper take him into custody and have him booked. If we couldn't convince Vitter that booking Shankar would wind up getting him killed, everything could fall apart. Hannah and McAvoy would escape, and Little Tony would go down for murdering the Russians. The only way to protect Shankar was to keep him in protective custody hidden from the Ruccis.

That also meant Vitter couldn't move against Hannah and McAvoy right away because if he did everyone would know Shankar had turned State's evidence. At some point, somebody would notice that Shankar was missing, and that would be it, but given Shankar's lonely life, it might not happen for a while. He'd be missed at work, but it would probably be at least a couple of days before anyone became worried enough to report it to the police. Even then, as long as Shankar wasn't in the system, what were the cops going to find?

With Chen's approval, I told Gracie to call Sebert and set up the meeting. In the meantime, I was putting together my own plan to make sure Shankar stayed with Chen and didn't go into the system. While Gracie was on the phone with Sebert, I called Chen and explained what I had in mind.

CHAPTER 60

We met at the New York Hilton on Sixth Avenue in a suite arranged by Joe Sebert using his wife's credit card. It was all very cloak and dagger, with District Attorney Vitter entering the hotel through the basement and taking a service elevator to the suite floor.

Sebert and Vitter were in the suite when Gracie and I arrived. Jack Connor was the next to arrive. After the introductions, Sebert asked when Shankar would be arriving. I said he'd be there soon, but first we needed to talk. Sebert and Vitter looked at each other, then at me, and Sebert accused me of playing games. I didn't dare look at Gracie who had no idea what I was doing, but I didn't have to look at her to know she wasn't a happy camper.

I said we were playing with Shankar's life, and we needed to discuss how we were going to protect him before we did anything else. I didn't need to say anything more because everyone in the room knew if the Ruccis found out Shankar was in custody they'd have him killed. To Vitter's credit, he didn't argue the point because he knew, as well as I did, that if the Ruccis wanted Shankar dead, they could have him killed at Rikers Island or any of the city's other jails as easily as they could have him killed on the street. That was a damn good reason for keeping Shankar's arrest secret and keeping him in protective custody at a safe house.

There was another reason we needed to slow things down. Shankar had waived his Miranda rights before speaking to Chen, and that was all well and good. But now he was being dragged before the district attorney and interrogated without a lawyer present. Whether he waived his Miranda rights or not, he was still entitled to a plea deal, and without a lawyer there to advise him, he'd probably lose whatever leverage he had in negotiating a deal. Sooner or later the whole story would come out, and when it did, Vitter might have some tough questions to answer. The mayor might be waging a war on crime that tolerated shortcuts, but the New York City media was still very liberal minded, especially when it involved civil rights.

I'm no politician, and even I knew the story wouldn't play well for Vitter. But Vitter is a politician, and he wanted no part of that story. So he asked what I had mind. I said Chen would bring Shankar to the suite, so he and Sebert could see him face-to-face while he read the statement he had given to Chen. That way they could decide for themselves whether he was telling the truth or not. But they couldn't ask him any questions, and he wouldn't give any information beyond what was in his statement.

Assuming they were satisfied he was telling the truth, Vitter would authorize Chen to take Shankar back to the safe house and to provide witness protection. In the meantime, I would arrange for a lawyer to represent Shankar and negotiate a plea deal.

Vitter didn't like being worked, and I was working him hard. But he knew I was right, and his political aspirations would be toast if he was seen as railroading Shankar. Left with no option, he agreed to my terms, and I called Chen who was waiting with Shankar in the parking garage and told him to come up.

While we waited for Chen and Shankar to arrive, I snuck a peek at Gracie, not certain what she thought of my little ploy. I suspected she might be angry with me, so I was mildly surprised when she smiled. I figured she knew I was right.

When Chen and Shankar arrived in the room, all eyes were on Shankar, mine and Gracie's included. For some reason, Shankar's appearance didn't conform to my expectations. I thought Shankar would be kind of geeky. A skinny guy with thick horn-rimmed glasses and a pocket protector filled with pens. But he looked nothing like a geek. He was tall, well-built, and fairly good looking, understanding that my idea of good looking might be different than your idea of good looking. Good looking or not, he was clearly nervous.

I made the introductions, then asked Shankar to take a seat and read his sworn statement. In a nervous cracking voice, he did as I asked. When he was done, I looked to Vitter and asked if we had a deal. Vitter looked first to Sebert who nodded in agreement, then to Cooper who did likewise. I then asked Vitter if we had his authority to return Shankar to the safe house in the custody of Detective Chen and his staff. Vitter said we did, and he would issue a formal order on Monday morning, referring to Shankar simply as John Doe.

Chen then left, taking Shankar with him, while I remained to iron out the details of arranging counsel for Shankar's plea bargain. Once that was done, I had no other business with the district attorney, and I left the suite. Gracie, on the other hand, would play an integral role in what happened next to Hannah and McAvoy, so she remained behind.

Later that night when we got back together, we talked briefly about the day's events, but knowing we were now back on different sides, it was a short conversation. Our joint effort was now concluded, and we'd each get back to our own business. It would be life as usual which was fine, but I'd miss working with Gracie.

CHAPTER 61

Monday morning, with Shankar back in the safe house, I now had to let Big Tony know what was going on. Sooner or later he was going to find out Shankar was in custody, and it was better if that news came from me. I was counting on Big Tony having been honest when he said he wanted his son acquitted. If he had been honest, he would see Shankar's arrest as a good thing. If he hadn't been honest, I'd probably wind up dead. I'm telling you this mob lawyer thing just kept getting less and less attractive. Yes, the money was good but not good enough for me to be doing the things I was doing.

I also needed Big Tony to smooth things with Silvio Rucci so he wouldn't kill me. I had no way of taking Junior out of Vitter's crosshairs but that was Gene Meyers' problem, not mine. Assuming Vitter was more interested in nailing Hannah and McAvoy, he might be convinced to cut Junior a deal since Junior was the one who could offer the best incriminating evidence against the two. But as I said, that was Gene Meyers' problem.

I called Joey Bats and told him I needed to see Big Tony as soon as possible, and we needed to meet somewhere privately. An hour later Joey called back and said Tony would meet me at noon at a little Italian restaurant on Hester Street. I had never heard of the place, but I told Joey I'd be there.

Then I called Joe Benjamin at the 18B Panel to ask a favor. Most times it was the other way around, so Joe was more than a little surprised when I asked him to represent Vijay Shankar. Joe was one of the few people I'd trust in this situation.

As I explained the circumstances to Joe, I skirted the part that made it sound as though we had kidnapped the man. When I was done explaining, Joe said he understood what needed to be done, and while he couldn't in good conscience put the case on the 18B Panel books, he'd handle it pro bono as a favor to me. With all the problems that went with the case, he was doing me a big favor, and I appreciated it. I just hoped we'd get through it without either of us being disbarred.

CHAPTER 62

It was just about noon when I arrived at the restaurant to meet Big Tony. The place looked like a hole in the wall; it was small, unremarkable, and not particularly inviting. I must have walked past the place a million times without taking notice. That was the kind of place it was.

Inside there were maybe ten tables, all empty. There was also a small bar, but no one was at it or behind it. The only person in the place was Big Tony who greeted me at the door, then locked it behind me. I followed him into a back room where we sat at a table facing each other. There was an espresso pot and two cups on the table. Tony poured a cup for each of us, then asked, "What's up, counselor?"

I still wasn't certain how Big Tony would take the news, and I wasn't particularly anxious to deliver bad news to a Mafia hit man. Especially when he and I were alone in the back room of a deserted restaurant. But I didn't have a choice, so I told Big Tony all about Vijay Shankar, leaving out only Shankar's location.

When I was done, Big Tony nodded, and much to my relief he didn't seem upset. I think he understood that Shankar was likely to implicate Junior, but if he didn't, I wasn't about to tell him. Then he surprised me and said that Silvio Rucci would take care of things.

When you're dealing with a Mafia hit man, you never really know what he means when he says that he'll take care of something. Truthfully, I didn't want to know. I just wanted to get this case over and done with, without getting myself killed.

Big Tony then asked when news of Shankar's arrest would break. There was more to the question than simple curiosity, and I was hesitant to answer, fearing the worst for Shankar. When I didn't answer right away, Big Tony said, "Relax, counselor, we're going to fix the problem while we can. So tell me when the news is going to break."

There was no direct threat in his words, but his tone of voice made it clear that I'd better answer his question, and I'd better answer it truthfully. I said that I couldn't be sure, but Shankar would probably cut a deal before the end of the week, and that's when it would all hit the fan. The two assistant district attorneys would likely be arrested just before Shankar was booked or just after he was booked. Then it would only be a matter of time before they turned on Junior. Big Tony gave me one those nods that said he understood everything perfectly.

Big Tony wanted to know what would happen in Little Tony's case. I could tell he was torn between his loyalty to Silvio Rucci and his love for his son. Old man Rucci might be unhappy with Shankar's arrest, but it played well for Little Tony's case.

I said a new assistant district attorney would be assigned to the case, and I'd make a motion to dismiss the charges based on the prosecution's misconduct in destroying exculpatory evidence. Unfortunately, I couldn't give Big Tony any assurances that the motion would be successful. All I could say was that I was confident even if the judge didn't dismiss the charges, he'd rule that negative inference charge was warranted. With that, I believed an acquittal at trial was in the cards. No guarantees, of course, but the odds were good.

Big Tony was apparently satisfied with my answer because I walked out of the restaurant alive and with all my bodily parts in place and working. I wasn't sure that would still be the case if the Ruccis had a say in it.

Donald L'Abbate

Walking back to the office, I felt more relaxed than I had in weeks. Just knowing I had done everything I could for Little Tony put me at ease. I was thinking it was now out of my hands, and over the next few days, fate would determine how things played out, but as usual I was wrong.

CHAPTER 63

The rest of the week started to unfold as expected. Joe Benjamin met with Shankar at the safe house, then over the next few days he negotiated a deal with Vitter. By Thursday afternoon, the terms of the deal were finalized. In exchange for Shankar's cooperation in testifying against his co-conspirators, the charges against him would be reduced to the lowest possible felony level. Upon pleading guilty, he'd have the choice of either serving a minimal prison sentence or having his green card revoked and being deported back to India.

It was a good plea deal, and everything seemed right on track. But then the unexpected happened. Over the objection of Joe Benjamin, but at the insistence of the Department of Corrections, Shankar was moved from the safe house to Rikers Island jail, where he was kept segregated from the general population.

On Friday at four o'clock in the morning, an NYPD squad of detectives led by the Investigator, Jack Copper, raided the apartment of Assistant District Attorney James Hannah and arrested him on an assortment of corruption charges. At the same time, another squad of NYPD detectives, this one led by Richard

Chen, raided the apartment of Assistant District Attorney Thomas McAvoy, arresting him on similar charges as those against Hannah.

Later that morning, District Attorney Jerome Vitter announced the three arrests, promising that all three would face justice. In a relatively short speech for Vitter, he reaffirmed his commitment to root out evil wherever it existed. No mention was made of Junior Rucci which was the second unexpected event and a tip-off that Junior wasn't going to be indicted.

Vitter may have been incorruptible and committed to rooting out evil everywhere, but that didn't necessarily go for the mayor, who had his eye on a higher office. Getting elected to higher office took a lot of money, and the mayor wasn't particularly concerned where it came from. I didn't have any proof that the mayor was on the take, but that was the only way Junior could skate on the charges. Somebody high up had been reached, and I was sure it wasn't Vitter. That left the mayor as the only person in the chain of command above Vitter with the power to quash an indictment against Junior.

Gene Meyers might not have had connections directly to the mayor, but I was sure he had connections to people who did, including a longtime friend of his who headed the Department of Corrections.

After our meeting, Big Tony tipped off Rucci as to what was coming, and that gave Meyers plenty of time to make things happen. Things like ensuring that no one would testify against Junior. It was a form of witness tampering, and it worked.

I had no doubt that just before they were arrested, Hannah and McAvoy were warned that if they tried implicating Junior Rucci, they'd be dead before they got to trial. Fingering Junior might get them a shorter sentence, but they'd never live to serve it. On the other hand, if they kept their mouths shut, they'd do their time protected by Rucci's guys inside, and once released, they'd still have the bribe money.

As for Vijay Shankar, he probably had a visitor while at Rikers Island who warned him what would happen to him if he fingered Junior. For Shankar, the decision must have been easy. So long as nobody was looking to jam up his mother, he'd be more than happy to forget he ever met Junior. So he changed his story, claiming he had been mistaken when he picked Junior out of the photo array.

Normally that would have voided the plea deal, but Shankar was able to get away with it because Vitter needed his testimony to nail Hannah and McAvoy. The plea deal remained in effect, and so long as Shankar testified against Hannah and McAvoy, he could do his time in prison and then remain in the country without fear of retaliation from the Ruccis.

Without the testimony from Hannah, McAvoy, or Shankar, the case against Junior was weak at best, and with pressure from the mayor, Vitter couldn't be criticized for not bringing charges.

The amazing thing about corruption is that everyone walks away happy because everyone gets something they want. Junior Rucci escapes indictment; the mayor gets campaign contributions; people in the Corrections Department make a little additional income; and Shankar, Hannah, and McAvoy get to live. It's the public that gets screwed in the deal, but they don't even know they're getting screwed, so everybody is happy.

The news wasn't all bad. Little Tony's case was reassigned to Sarah Washington with instructions from Vitter that she handle it herself. With everything back on track, I prepared my motion to dismiss the charges against Little Tony.

CHAPTER 64

I spent most of the next week finalizing the motion to dismiss the indictment against Little Tony. It was a long shot, but I had some strong arguments, the strongest being that the prosecutor's misconduct had deprived Little Tony of his right to a fair trial. How successful the arguments would be depended in no small part upon which judge was assigned to hear the motion. A more liberal judge would be more open to those arguments than a conservative judge. It all came down to the luck of the draw.

Then, as luck would have it, the motion was scheduled before Judge Paul O'Donnell, who you may recall is commonly referred to as "Hang 'em high Paul." If I had been facing an uphill battle before, it became a little bit more of a climb.

There was a lot riding on this motion for both sides. Obviously, if the motion was granted, the case against Little Tony would be over, ended due to the misconduct of both the Medical Examiner's Office and the District Attorney's Office. District Attorney Vitter knew only too well he'd be crucified by the media if that happened, and he was doing everything possible to protect his image.

Donald L'Abbate

To the surprise of many, but not to me, Vitter himself handled the arraignment hearings for Hannah and McAvoy. Since both were charged with felonies, little or nothing of substance, other than the setting of bail, occurs at the initial hearing. But it gave Vitter an opportunity to make a speech and establish himself as a man intent on rooting out corruption in his office. After the arraignments, Vitter held a press conference at which he further portrayed himself the virtuous but duped employer, intent on making everything right. A regular Sir Galahad on a quest.

Apparently, Sir Galahad's courage didn't extend to the actual battlefield because he sent Sarah Washington to argue against the motion. It was strictly a political move. He knew if I won, and there was a good chance I might, he'd look bad, so rather than take a chance, he sent Sarah. If she won, he'd take all the credit, but if she lost, she'd be the sacrificial lamb.

The morning that the motion was being argued, I met Little Tony and Big Tony at the Worth Street Coffee Shop for a last minute prep session. Neither had to testify; I just wanted to make sure we were all on the same page which we were.

When we arrived at the courthouse, we found the media out in full force. Television camera crews were set up on the courthouse steps, and reporters pushed microphones in our faces as we made our way up the stairs to the courthouse door. Both Little Tony and his father said nothing as I had instructed them to do. As for myself, I just smiled and kept repeating, "No comment."

The hallway outside Judge O'Donnell's courtroom was filled with more media people, as was the spectator gallery inside the courtroom. If the judge denied my motion, Vitter would miss a golden opportunity to play hero to a big audience. Of course, if the judge granted my motion, Vitter wouldn't want to be within a hundred miles of the courtroom. The fact that he wasn't taking a chance and had sent Sarah in his place made me think I had a better chance at winning than I thought.

Sara, who was already seated at the prosecutor's table reading her notes, looked up and smiled as Little Tony and I walked into the courtroom well and took our seats. Smiling back, I wished Sarah good luck, and she returned the sentiment. It was a big day for both of us, and I think we were both a little nervous. At least I was.

239

For a trial lawyer, being a little nervous is a good thing; it keeps you sharp. The day I don't get excited and a little nervous starting a trial or a hearing is the day I'll know it's time to quit.

Once settled in, I opened my trial bag and pulled out my files, plus the couple of law books I'd brought with me. The books were mostly for show because I had Xeroxed copes of the cases in folders. Still, I liked the idea of having the actual books on the desk.

The hearing involved a two-step process, or at least I hoped we'd get to step two. The first step was to convince the judge that there had been enough misconduct on the part of the prosecution to warrant a hearing. If the judge didn't buy the argument, the whole proceeding could be over in twenty minutes, and the spoliation defense would be dead. But if the judge was convinced there was merit to the argument, then he'd allow me to call witnesses to prove that Little Tony's defense was harmed, perhaps irreparably by the misconduct.

I would have been more confident if we had a different judge, but you play the cards you're dealt. All I could do was give it my best and hope it was good enough.

Little Tony was seated at the counsel table next to me, and Big Tony was seated in the gallery right behind his son. Also seated in the gallery among the media people were two goons who I presumed were there as the eyes and ears of one or more of the Ruccis, or maybe the Russians. It really didn't matter, but I was curious, so I asked Big Tony who they were. He said they were Junior's boys. I looked at the two, then smiled and nodded my head. Neither acknowledged my little gesture. I couldn't help but wonder if they'd be the ones that would kill me if things didn't go right.

Theo, who I planned on calling as a witness, sat outside the courtroom. As a witness, he wasn't allowed into the courtroom until it was time for him to testify. I had subpoenaed Vijay Shankar who was now being held at a new safe house guarded by Vitter's investigators. Vitter claimed that bringing Shankar to court to testify created too great a danger to his life, and he had, with the judge's permission, arranged for him to testify via closed circuit television. I only hoped we'd get that far.

The door to the judge's robing room opened, and the judge's law clerk entered the courtroom with Judge O'Donnell right behind. The

Donald L'Abbate

court officer announced the judge's arrival, commanding us all to stand. As he took his seat, O'Donnell told us to do the same, smiling at both Sarah and me. We were no strangers to Judge O'Donnell, but familiarity would do neither of us any good. However, if the judge's memory went back far enough, I might be at a slight disadvantage. After all, I wasn't always the model of decorum in the courtroom.

The clerk read the case name and docket number into the record, and with the formalities out of the way, the judge called on me to state the nature of my motion. I said the defendant sought a dismissal of the indictment based on the prosecutor's misconduct, culminating in the intentional destruction of exculpatory evidence. Evidence that would have proved that the gun used to kill the two victims in the case was not the same gun confiscated by the police when the defendant was arrested. Thus, disproving a theory of the case advanced by the district attorney.

At that point, Judge O'Donnell interrupted, saying it appeared to him that if the district attorney's theory had been correct and there was a match, then the disappearance of the evidence would benefit the defendant. I acknowledged that was true, but I countered by saying we were prepared to offer expert testimony that there was no match. Testimony from a renowned medical examiner that the size of the entry wounds shown on the x-rays of both victims' skulls did not match the caliber of the defendant's gun. I had to admit the opinion was subject to rebuttal, whereas a ballistic test of the slugs would scientifically settle the matter.

Satisfied that I had at least gotten Judge O'Donnell's attention, I took my seat. The judge then turned to Sarah and asked if she'd care to reply. Sarah was wise enough not to sugarcoat the situation. Right up front she admitted that two lawyers in her office had conspired with a clerk in the Medical Examiner's Office to destroy evidence.

But and it was a big but, the two lawyers weren't talking, so no one could be sure on whose behalf they were acting. Perhaps the evidence wasn't exculpatory at all. Maybe it was damning, and it was the defendant or someone on his behalf who had paid the two lawyers to get rid of the evidence. The expert testimony was simply an opinion, perhaps a well-qualified opinion, but an opinion nonetheless. Besides, even if it was all true and the slugs didn't match the confiscated gun, that didn't prove the defendant hadn't

241

killed the two victims. All it proved was he hadn't killed them with that gun.

It was a good argument and one I had expected Sarah to make. Fortunately, I had a rebuttal, and I needed one because Judge O'Donnell was obviously impressed with Sarah's argument. He looked at me and asked if I cared to reply. Realizing I was losing the argument, I got right to my point. I said the autopsy report on victim number one stated that he suffered a traumatic injury to the knee, resulting in a shattering of the patella or kneecap. I reminded Judge O'Donnell that such an injury was commonly called "kneecapping" and was generally done by a gunshot through the patella.

I said that our expert medical examiner would testify that the kneecapping was, in fact, done with a gun, but a gun of a different caliber than the one used to kill the two victims. That meant either the killer used two guns during the attack, or there were two gunmen, one who shot the two victims in the head killing them, and the other who only kneecapped victim number one. That raised serious reasonable doubt issues as to my client's guilt. But by intentionally disposing of the slugs, the State had made it more difficult, if not impossible, to prove reasonable doubt existed; thus, my client was being deprived of his right to a fair trial. Deprived of that right by the willful wrongful conduct of the prosecution team.

Sarah wanted to say more, but the judge cut her off, saying he had heard enough. Looking from Sarah, then to me, and then back to Sarah was a clear sign that the judge had made up his mind and was going to issue his decision from the bench. Judge O'Donnell may have been a law and order judge, but he'd always been fair when applying the law, and I was hoping my legal argument had persuaded him to rule in Little Tony's favor. But it didn't happen.

The judge called my argument persuasive, but not sufficiently compelling to warrant a dismissal of the charges, even if I proved the evidence had been intentionally destroyed. Needless to say, I was disappointed with the decision, figuring the two-gun defense was dead, but then the judge added a "however." Maybe we were back in the game.

Still looking in my direction, the judge said that a jury might be more sympathetic to my position than he was, and he would order a negative inference charge be given to the jury. The two-gun defense was still alive, wounded but alive.

With the motion decided, the case was put on the trial calendar. It was time to prepare for trial which meant I had some long days and nights ahead of me.

CHAPTER 65

The case was assigned to Judge Moore for trial. Moore was a no-nonsense judge, who ruled his courtroom with an iron fist. He had no tolerance for histrionics or showboating, as many of my more flamboyant brethren learned the hard way. With Moore you played by his rules, or he'd make your life miserable.

I wasn't worried. I understood Moore and got along with him, at least as well as any lawyer gets along with a judge. Moore had come on the bench after I got sober, so he hadn't witnessed any of my nasty outbursts that were all too common when I was drinking.

Once again Vitter had chosen to exit the battlefield and had sent Sarah Washington to try the case. I had hoped Vitter would try the case himself because it would have brought my corruption pitch a little closer to home. If anyone was seen as a devil in all of this, it would be Vitter and not Sarah. The jury might tolerate my unloading on Vitter, but they might not look so kindly on my doing the same to Sarah.

When Sarah and I met with Judge Moore for a pretrial scheduling conference, the first thing he did was issue a gag order and make it abundantly clear that this case was going to be tried in his courtroom and not in the media. Ever since Hannah's and McAvoy's arrest, the media had been all over the case, and the coverage was likely to intensify once the trial started.

I expected Moore would do everything he could to keep the trial from becoming a circus, and a gag order was a good start. But Moore knew that with any high-profile trial, leaks were bound to occur. The media would be hounding anyone and everyone associated with the trial, and some clerk or low-level employee was bound to talk to a reporter. The reporter will describe the source as "someone with knowledge" or "someone close to the case." Most times the information is bullshit, but occasionally it's accurate. In either case, most judges get really pissed off when it happens, and Moore was no exception.

I had enough problems with the case without having Moore pissed off at me, so I had no intention of leaking any information, and I'd make sure no one on the defense team did so. I was sure Sarah felt the same way, so I didn't expect any leaks coming from the prosecution.

Of course, if as expected, the media coverage included cable television, there'd be no shortage of "talking heads" offering all sorts of opinions and insights into the court proceedings. Most of what was said would be bullshit served up by lawyers who probably never tried a criminal case in their lives.

The best way to reel in the media mob and keep the trial from becoming a three-ring circus was to get it over quickly. When Judge Moore asked Sarah how long it would take to present her case, she said two to three weeks. Then Moore asked me how long I expected to take presenting the defense. It was a tough question to answer because much depended on how well Sarah's case went in, but the judge wanted an answer, so I said two weeks tops.

Moore thought about it for a moment, then shaking his head, he said that was much too long. He wanted the trial over in no more than two weeks. He cautioned both of us that he wouldn't tolerate delays, repetitive witnesses, or requests for adjournments that he thought frivolous. To be honest, I was happy with the time restraints because they were more of a detriment to Sarah's case than to mine.

After reviewing witness lists and proposed exhibits, and agreeing to Moore's basic ground rules, the judge set the matter down for trial in five days. We'd begin jury selection the following Monday and begin the trial on Wednesday morning. That left only two days to select the twelve jurors. When I mentioned that the jury selection period seemed too brief, Judge Moore said he would be sitting in on the voir dire, which is the technical name for the process, to insure it moved along at the proper pace.

We were done. In three days, we'd select a jury, and the following day we'd start the trial. I now knew how I'd be spending the next five days and probably the next five weeks after that.

The key to success in any trial is preparation, preparation, and more preparation. I've seen many lawyers lose cases they should have won because they weren't prepared. I've even won a few cases I should have lost because opposing counsel wasn't prepared. Most times the jury does the right thing, and no lawyering skills are going to produce a winner out of a sure loser. But in cases that can go either way, preparation is often the difference between winning and losing.

That was why I spent the next three days locked in my office making sure I knew every detail of Little Tony's case. With the facts fresh in my head, I could outline my strategy and game plan. Then I'd prepare my witness outlines and begin drafting my opening statement. It was the same process I had used in all my prior trials. At least those when I was sober. When I was drinking, there may have been a little slippage here or there, but if there was, it wasn't much. I say that with confidence only because the process was so ingrained in me it had become second nature.

CHAPTER 66

With Judge Moore overseeing the process, we selected the jury in less than the two days the judge had allotted. Had the judge not been present, it would have taken four days at least. Why? Because lawyers overthink when selecting jurors. It's not that we believe asking enough questions will enable us to read a potential juror's mind. It's more a reluctance or maybe a fear of deciding. I'm unable to make up my mind, so I put off deciding by asking more questions.

But the judge limited our questioning, and by two o'clock on Tuesday afternoon, twelve jurors and three alternates had been selected, sworn in, discharged, and told to return the following morning at nine thirty sharp. The jury was comprised of eight men and four women, ages ranging from eighteen to sixty-eight years old. The three alternates were males.

The jury selection process is important because it's my first chance to interact with the jurors. It's also my last opportunity to address them until after Sarah Washington made her opening statement laying out the prosecution's case. Being the first to address the jury gave Sarah a definite advantage, and I hoped to limit that advantage by using the voir dire to introduce at least a bit of Little Tony's story. I couldn't turn the voir dire into an opening statement, especially with Judge Moore overseeing the proceedings, but experience had taught me how to subtlety make my point.

It starts with understanding that while not all people in a group think alike, they do share some ideas. So, for instance, young people tend to be more liberal than older people, and in most instances, women tend to be more sympathetic than men. Depending on the nature of the case and the defense, I might want young jurors, or I might prefer women jurors over men jurors.

I intended to turn Shankar into the poster child for government corruption and wrongdoing, so I wanted jurors with a healthy skepticism of government who might be offended enough by Shankar's conduct to acquit Little Tony. With that in mind, my target jurors were young and preferably minority members. I hit my target with six of the twelve jurors which meant if I didn't get an acquittal, I had a better than average chance of getting a hung jury.

An acquittal is, of course, better than a hung jury, but a hung jury is better than a conviction. In most cases when a jury hangs and a mistrial is declared, the district attorney will retry the case. But the second time around, the district attorney is generally more generous when plea bargaining. The last thing the DA wants is another hung jury.

I had another objective while selecting the jury in Little Tony's case. I needed to make the jury comfortable with Little Tony's appearance. Knowing Sarah would portray the case as a Mafia hit man, Little Tony's appearance could work against him. I mean, he looked like a Mafia hit man or what everyone probably thinks a Mafia hit man looks like. I couldn't change his size or the impression it made, but I could get the jury accustomed to seeing him, so it wouldn't come as a shock when the trial started, and that's why I had him sit next to me during jury selection.

It's called desensitizing, and it's a tactic used by most criminal defense lawyers. I use it all the time with autopsy photos. Autopsy photos are gruesome, and the prosecutors use them simply to inflame the jury's passion. Knowing I can't keep them out of evidence, I do the next best thing, I make them less shocking. I talk about them during jury selection by warning prospective jurors they'll be presented with very gruesome photographs. That way, when the jurors see the photographs, they expect them to be gruesome, and that takes away much of the shock value. Often the photographs turn out to be less gruesome than the jurors expected.

I should mention that Sarah Washington is no rookie when it comes to trial tactics, and she was sending her own messages during jury selection. Knowing I'd be working the corruption angle, she brought it up herself. She was desensitizing the jury to the corruption angle, the same as I was doing with Little Tony's appearance. But she had another reason for doing it as well. She didn't want the jury thinking she was hiding it from them. With all the media attention that had been given to Hannah's and McAvoy's arrest, not to mention Shankar's, someone would have to be living in a bubble not to have heard or seen something about the scandal.

A good rule in any trial is to get ahead of bad news, meaning if you know something bad is going to come out, get it out yourself. That way, you steal the prosecutor's thunder, and you get to frame it in your terms. It now remained to be seen if either of us had accomplished our goals.

CHAPTER 67

Wednesday morning at nine thirty, the twelve jurors and three alternates were seated in the jury box waiting patiently for something to happen. Sarah Washington, seated alongside her young associate, stared intently at a legal pad, presumably studying notes for her opening remarks. I sat next to Little Tony at the other counsel table, and after studying the jurors, I briefly turned my attention to the visitors' gallery.

Not surprisingly, it was packed with the media and a couple of familiar faces. Of course, Big Tony was there sitting in the front row behind his son. I also recognized a couple of regular court sitters, people who with nothing better to do than hang out in the courthouse and sit in on trials. For them it's a free form of entertainment. Most of the remaining spectators I took to be media people, some of whom I recognized. Then there were four guys who were definitely mob guys.

Two of them sat a few rows behind me and Little Tony, so I figured they were Rucci's guys. The other two sat on the opposite side of the aisle. That and the way they were dressed made me believe they were Russian goons. Unlike the Mafia guys who wore suits and ties, the Russian guys wore tee shirts and leather jackets. When it came to class, the Mafia had it all over the Russian mob. Of course, when it came to viciousness, it was the other way around.

At nine thirty five, Judge Moore made his entrance, and after giving the jury their preliminary instructions, he told Sarah to deliver her opening statement.

As I expected, Sarah did a good job of laying out the case. First, she stated the simple facts: two victims known as bookies killed in Brooklyn, shot gangland style, their bodies found in the trunk of a car two days later. Then she brought Little Tony into the case. A man with known Mafia connections, his fingerprints found at the murder scene, and on the car in which the bodies were stuffed. His skin found under the fingernails of one of the victims.

Sarah was doing a great job, and she had the jury sitting forward in their seats, a sure sign they were paying attention, and they were with her. Next, Sarah introduced motive into the story. A dispute between the Russian mob and the Mafia over territory. Finally, a warning that the defense would try to distract attention from the clear facts with a claim that there had been evidence tampering. Yes, there had been wrongdoing, but the facts remained the facts.

It was a good opening statement, not too long and well delivered. Now it was my turn. First order of business was to reintroduce Anthony Savino to the jury, not that they were likely to have forgotten him. Trials may involve hard cold facts, but in the end, trials are about people, and jurors need to be reminded of that. They needed to see Little Tony not just as a defendant but as a person whose life was in their hands.

The next step was reminding the jury that the law requires them to find a defendant guilty beyond a reasonable doubt, and that "maybe and could be," didn't cut it. Anthony was charged with murder which would require the jury to be convinced beyond a reasonable doubt that he had murdered the two victims.

Then I wanted the jury to focus its attention on the lack of evidence proving murder. There was no direct evidence in the case, only circumstantial evidence, and I wanted the jury to understand from the start what that meant and why it was important. Pushing the limits a bit and hoping the judge wouldn't call me for it, I referred to "real" evidence, as opposed to "maybe" or "could be" evidence. Fingerprints don't come with time stamps, so by themselves they can't tell you when they were left there. Skin under a victim's fingernails only tells you that he scratched someone. but not when and not where it happened. None of it proved a murder, no less who had committed it.

Then I mentioned what Sarah Washington had failed to talk about. The lack of "real" evidence. No witnesses, not even a murder weapon. Then I laid out the two-gun defense, telling the jury what they would hear from Theo. I explained how two corrupt assistant district attorneys, who formerly handled the case, and a corrupt clerk in the Medical Examiner's Office had disposed of evidence relevant to Anthony's defense. I concluded by saying, "Ms. Washington will probably tell you the missing evidence was not conclusive. But when she does, you ask yourselves if that was so, why would the assistant district attorneys originally handling the case want it destroyed?"

It was part of my strategy to force Sarah to call Shankar as a witness so I could cross-examine him before we began our case. If nothing else, by cross-examining Shankar in the middle of Sarah's case, I'd break up any momentum she had going for her.

It was risky because Sarah could play it one of two ways. She could ignore the bait and let things play out, or she could call Shankar and have him testify that the Mafia made him do it. The implication would be that the slugs matched Little Tony's gun. That's where the risk came in. But common sense said, if that was the case, I wouldn't use it as a defense, and Theo, a well-known and respected expert witness, wouldn't back me up. I believed getting Shankar on the witness stand as early as possible made the risk worthwhile.

CHAPTER 68

Sarah called Detective Michael Rojas as her first witness. Detective Rojas, along with his partner, Detective Joyce Barnes, both from the Fifth Precinct, had been dispatched to the location where the two dead bodies were discovered in the trunk of the Cadillac. Aided by photographs of the two bodies taken by a crime scene investigator, Detective Rojas described the scene in graphic detail. It was definitely a dog and pony show aimed at inflaming the jurors. I could only hope my earlier warning to the jurors about gruesome pictures was blunting some of the shock value of the photographs.

When Sarah tried taking a double bite of the apple by having Rojas refer to the photographs that she had already shown him, I objected on the grounds that it was repetitive. Judge Moore agreed and sustained my objection. Moore was determined to finish this case in two weeks, and he was going to keep us moving along no matter what it took. For me, that was a good thing. The less time spent with these dog and pony shows, the better.

When Sarah finished her direct examination of Detective Rojas, it was my turn to cross-examine him. But I had nothing to cross-examine him about. He had simply described what he saw, and from everything I knew, he had done so honestly and correctly. I could have run him around the block a few times, but there was no reason to do it. He wasn't my target and rather than just have him repeat his testimony unchallenged, I chose to ask no questions.

Typically, the next witness called is the medical examiner to establish the cause of death and to introduce those damn autopsy photos. The name of the doctor who had performed the autopsy was on Sarah's witness list, along with Vijay Shankar's name, and the name of another clerk, Dennis Petrino. I wasn't sure why Petrino's name was on the witness list, but I sensed it was going to be a problem, and I was right.

When Sarah called Dennis Petrino as her next witness, I asked for an offer of proof because I had no idea why this witness was being called or what he had to say. In a side bar conference out of the jurors' earshot, Sarah said Petrino was there to simply introduce and authenticate the two autopsy reports. It was clear that Sarah didn't want either the doctor who had performed the autopsies or Shankar on the witness stand during her case. It was a smart move, but I couldn't let her get away with it.

I objected, stating that as far as I knew from the discovery provided by the District Attorney's Office, Petrino had neither performed the autopsies, nor had he prepared the reports, and as such, he could not verify their authenticity. Sarah argued that the autopsy reports were official documents kept in the ordinary course of business, and therefore, they were admissible on that basis alone. I agreed, but only insofar as they were an exception to the hearsay rule. Their authenticity, however, was another thing, and I demanded that the person who prepared the reports was needed to authenticate them. Fumbling through my notes as though I was looking for a name, I said, "I believe, Your Honor, that the reports were prepared by someone named Vijay Shankar, who is listed as a witness."

Sarah tossed me a nasty stare which I probably deserved. But I didn't care because the judge agreed with my argument and ruled that the reports had to be authenticated by the individual who had prepared them. Then came the fun part. The judge, looking at his watch, suggested we break for lunch, saying that should give Sarah enough time to arrange for Mr. Shankar's appearance that afternoon. I tried my best not to grin when Sarah had to explain to the judge that things weren't quite that simple because Mr. Shankar was locked away in protective custody. Sarah suggested that we adjourn for the day, so she could arrange to have Shankar in court the next morning. Unfortunately for Sarah, Judge Moore was not sympathetic to her plight and ordered her to have Shankar in court that afternoon or plan on calling a different witness. He did, however, extend the lunch recess from his normal forty-five minutes to an hour and a half.

After the jury was dismissed, and as we were leaving the courtroom, Sarah pulled me aside and complimented me on how I handled the Petrino business. She admitted that she didn't want to call Shankar, but anticipating my reaction to Petrino, she had arranged for him to be on call. He'd be in the courtroom on the witness stand that afternoon. The fun was about to begin, only I didn't know how much fun it was going to be.

CHAPTER 69

It started innocently enough with Sarah calling Vijay Shankar to the witness stand.

Escorted into the courtroom by two detectives but not wearing handcuffs, Shankar looked more composed than when I had last seen him in the hotel suite. With his plea deal in place and having refused to implicate Junior Rucci in the corruption scheme, he had little to worry about. The Mafia no longer had a reason to kill him, and he could either do his short prison time or return to India. All that remained was his testimony today, and then his nightmare was presumably over.

Sarah took Shankar quickly through his direct testimony. His position at the Medical Examiner's Office and what role he played in preparing autopsy reports. She moved quickly to the two autopsy reports, having him identify them, which he did. Sarah then asked for the reports to be admitted into evidence. We had reached the crossroads, and I had a decision to make.

I could simply offer no objection and allow the reports into evidence, or I could call for cross-examination of the witness outside the presence of the jury. It's called a voir dire on the document, and it can be very effective in discrediting documents, especially in these circumstances. If I succeeded in keeping the reports out of evidence, it would put Sarah in a real bind, but it wouldn't necessarily be fatal to her case. On the other hand, with the reports out, there'd be no reason for me to cross-examine Shankar in front of the jury, and even if the judge allowed it, he might be inclined to limit the scope of the cross-examination.

My goal wasn't to discredit the reports; it was to discredit Shankar, so rather than take a chance on the voir dire, I simply said that I had no objection to the autopsy reports being admitted into evidence. It was then my turn to cross-examine Vijay Shankar, and as I stood to do it, I glanced over at Sarah who clearly wasn't a happy camper.

Shankar, who had appeared very much at ease during his direct examination, was now looking a little less comfortable. I knew Sarah had prepped him for what was coming, but there is only so much you can do to prepare a witness that you know is going to be crucified on cross-examination.

I started off with a few friendly warm-up questions. It's important when cross-examining a witness not to start off with an attack, no matter how vile the witness might be. To the jurors, Shankar was simply a decent guy called as a witness to introduce the autopsy reports. They had no reason to think otherwise, so if I was hostile toward Shankar from the start, I'd risk antagonizing them. My first job was to give the jurors a reason to dislike Shankar.

After a couple of friendly introductory questions, I asked Shankar to explain how autopsy reports are prepared in the Medical Examiner's Office. I departed from my usual practice of asking only leading questions because I wanted the jury to hear the process from Shankar's mouth.

When Shankar was done explaining the process, I asked him if there was a standard procedure which he was required to follow when he transcribed the doctor's tapes and handled evidence. That was a leading question because the facts were in the question, and the answer required only a yes or no response.

Shankar answered, yes, there was a standard procedure, and I had him describe it in detail. Then came the question I had been waiting to ask, "Mr. Shankar, in this case, did you follow the required procedures when you transcribed the doctor's autopsy tapes and handled the evidence?"

Of course, Shankar's answer was a simple no. Glancing at the jury, I could see them sitting up a little straighter, and some were even leaning a bit forward. They were definitely intrigued, and they were beginning to have a reason to dislike Shankar.

With the jury watching intently, I asked Shankar, "Why didn't you follow the required procedures in this case?" A simple question, but the answer turned out to be more than any of us expected.

In an even tone of voice, Vijay Shankar replied, "Because I was paid one-hundred-thousand dollars to change the reports and get rid of evidence by Willie Rucci who told me he killed the two victims."

It was as if a bomb had exploded and pandemonium filled the courtroom. The gallery was in chaos. The media types were pushing and shoving their way to the doors trying to reach the hallway to call in the news. A couple of brazen reporters weren't waiting until they left the courtroom to make their calls and were talking on their cell phones. The two Mafia guys and the two goons I suspected to be Russians remained seated and were talking to each other.

Sarah was screaming over and over, "Objection! Move to strike!" But the judge was too busy banging his gavel and calling for order to pay attention to her objection.

I glanced at the jurors to see their reaction and wasn't surprised that they looked dumbfounded and obviously unsettled by the commotion. With it all, I was sure they knew that Shankar had just torpedoed the prosecution's case. That was if the judge didn't declare a mistrial.

Finally, I looked to Big Tony for his reaction, but he remained expressionless. Talk about a poker face; Big Tony had one in spades. I couldn't tell whether Shankar's testimony came as a surprise to him or not. My guess was it hadn't. I couldn't figure out exactly who had inspired Shankar's sudden revelation, but the presence of the two Mafia goons in the courtroom made me believe it was somebody in the Mafia. But who? Was it Big Tony acting in defiance of the Ruccis, or was it one of the Ruccis? It didn't matter. It was what it was, and it was good for Little Tony.

Finally, order was restored to the courtroom and Judge Moore ordered the jury to be removed to the jury room. Then his face still red with anger, he adjourned proceedings and told Sarah and me to follow him into his robing room.

CHAPTER 70

As soon as we were seated, the judge demanded to know what was going on. I said I had no idea; Shankar's testimony was as much a shock to me as it was to everyone else. Sarah said the same, adding that Shankar's testimony contradicted everything he had said to her in the past, all of which was contained in signed sworn statements.

Apparently satisfied that we were both telling the truth, the anger drained from Judge Moore's face. Then, in a calmer, friendlier tone, he said that we obviously had a problem, and he asked how we proposed to fix it. Sarah jumped right in and asked for a mistrial which is exactly what I thought she would do. I was prepared to argue against declaring a mistrial, but before I could state my objection, the judge denied the request, at least for the time being.

Judge Moore was convinced he could get the trial back on track without prejudicing either side. He said the first thing he had to do was to advise Shankar of his Fifth Amendment right not to incriminate himself. Shankar's plea bargain covered the bribery charge, but if when he took the money, he knew it was to cover up a murder, he'd be implicated as an accomplice after the fact.

Judge Moore was prepared to adjourn the trial to allow Shankar to confer with counsel and to have counsel in court during his testimony if Shankar so requested. The judge asked if either of us objected to proceeding in that fashion. I didn't like the idea, but there was nothing I could do about it, so I didn't object. Sarah, likewise, had no objection, so we moved on to the next point.

Judge Moore said once Shankar had been advised of his rights, if he agreed to continue testifying without conferring with counsel, I would be allowed to continue with cross-examination.

Sarah voiced an objection, saying she wanted the judge to rule on her earlier request that Shankar's statement be stricken from the record. I was starting to respond when the judge held up his hand to silence me, and he asked Sarah the basis for her request. She said the answer far exceeded the scope of the question, and those portions of the answer that were non-responsive to the question should be stricken.

The judge smiled and said, "You're right about that, Sarah, but the cat's out of the bag, and even if I strike the answer, Jake's going to ask the question properly, and the answer will come back in. Why waste the time striking the answer?"

Next, Sarah asked for an adjournment so she could confer with Shankar and prepare for her further redirect examination, once I concluded my cross-examination. Now I objected. It was a longstanding rule that counsel could not consult with a witness during cross-examination. The judge agreed, saying he'd give Sarah time to consult with Shankar after I completed my cross-examination. That was assuming there was anything left of him after I was done cross-examining him.

Returning to the courtroom, I was in a good mood, and why not? There'd be no mistrial and no stricken answer. Things were looking good for Little Tony. Then it dawned on me that not knowing who was pulling the strings meant I could still wind up dead.

There's nothing like the thought of being killed to ruin a good mood. If this was what being a mob lawyer was all about, then count me out. After years of representing scumbag violent felons and a couple of good guys, all for peanuts, I'd be memorialized in a *New York Post* headline, "*MOB LAWYER SLAIN IN MOB DISPUTE.*"

Donald L'Abbate

But I didn't have time to dwell on my passing. I'd soon be resuming my cross-examination of Vijay Shankar, and I had a whole new line of questions to prepare.

CHAPTER 71

The courtroom gallery was again packed with the media. The two Russian goons were there, but the two Mafia types had not returned. Shankar remained seated in the witness box, being watched carefully by the two detectives.

With the jury still out of the courtroom, Judge Moore advised Vijay Shankar of his Constitutional rights and the consequences he could face in waiving them. After acknowledging that he understood what the judge had told him, Shankar waived his rights and agreed to continue his testimony.

Before having the jury brought back into the courtroom, Judge Moore cautioned the gallery against any further outbursts, warning that he would empty the gallery if there was any disruption. The gallery fell silent, the judge's words sufficiently stern to quiet the murmuring that had been going on even as he spoke.

The jury was brought back into the courtroom and Judge Moore explained they should ignore the commotion that had erupted earlier, and it should play no role in their deliberations. Then he invited me to continue my cross-examination of Mr. Shankar.

I don't think I have to tell you that the first item on the agenda was getting Shankar to repeat his last answer which he did quite willingly. Having now established twice that he had been paid by Willie Rucci to falsify the autopsy reports and get rid of evidence, I had him explain how he had accomplished all of that.

After having Shankar admit he was presently under indictment for his criminal actions and being held in protective custody, I turned to motive. Not his motive, which was clearly money, but Willie Rucci's motive for wanting the evidence destroyed. Shankar said Willie Rucci told him he wanted Tony Savino convicted of the two murders because he, Willie, was the one who had killed the two victims.

Naturally Sarah objected on the grounds that the statement was hearsay, and she was right. However, an admission, which Willie's statement was, is an exception to the hearsay rule. Sarah knew that, and she knew her objection would be overruled as it was, but she made the objection simply to break my momentum.

There wasn't much more I could get from Shankar. God knows he had given me the world, but I knew Sarah would make some dents in his testimony, and I decided to blunt some points by hitting them first. As I've said many times, you're better off putting out the bad news yourself, so you can control the narrative.

I asked Shankar if he had identified Junior Rucci, and not Willie Rucci, as the person who had bribed him. He said that he had, but he was confused at the time. Then I asked if he recanted that identification and subsequently swore that he didn't know the identity of the man who had bribed him. Again, he acknowledged that was true, claiming he did so out of fear for his life. I asked if he feared for his life, then why tell the truth now? He said it was because he was offered witness protection.

All good answers, but they didn't explain why he hadn't told the cops or Sarah about Willie when he was offered witness protection and why he chose this particular moment to do so. I suspected the answer to that question had something to do with the two Mafia goons who had been in the courtroom earlier. Not sure how Shankar would handle the question, I thought it best left for Sarah to ask. I had everything that I needed, and I had gotten it without attacking Shankar. If Sarah was going to shake his testimony, she'd have to go at him hard, and since he was her witness to begin with, the jury might not like her attacking him.

By the time I had finished my cross-examination of Shankar, it was just after four o'clock. Judge Moore, true to his word, asked Sarah if she'd like an opportunity to confer with Mr. Shankar prior to her redirect examination. When Sarah said she would, the judge decided to adjourn the case until the following morning. Then, after instructing the jury that they were not to discuss the case either amongst themselves or with anyone else, the judge sent them home, telling them to return the next morning at ten o'clock sharp.

Judge Moore's normal starting time was nine thirty, so having the jury report at ten o'clock was unusual. He probably expected Sarah to raise further legal objections that needed to be dealt with outside of the jury's presence. It was better having the jury report later than having them wait idly in the jury room.

Sarah was in a bind, and the judge and I knew it. Unless Sarah could convince the judge to declare a mistrial or strike Shankar's testimony from the record, this case was all but over. Shankar's testimony had created more than enough reasonable doubt for the jury to acquit Little Tony in a New York minute. In fact, his testimony was so devastating to the prosecution's case that the judge might even dismiss the charges himself as a matter of law.

I had no doubt that Sarah and the district attorney would hammer Shankar to recant his testimony. Normally they'd simply threaten to withdraw the plea bargain, but in this case, they couldn't do that, not if they wanted to nail Hannah and McAvoy, and nailing them topped Vitter's list. Besides they weren't losing the murder charges, they were simply swapping out defendants, with Willie the Worm Rucci replacing Little Tony. When you looked at it that way, it was still a win win for Vitter.

To be honest, never in my life have I ever had a day like that in court, and I'm not likely to have another one in the future. Had it been the old days, I'd have been in a bar buying drinks for everyone. But it wasn't the old days, so I was at Ecco having dinner with Gracie.

Gracie had mixed feelings about the day's events. She hated to see cases being manipulated, and this case was certainly being manipulated, but she wanted Hannah and McAvoy convicted, and that was all that mattered. Manipulated or not, I said justice was being served because Little Tony was innocent. Gracie laughed and said he might not be guilty of killing the two Russians, but Little Tony was far from innocent. I had to admit she had a point.

CHAPTER 72

The next morning, Sarah argued furiously for a mistrial. Given the number of cases she was citing in support of her argument, I figured Vitter had half the office up all night researching the law. But it was all to no avail. In the end, Judge Moore refused to declare a mistrial, and at ten o'clock the jury was brought into the courtroom, and the trial continued.

Sarah called Shankar back to the witness stand. After confronting him with his sworn statement in which he said that he couldn't identify the individual who had offered him the bribe, Sarah asked the judge for permission to treat Shankar as a hostile witness. That meant she could use leading questions, and she could challenge the truth of Shankar's testimony, even though she had called him as her witness. The judge granted Sarah's request, and the fireworks began.

Sarah went after Shankar with everything she had. She confronted him with three additional sworn statements which directly contradicted his earlier testimony. She repeatedly called him a liar and questioned his motivation. Normally I would have objected to the repetitious nature of the questions and Sarah's badgering of the witness, but so long as Shankar wasn't changing his testimony, I didn't care if she beat him with a hammer.

Sarah was smart enough to know that beating the crap out of her own witness wasn't winning her any points with the jurors who were beginning to look at her as though she was a she-devil. But the entire case rested on Sarah getting Shankar to change his testimony or proving him to be totally unbelievable. If she didn't crack Shankar, the game was essentially over.

After more than a half hour of Sarah beating, badgering, and belittling Shankar, the judge called an end to the massacre. Clearly Shankar was done. I think even the jurors who had started to hate Shankar were now feeling sorry for him.

With nothing more to gain, I passed on further cross-examination, and Shankar was allowed to leave the courtroom. As he walked from the witness box escorted by the two detectives, the jurors glared at him with an intensity reminiscent of the villagers in the *Frankenstein* movie.

Next came the biggest moment in the trial when Judge Moore told Sarah to call her next witness, and Sarah said the prosecution rested. Her answer took me by surprise because, as things stood, her case was in shambles, and I would have thought she'd at least try to rehabilitate it. She still had the eyewitnesses who put Little Tony at the office around the time of the murders, unless they also had a change of heart.

It was a simple matter of risk versus reward. The eyewitnesses alone weren't enough to rescue the case, and if they waffled at all under cross-examination, they could do more harm than good. Seeing how the jury reacted to Shankar, Sarah knew the risk of putting another disastrous witness on the stand. Whatever her reason for throwing in the towel, I was just happy that she did.

Typically at the close of the prosecution's case, the defense makes a motion for a dismissal of the charges, claiming the prosecutor has failed to prove a case. Alternatively, the defense can ask for a directed verdict. That's when the judge instructs the jury that the evidence presented is insufficient as a matter of law, and they are directed to find the defendant not guilty. In Little Tony's case, I wanted to make both motions.

Donald L'Abbate

The judge sent the jurors to the jury room, and I made my pitch. My argument was short, simple, and sweet. Shankar's testimony had raised sufficient reasonable doubt about Little Tony's guilt to warrant a directed verdict or a dismissal of the indictment.

When I was done, Sarah argued that although the case had taken a hit with Shankar's testimony, she had still offered enough evidence of Savino's guilt to warrant the case going to the jury. It was a stretch, but that was all she could say. She was relying on the fact that judges generally hate to take cases away from juries. It's perfectly legal for them to do so; it just seems like it shouldn't be.

From what I knew about Judge Moore, I wasn't confident that he'd take the case away from the jury. Although Shankar's testimony gave solid grounds to do so, the safer course for him was letting the jury decide. If the jury returned a guilty verdict, he'd still have a chance to correct the situation by setting the verdict aside.

That was essentially how the judge ruled and why I was neither surprised nor upset with his decision. He said the case against Savino was, at best, paper thin, but he'd allow it to go to the jury, adding he'd revisit the matter if the jury returned a guilty verdict. In other words, I could still win even if the jury convicted. At that point, I figured unless something unexpected happened, the odds were ninety-nine to one that the judge would set aside a guilty verdict.

Now I had a decision to make. Did I put on a defense or not? Should I go with the two-gun defense or rely on Shankar's testimony having created enough reasonable doubt to acquit Little Tony? I had Theo all prepped and ready to go, but why chance something bad happening when we were riding a high? It was a tough call with a lot riding on it.

For some reason, lawyers love overdoing it when it comes to proving a point. I can't tell you how many times I've seen lawyers argue themselves out of a win because they didn't know when to shut up. The point being, you have to know when to shut up, and my gut was telling me this was one of those times. Relying on my gut instinct, I told the judge that the defense rested.

I think Judge Moore anticipated my decision because he immediately dismissed the jury, telling them to return the next day at noon, at which time they would hear closing arguments. He

269

reserved the morning for a charge conference during which we would discuss the instructions he would give to the jury.

CHAPTER 73

It took less than two hours to hammer out an agreement on the jury instructions. The only real bone of contention was whether the judge should give the jurors the negative inference charge I requested. Sarah did her best, arguing against giving the charge, but after Shankar's testimony, there was no way she could win that argument.

So, why did Sarah argue knowing she couldn't keep the judge from giving the charge? Because it was her last chance to salvage her case. It was all coming down to a question of reasonable doubt. Had Sarah done enough to convince the jurors that Little Tony had committed the murders, or did they have doubts?

Creating doubts and turning them into reasonable doubts is the job of a criminal defense lawyer. Most times we do it using logic and reason, but other times we're forced to use smoke and mirrors. You'll probably be relieved to hear that smoke and mirrors rarely work as well as logic and reason. But no matter what tactic a criminal defense lawyer uses, it all comes down to persuading the jurors to question and doubt the prosecution's case.

I would give the jurors plenty of reasons to doubt Sarah's case, but what I offered was just argument. The jury was free to buy it or not. But when the judge casts reasonable doubt on a case, that's a whole different story, and that's what would happen when the judge gave the jury the negative inference charge.

He'd tell them that they could, if they chose, assume that the evidence Shankar had destroyed or tampered with would not have supported the district attorney's theory of the case. The jurors might question my take on the case, and rightfully so, but they wouldn't question the judge's take. That was why the negative inference charge was so important. It was a judicial affirmation of my reasonable doubt argument.

With the jury instructions agreed upon, we returned to the courtroom and waited for the jurors to arrive. The courtroom was again packed mostly with media people who were talking amongst themselves. The two Russian goons and the two Mafia goons sat in silence on their respective sides of the aisle. Big Tony was in his seat behind Little Tony.

The jurors arrived on schedule, and by one o'clock we were back in session. Final arguments are done in the opposite order of the opening statements, with the prosecutor going last. Since the prosecutor has the burden of proving the defendant guilty, the prosecutor gets the last word. That means the defense must present its argument not knowing exactly what the prosecutor is going to say. Actually, it's not that big of a problem. The defense has its own story to tell and sell, and most times the defense knows what the prosecutor is going to say, at least in general terms.

Every prosecutor has his or her own style when making a final argument to a jury, but all closing arguments still tend to follow the same pattern. If the evidence of guilt is strong, which very often it is, most prosecutors will spend time talking about the evidence. They'll use the evidence as a prop to punctuate points in their arguments, like holding up the gun while describing how the defendant callously fired six shots into the victim's body. In murder cases, the prosecutor will often have poster size copies of the damn autopsy photos displayed on easels to remind the jury of the brutality of the crime. Much of it is theater, but theater only gets you so far, and in the end, it comes down to the quality of the evidence.

Donald L'Abbate

When the evidence is weak, a prosecutor will usually appeal to the jurors' emotions, hoping anger or sympathy for the victim will get them past reasonable doubt. Sometimes it works, but often it doesn't. In my experience, I've found that a good jury will always try to do the right thing. Being human, it's only natural for them to be swayed by emotion, but most take their oaths seriously and will set aside emotions as the judge tells them what they must do. As a defense lawyer, I remind the jurors that they took an oath, and for justice to prevail, they must honor that oath and decide the case on the facts, not on emotions.

In Little Tony's case, sympathy wouldn't be an issue. The victims had been identified during the trial as Russian mobsters killed in a territorial dispute, so, naturally, they weren't portrayed as innocent victims. This case was all about the evidence, or more precisely, the lack of evidence.

That was my thinking when Judge O'Donnell invited me to deliver my closing argument.

My strategy was to start with an attack on Sarah's weakest point, namely Vijay Shankar. It would be a very strategic attack because I needed the jury to believe his lie that Willie Rucci confessed to murdering the two victims. Yes, Willie had killed the two Russians, but there was no way in the world he ever admitted that to Shankar. I just needed the jury to believe it was true, or that it was possible, and that would create reasonable doubt as to Little Tony's guilt.

After thanking the jurors for their patience and attention, I turned immediately to Vijay Shankar, calling him a despicable human being. I said he was a liar, and a soon to be convicted felon. He had intentionally destroyed and altered evidence, evidence that the judge would tell them wouldn't support the story that the prosecution wanted them to believe. Evidence that wouldn't prove Anthony Savino had been the one who murdered the two victims. But evidence that could, in fact, prove Anthony innocent. But it wasn't my job to prove him innocent; it was Sarah's job to prove him guilty beyond a reasonable doubt, and to do so with the evidence she had introduced. But she had failed to do that.

Then I launched into my standard speech about reasonable doubt. Over the years, I've made it a practice to talk with jurors when a case is over to find out which points were effective and which weren't. Now after almost thirty-five years of practice and talking with hundreds of jurors, I have a pretty good idea of what works and what doesn't.

After putting the idea of reasonable doubt front and center in the jurors' minds, I attacked the little evidence Sarah had and highlighted the evidence she failed to produce. I reminded the jurors that the prosecution had failed to produce a murder weapon, an eyewitness, or even a motive.

Then I returned to the negative inference charge, asking the jurors to listen closely to the judge when he instructed them on the law and to pay special attention to what the judge had to say about the evidence and how they should view it. I was getting close to the borderline with that comment, but it wasn't so clearly out of bounds that Sarah would call me on it. It had nothing to do with our relationship, but her knowing the judge would overrule her objection and make her look bad in the jurors' eyes.

Finally, I returned my attention to Shankar with the most critical part of my argument. This is what I told the jury.

"Remember, even liars sometimes tell the truth, and that goes for Mr. Shankar. Would he and did he lie to protect himself, yes. But when he sat there on the witness stand, he was beyond protecting himself. He was already a convicted felon, soon to be put in prison. He had no reason to lie. So when he sat in that witness chair in front of the judge and you, and testified under oath, was he telling the truth? Yes, yes, he was. How do I know? The facts tell us so. What facts? The facts that he swore were true when he pleaded guilty to felonies. Common sense tells you that no one swears to facts that send you to jail if those facts aren't true.

What are those facts? Mr. Shankar took a bribe; he destroyed evidence; and he altered other evidence. Those were all facts, facts that he's confessed to and it's on those facts that he's going to prison.

Why did he do it? For the money obviously. But why would someone pay him $100,000 to destroy evidence? Mr. Shankar told you why. Because the evidence he destroyed would have exonerated Anthony Savino, and Willie Rucci didn't want that to happen. Willie Rucci wanted Antony Savino convicted of the murders that he, Willie Rucci, had committed. That's what Mr. Shankar said right here in front of you and under oath. Mr. Shankar destroyed evidence which

*would have proved Anthony Savino innocent in order to frame him
for the murders he didn't commit. Those are the facts.*

*It's true that Shankar hadn't mentioned Willie Rucci in earlier
statements. Had he given those statements under oath? Yes, he had.
Were they lies? Yes, they were. So, why should you believe him now?
Because today he said these things to you. Don't judge Mr. Shankar's
words on pieces of paper. Pieces of paper signed under conditions
about which you know nothing. Why did he choose to lie then? I don't
know; I wasn't there and neither were you. We weren't there to look
him in the eyes, to see his face, and to judge for ourselves if he was
lying.*

*But we're here now. We've looked Shankar in the eyes, and we've
seen his face while he testified, so judge his credibility on what you
observed when he sat in that witness chair and spoke to you. When
you judge him, ask yourself, why would he lie? He's confessed to his
crimes; he's going to jail; and he has nothing to gain by lying to you.
So why lie under oath and risk a perjury charge on top of his other
felonies?*

*Ms. Washington will undoubtedly attack Mr. Shankar's
credibility. The credibility of the witness she called, a witness she was
relying on to prove beyond a reasonable doubt that Anthony Savino is
guilty. Why will she attack his credibility? The answer is obvious
because Mr. Shankar's testimony exonerated Anthony Savino.*

*Must you believe everything Mr. Shankar said in order to find
Anthony Savino not guilty? No, you don't have to believe anything he
said. All you must believe is that what Mr. Shankar told you under
oath was possibly true. If you believe that it is possible Willie Rucci
committed the murders for which Anthony Savino is being tried, then
you have reasonable doubt that the murders were committed by
Anthony Savino, and you must acquit Anthony Savino."*

After again thanking the jurors for their attention, I was done. As
I returned to my seat, Big Tony gave me a slight nod which I took as
a sign that he was pleased with my performance. As for Little Tony,
he remained stoic, apparently doing as I had instructed by not
showing any emotion.

I thought it had gone well. The jurors seemed attentive, and once
or twice I saw a couple nod in agreement. Now it was Sarah's turn,
and she had a real uphill battle. It wasn't so much my closing

argument that made her job tough, it was the fact that her case had fallen apart. But Sarah is a fighter, so I didn't expect her to just fold, and of course, she didn't.

Sarah opened her closing argument talking about Vijay Shankar. If she had any hope of winning, she had to convince the jury to ignore his testimony. Being forced to take that approach put Sarah back on her heels. The prosecutor's unspoken rule for closing arguments is to start strong and finish strong. Beginning your closing argument with an attack on your own witness doesn't qualify as a strong start.

Methodically, Sarah went through each of Shankar's sworn statements, pointing out his lies. Repeatedly, she called him a liar and a disgrace to the Medical Examiner's Office, the City of New York, and the human race. She concluded her remarks about Shankar with the comment that he wasn't worthy of belief, and she pleaded with the jury not to judge the case on this one man's despicable conduct. Rather, she said they should look at the untainted evidence.

That was the heart of Sarah's argument, but she was in a difficult spot. What little untainted evidence she had implicating Little Tony was circumstantial and not very convincing. Her best evidence was Little Tony's skin having been found under one of the victim's fingernails, and she leaned heavily on it during her closing.

Then she turned to the fingerprint evidence which, again, was untainted by Shankar's conduct, but it was still only circumstantial and explainable.

In closing, Sarah asked the jurors to ignore Vijay Shankar's fabricated and unreliable testimony, and for the sake of the victims, to focus on the untainted evidence which demanded a guilty verdict.

Under the circumstances, it was a good argument. Watching the jury while Sarah spoke, I sensed she might have reached one or two jurors, but I wasn't concerned. Most of the jurors were sitting with their arms crossed or slouched and partially turned in their seats, all signs they were reacting negatively to Sarah's argument.

I don't generally buy into the body language nonsense touted by the professional jury consultants, but back in my early days, I had read a little bit about it. Over time and with experience, I came to realize that there was some truth in what they were preaching. Not that there is some universal body language, but that certain poses correlate to certain moods or attitudes. It's not always true, and I never take it as gospel; it's more of a guidance thing.

CHAPTER 74

By the time we were done with final arguments and Judge Moore had given the jury their instructions, it was late afternoon. Looking at the time, the judge offered the jurors the option of beginning deliberations right away or waiting until the next morning to start. After conferring amongst themselves, the foreman announced they'd prefer to start deliberations immediately, and if possible, remain working into the night if they could. Apparently, they wanted to be done and finished quickly.

The judge told them they could start deliberating immediately, and he would make arrangements for them to be served dinner in the jury room. He said if they couldn't reach a verdict that evening, they should simply let the court officer know when they were done for the night. Then they could leave and return in the morning to continue deliberating.

Once the jurors left the courtroom, the judge adjourned the case and headed off to his chambers. I glanced over at Sarah Washington who gave me a shoulder shrug. Neither of us knew what to make of the jury's request. As I packed away my papers, I told Sarah that I thought she had done a good job with her closing.

Sarah and I are friends, and I felt badly for her. She was left to pick up the pieces after those scumbags Hannah and McAvoy had sold out the District Attorney's Office. And if that wasn't bad enough, Shankar turns on her in the middle of the trial, leaving her in the worst bind a trial lawyer can find herself in. It definitely hadn't been a good week for Sarah.

Sarah returned my compliment, adding the words "as usual." Now we just had to wait for the verdict.

By then, Big Tony had made his way through the railing and was talking quietly with his son. The media crowd was thinning out, and the four goons were gone. I turned to the Tonys and said we should grab a quick bite in case the jury came back quickly. Big Tony asked if it would be better for us to wait in the courtroom, but I told him that wasn't necessary. The court clerk had my cell number, and when the jury announced it had reached a verdict, she'd give me a call. Of course, we couldn't go too far, but the Worth Street Coffee Shop was easily in range.

Needless to say, I was dying to know what had caused Shankar to suddenly turn on Willie Rucci, but I wasn't sure how to broach the subject. I was hoping Big Tony might tell me without my having to ask, but so far that wasn't happening. Maybe over dinner.

CHAPTER 75

While we ate our hamburgers at the coffee shop, nothing much was said about the trial. All Big Tony said was that he thought I'd done a great job, and Little Tony nodded in agreement with his father, but that was about it. I was still dying to know what had gone on with Shankar but was afraid to ask.

When we were done with the meal and having our coffee, I couldn't hold out any longer. I had to ask what the hell had happened with Shankar. Who put Shankar up to lying and why?

Big Tony just nodded and said, "In time, counselor. In time. For now, all you need to know is that you're in the clear."

It didn't answer my question, but knowing I was in the clear made me feel a lot better. I wasn't sure what that meant exactly, but it sounded good, and my hope was that it included the Russians.

With nowhere else to go, we hung out in the Worth Street Coffee Shop chatting. Earlier I had called Gracie and explained I wouldn't be around for dinner. Now it was just past nine o'clock, and I was about to call her with an update when my phone rang. It was the court clerk; the jury had a verdict.

It took about twenty minutes to get everybody back into the courtroom. The media people who had all left the courtroom earlier were back in full force. Apparently, they had drawn straws, and the losers remained behind and alerted the others when it was announced that the jury had a verdict.

Judge Moore took to the bench and before calling in the jury, he addressed the crowd. He said that he expected silence when the verdict was read, and no one was to leave their seats until the jury had been discharged. To ensure no one was tempted to disobey his orders, he instructed one of the court officers to lock the courtroom doors.

As the jury returned to their respective seats in the jury box, a few of them were looking at Little Tony. I took that as an encouraging sign. Usually when a jury convicts a defendant, they don't look at him until after the verdict is read. Sarah must have noticed the same thing because she shook her head slightly.

After confirming that the jury had reached a unanimous verdict, Judge Moore instructed Little Tony to stand. Standing with him, my heart was beating a little faster, and adrenaline was starting to run through my system. This was the moment trial lawyers live for.

Then came the question, "In the case of *New York State vs. Anthony Savino*, on the charge of murder, how do you find?"

My heart was racing, and the adrenaline was surging.

"We, the jury, find Anthony Savino not guilty."

I turned toward Little Tony. He was smiling for the first time since I'd known him, and he gave me a hug. Feeling a hand squeeze my shoulder, I knew it belonged to Big Tony.

We took our seats while Judge Moore thanked and dismissed the jury. As they left the courtroom, I smiled and added my own thanks. Then I looked over at Sarah and gave her a sympathetic nod. She smiled back.

Leaving the courthouse, Big Tony invited me to join him and Little Tony in a celebration at the Bocci Club. I was tempted to accept the invitation, but then I thought better of it and politely declined. As Big and Little Tony walked off heading for the Bocci Club, I called Gracie and told her the news. She said if I hurried home, we'd have an ice cream party to celebrate my victory.

I didn't consider the outcome a real victory. Yes, Little Tony was acquitted, and for him, it was a victory. But the acquittal wasn't the result of my legal skills. It came about from witness intimidation; I was just along for the ride.

It's funny how your life can change. It wasn't really that long ago that I'd have considered the win a victory and gone without question to the party at the Bocci Club. Instead, I was heading home for ice cream.

That night two things ended, the trial of Little Tony Savino and my career as a mob lawyer.

CHAPTER 76

The day after the verdict, I was walking on Mulberry Street when the two goons who had kidnapped me weeks earlier stepped in my path. This time they were a lot friendlier, explaining that Mr. Rucci would like to see me.

Following the same route we had taken previously, we wound up at the same shabby bar. This time I was escorted and not shoved into the place, and I wasn't even frisked.

Entering the back room, I found Silvio Rucci seated at the table next to Big Tony Savino. Both men stood as I entered and shook my hand. Rucci invited me to be seated and signaled his men to leave the room.

There was a pot of espresso on the table, along with a plate of pastries. Rucci poured coffee and passed the pastries. Then Big Tony said something to Rucci in Italian, who replied with a nod. Rucci took a sip of his coffee, and looking at me, he said, "Counselor, you've done a good job and probably have some questions. My friend, Big Tony, thinks you deserve some answers, and I agree."

With that, Rucci told me the following story. He and Big Tony had been friends going back to their first days as soldiers in the Gambino family. When he took over as boss of the family, he appointed Big Tony his consigliere. A number of years earlier, he learned of a possible coupe brewing in the ranks of the Stagliano crew. On learning this, his first instinct was to take out the entire Stagliano crew. But Big Tony warned him that doing so would make their territory vulnerable to a takeover by outsiders, most notably the Russians. A more subtle plan was needed, and Big Tony had such a plan. The plan would give Rucci a pipeline into the street crews so that he could make surgical preemptive strikes against any treachery. But it meant he had to demote Big Tony and banish him to the Stagliano crew. Big Tony would be his eyes and ears on the street.

For the plan to work, no one, not even his sons, could know about it. It hadn't been easy, but they managed to keep it all secret. At the start, with everyone knowing how close Silvio was to Big Tony, they needed to feign a major falling out. But it couldn't happen suddenly because that would be too suspicious. So, he and Big Tony started arguing publicly over small things. The arguments grew more frequent, and after a few months, there was open hostility. Finally, after a particularly nasty public blowup, he demoted Big Tony and sent him off to be Sally Boy's second in command.

While it was a humiliating public demotion, in actuality it changed nothing between him and Big Tony. Big Tony continued to receive his share of the family money, and by way of secret phone calls, Big Tony continued to give him advice. The original threat to the family was eliminated, but he and Big Tony thought it was a good idea to keep their little plan in place, and it had remained in place until now.

At that point, Silvio Rucci smiled and said it was time for another cup of coffee. When we were finished, he leaned forward, and looking at me with the same deadly look I had seen the last time we met, he said, "Counselor, what I'm about to tell you next must never pass your lips. I'm telling you this because I believe you're a man of honor, a man I can trust. I don't have to tell you what will happen if you ever reveal any of what I'm about to tell you."

He wasn't looking for a response because he knew his words were threatening enough that a response wasn't needed. Sitting back, he continued with his story.

He had three sons. His two older boys, Silvio Junior and Jimmy, were good men, but his youngest, Willie, had gone wrong. He loved all three, even though they plotted to take over the family. It was a threat he was used to because somebody was always looking to take over. It didn't matter that it was his sons; business was business. The only difference being his sons probably wouldn't kill him if they succeeded in deposing him, just as he had no intention of killing Junior or Jimmy now that he had won.

But with Willie, it was different. Willie was wild, and he was always causing trouble. As he had told me at our last meeting, it was Willie who had killed the two Russians. It was Willie who first suggested framing Little Tony for the murders. His other sons, not knowing of the relationship with Big Tony, agreed to go along. Junior took charge and came up with the plan. But what neither of his older sons knew, and what he only recently learned, was that Willie intended to kill his two brothers as well as him and take over the family.

It wasn't the threat against him that bothered him; it was that Willie would kill his brothers. Silvio promised his late wife on her deathbed that he would always protect their sons, and he kept that promise. After he and Big Tony secured the confession from Willie, they turned him over to the Russian mob. It broke his heart to do so, but Willie had left him with no choice.

It was a frightening story. But what scared me the most was how calmly and matter-of-factly Silvio Rucci had told it. I don't remember much about my father, and I hate him for abandoning me and my mother, but I'm not sure I could turn him over to be killed. Kick his ass, spit on him, and curse him out, yes, but arrange for his murder, I don't think so.

I found it hard reconciling the gracious Silvio Rucci who served espresso and pastries with the Silvio Rucci who turned his son over to the Russians. I had met plenty of men who would have no problem killing their own children, but they had all been wildly crazy sociopaths. None of them had a sympathetic bone in their body, and certainly none of them had been gracious. Just as I'd never know what made those sociopaths the way they were, neither would I know what made Silvio Rucci, Silvio Rucci.

When Rucci was done with his story, Big Tony reached for something on the chair next to him, making me more than a little nervous. But he came up with a thick Manila envelope, not a gun. He tossed the envelope on the table in front of me and said, "It's the rest of your fee. You earned it, counselor."

Picking up the envelope, I barely had time to say thank you when Rucci signaled one of his goons, and I was ushered out of the place. This time when offered a ride, I accepted and was pleasantly surprised when no one joined me in the back seat. After telling the driver to drop me at Mott and Canal Streets, I sat back, and making sure I wasn't in the line of sight of the rearview mirror, I peeked into the envelope. It was filled with one-hundred-dollar bills. Later in the privacy of my office, I counted the money. There was another one-hundred-thousand dollars in that envelope.

EPILOGUE

A week after my meeting with Silvio and Big Tony, I read in the newspapers that Sally Boy Stagliano and three of his associates had been killed outside an Italian restaurant in Brooklyn. Later that month during a lunch with Chen, I learned there had been a shake-up in the Rucci mob family with Junior and Jimmy being demoted to crew capos and Big Tony returning to his role as consigliere.

After Little Tony's trial, a warrant was issued for the arrest of Willie Rucci, but no one could find him. A couple of months later, body parts were discovered at a construction site in Brooklyn. They were eventually determined to belong to Willie Rucci. To the surprise of many, but not to me, there was no big Mafia funeral for the youngest son of the Don, and more importantly, there was no retaliation. Scores had been settled, and life carried on.

Last year, a close associate of Silvio Rucci got himself in a jam and turned State's witness to save his ass. Once safely in the Witness Protection Program, he wrote a book, a best seller, revealing all the secrets of the Rucci family, including everything Silvio had told me at our last meeting. That's why I'm able to tell you this story without fear of being killed.

I learned something from all of this. Being a mob lawyer might pay well, but it was hard on the nerves, and it came with a price. In this case, the price was Gracie choosing the vacation I had promised her and hoped she had forgotten. It's not that I welsh on my promises; it's just that I hate traveling. Since I've never actually done any traveling, you'd probably agree with Gracie and Doug that I should at least give it a try. Well, this time I had no choice.

Gracie booked us on a seven-day Caribbean cruise, of all things.

AUTHOR'S NOTE

All proceeds from the sale of this book, as well as the proceeds from the sale of the other *Broken Lawyer* books, are donated to three charities. The Lowcountry Food Bank which feeds the hungry in the low counties of South Carolina; the Veterans Welcome Home and Resource Center which provides help and services to our veterans; and Providence Home which provides support and services to abandoned and troubled teenagers.

On behalf of those organizations, I thank you for having read this book and hope you enjoyed the story.